Voices of Angels

Darlene Oakley

To: Lois
Enjoy the journey
with Julia

Ps. 139:4

Lanico Media House
Celebrating literary lessons and legacies
ARKANSAS · TEXAS · LOUISANA

VOICES OF ANGELS

Lanico Media House
Lanico Media House is an imprint of Lanico Enterprise.

The text of this book is set in Garamond, Adobe Garamond Pro, Homemade Apple, Rage Italic, Mistral, Old Script, and Verdana.

First U.S. Paperback Edition: December 2016

ISBN: 978-0-9967799-5-1

Printed in the United States of America.

Reviews for Voices of Angels

I love a good mystery with a hint of romance. *Voices of Angels* by Darlene Oakley does both very well. With various cities and rural settings in Canada as the setting, this Canadian was truly blessed. The more guess work in a mystery, the better! Oakley kept me guessing right up until the final chapters as she unraveled the layers surrounding the villain and the reason for his actions. It took a message in a bottle and tragic experiences to bring Julia and Dany together. As they sort through their tragedies and aid one another, the villain continues to elude them and the local authorities. I look forward to future books in this series with Julia and Dany and perhaps there will be more messages in bottles.

- JennyEBurr

Voices of Angels by Darlene Oakley is a wonderful Christian fiction novel I found uplifting, well written, with just the right mixture of suspense, romance and faith. The realistic plot was easy to read and kept me engaged. I fell in love with and truly cared about the primary characters Dany and Julia. The story ends very poetically and left me feeling satisfied, inspired, and reinforced my belief in the power of forgiveness.

-Loretta Paszkat

I will start off by saying that I am a Christian and I do read Christian fiction, but I rarely read contemporary Christian fiction including Christian romance. My reasoning behind this is that I don't find the characters relatable. The Christian characters always seem ideal and perfect even when things are going bad. I am so happy to say that this is not the case with Darlene Oakley's book *Voices Of Angels*!

The characters, Dany and Julia, are well written. They have the right blend of human emotions and reactions mixed into their faith to allow for characters that are not only believable, but also relatable. They struggle with their initial reactions like normal people, but then work through their reaction and thoughts to respond in a way that is pleasing to God. Their love story, although somewhat quick for some people, is extremely believable and is understandable to those of us who fell in love quickly with the spouse that God had designated for them.

Darlene is able to weave a mystery that is full of suspense without getting boring or foreshadowing the conclusion. She keeps you guessing right to the end. I couldn't put this book down.

I highly recommend this book and can't wait to read more of Darlene's books.

-Twilah St. Cyr, Ottawa

Other Works by the Author

Inner Sanctum

Finding Your Voice: When Life Seems to Have Stolen Yours
A Devotional Companion to Voices of Angeles

The Connected Voice Journal: Connecting Your Voice with God's
A Journal Companion to Voices of Angels

Dedication

One of the main themes in this book is dealing with the hardships that come along in our lives. While these experiences may seem daunting to most of us, they have a tremendously different effect on those with mental illness.

This book is dedicated to John Konrad. John always greeted everyone with a broad smile, was not afraid to hug, an astonishingly open evangelist, and had a heart for missions and helping people. What many people didn't realize was John's struggle with mental illness. John was bi-polar.

Though I'd heard the term applied to me before from several people, I came to associate "voice of an angel" with John who never missed an opportunity to tell me how much he loved to hear me sing. Later, when I learned of his mental health struggles, I discovered what kind of an impact the voice of an angel could have.

Sadly, during a period of depression, John took his own life in the fall of 2015. He leaves behind a legacy of evangelized hearts, a loving and excellent hugger of a wife, Joy, and a huge, gaping hole in the hearts and lives of those he came in contact with.

He's certainly hearing the voices of angels now.

Chapter One

Halifax police officer Daniel Howard peered around the corner as his fellow officers raced up behind him.

He and his partner, along with two other on-duty cruiser patrols, were responding to a burglar alarm at one of the local downtown businesses. Seeing no one in the front of the building but hearing smashing glass, the banging of the cash register drawer, and the high-pitched tinkle of jewelry inside, Daniel inched his way around the corner, then toward the front door and broken-in store-front window. A glance into the store revealed two people in hooded sweaters and dark-colored jeans the bottoms of which wobbled about mid-thigh.

How could young people even walk that way, and what was so impressive about Fruit of the Looms that they felt compelled to advertise to the world they were wearing them?

Dany relayed a description of the burglars to Dispatch from the radio clipped to the epaulet on his left shoulder.

With the teams ready on both sides of the building, Dany shouted, "You in the store! This is the police! We know you're in there! Come out now with your hands above your heads!"

Curiously, there was no response. No swearing. Nothing.

He peeked in the store again as the two men continued their burglarizing without noticing – or at least choosing not to acknowledge – the troop of police about to arrest them.

Dany raised his weapon to just below his chin. There was no way to know for sure if these men were unarmed. Even if they didn't have guns, they had to have used something to break in the window, and whatever that was could still be used to hurt him and the other responders.

Keeping his gaze trained on the two men he repeated his instructions. "This is the police! Come out now with your hands where I can see them!"

Still no response. Not even a turn of the head. Were they deaf? How had they not heard him?

He nodded to his fellow officers, then crept out in front of the window. One of the burglars turned his head, his face hidden by a ski mask, but his eyes widening in recognition and then fear. The man's jacket bulged with likely the haul from the cash register and goods from the shelves around them.

"Turn around now! Put your hands in the air!"

The first burglar who had turned his head, nudged his partner who now looked up. They stared at the gathering of police officers hovering around their only escape route.

Dany knew they were trying to determine their chances of eluding capture. Given the amount of officers who had responded, there was little likelihood these two would get away, and hopefully the burglars had come to the same conclusion.

What happened next Dany would later replay over and over in his mind, and recount seemingly hundreds of times to his superiors and counsellors. The first burglar dashed out from behind the cash counter, hands buried in his swollen jacket pockets.

"Stop!" Dany shouted when the thief was about halfway to the window. "Let me see your hands!"

In the millisecond Dany made eye contact with the first man, the only emotion he saw there was sheer panic, not survival as he'd seen in the eyes of countless other criminals he'd apprehended over the years.

"Let me see your hands!"

But the man's hands remained buried in his pockets as he neared. Was he trying to keep his stash safe, or concealing a weapon? Perhaps the very weapon they used to break into the store. Perhaps a different weapon they'd brought with them in the event the police showed up.

The man's hand wriggled free of the pocket, and in that same second Dany's service weapon discharged and the man fell. Once he was down, the second burglar stopped running and threw up his hands as the other officers swarmed around them.

"You bastard! You shot him! He was just a kid!"

Dany knew he would never forget the words or the hatred which spewed from the second man's mouth as the other officers dragged him away, expletives filling the air. Dany turned and knelt beside the body of the first one, his heart filled with horror at the thought of the possibility.

It couldn't be true.

Dany lifted off the mask and what he saw would haunt him the rest of his life. The look of panic he'd seen in the man's eyes, hardly the kind of thing he'd see in the eyes of a career or hardened criminal, was because he wasn't a man at all. But a kid. No more than 15 years old. As the earbuds tumbled to the ground with music emanating from them, Dany finally understood why the boy had never responded to his demands.

Dany looked at his partner who had joined him.

"So, it's true. He was just a kid."

Dany nodded. He pinched the corner of the kid's jacket and shook out the contents of the pockets. Money from the till, several necklaces and gold bangles, some cigarettes, a few candy bar wrappers, a lighter, and a flashlight.

The months that followed whirled blurrily by, as Dany found himself caught in the nightmare that all police officers fear. No one liked to discharge their weapons. They were supposed to be used as a last resort. They all feared that one day they would make the mistake of shooting a kid while carrying out their duty.

The media and community had a way of keeping incidents like these front and center, which made the crippling heartache that came with such a burden even heavier. The media and ensuing public response were seldom compassionate about it, either. Everything focused around how terrible a police officer was for making such a mistake, and every officer felt the impact of that mistake in the very core of their being. Everything was compounded by the fact that the young man had been black. Descendents of the African slaves who had been brought over to the U.S. and then eventually settled in Nova Scotia with the promise of freedom. But Nova Scotia also had a dark history of racism, and incidents like this always brought that to light.

Dany's job -- every officer's job -- was to protect life, not to take it. He had reacted to the possibility that the boy may have been about to draw a weapon which would have posed a direct threat to him or his fellow officers. The fact that the contents of the black boy's pockets didn't include a gun did little to support his side of the story.

Endless meetings, hearings, and counseling sessions concluded with him being cleared of any needed disciplinary action, physically capable of returning to duty, but not emotionally capable. So the decision was to place him on stress leave for a year.

Dany paced back and forth in his apartment like a caged lion. He was on the 12th floor, but felt like every eye was on him. Everyone knew his name and knew what he had done. He'd never be able to come to any sort of peace with people judging him every time they looked at him. The unspoken accusations, hatred, mistrust.

The vision of Jayson's mother wailing over her son's casket at the boy's funeral screamed through his dreams and made him dread even going to sleep.

He had to get away. And there was only one place he could go.

As he looked out at the ebb and flow of the mighty Atlantic in the Bay of Fundy from Nan's verandah, hip-high grasses swaying all around with gray rocks jutting through, Dany took a deep breath of the salty air. There was something completely intoxicating and relaxing about the smell and watching the waves rolling beyond the cliff edge. He'd spent many summers in this old house. The tranquility of the water and the warm, hominess of Nan's Victorian from times gone by started to ease the tension from his body.

The town of St. Martins, New Brunswick, had once been the third largest producer of wooden sailing vessels on North America's eastern seaboard. His grandmother's house was one of the few to have survived the fire of May 31st, 1900, which destroyed over 68 buildings in the village.

Its rustic covered bridge and red-sand beach drew thousands of visitors each year to St. Martins. He'd spent many childhood afternoons on that beach and in the caves that became accessible when the tide was out, the red sand squishing between his toes and hundreds of tiny snails huddling in tide pools.

It was too cold to do that now though. The beach had closed months ago, and he shivered at a blast of the cold, salty Atlantic wind. Time to go in.

Hands in his jacket pockets, he hunched his shoulders against the biting cold and entered the house. It was just as he remembered it. A little dustier maybe with cobwebs Nan never would have allowed, but until this latest bit of assigned time off, he'd had very little time to come down and take care of the place like he'd promised.

His heart and mind raged over whether to start cleaning now or put it off, but eventually the cleaning won out. Nothing better to distract a person's mind than house cleaning – at least that's what Nan would have said.

He found some rags under the sink and Nan's standard PineSol, and set to wiping down counters, sinks, stovetop, and table, then scrubbed the floor on his hands and knees. "The only way to properly clean a floor," Nan's voice said, and he almost turned to see if she were standing there watching him, but of course she wasn't. She was in Heaven with his father now. She had passed on a few years back after spending 54 years mourning her husband, Wilmot Howard, and 20 years mourning her son, James Howard, who'd died in the Westray mine disaster back in '92. His mother, Ada, also passed on, not long after the death of his father, so Nan's house had come to him as he was the only remaining living family member.

He'd heard it said that the death of a child guts you in a way that no other death does and Dany supposed that were true. Nan had never been the same after the death of his father. He was never sure if Nan had taken care of him out of a sense of duty because he was her only grandchild and there was no one else to do it, or because she truly did love him. She'd always been very loving toward him, but he couldn't help but wonder if she saw his father every time she looked at him. The pain of that loss never left her eyes.

The same kind of haunted, grief-stricken look he'd seen in Jayson's mom's eyes every time they encountered one another. His memory assaulted him with visions of discharging his weapon, removing Jayson's mask, and the virtually debilitating pain that came from not only taking the life of another person, but the life of a child. A child was dead because of him. A mother's heart was broken because of him.

Dany collapsed into Nan's recliner under the crushing weight of emotions. The grief counselor and chaplain had both told him to expect these emotions and how they might affect him. It was one of the reasons for recommending he take a year off. He'd heard philosophies that encouraged getting "right back on the horse again." Perhaps it would have helped him work through those feelings if he kept himself occupied, doing things duty habitually required of him. There would have been something comforting about the routine. But he couldn't even bring himself to look at his service weapon since the shooting and didn't want to be stuck behind a desk. That would have been worse and given him ample time to replay all the events in his head until he drove himself mad.

No, the year off was a better idea, and coming to Nan's was really a good idea. The media coverage following the shooting meant there was no refuge for him in Halifax. Only a few close friends knew about Nan's house, and for the moment, Dany relished the solitude. Here he'd be able to grieve in his own way, in his own time. He saw the boy's face virtually every waking moment and he needed to find something else to do. Cleaning for Nan was always therapy, what she did to maintain some control over a life that seemed out of her control. That's what he needed right now. There was something comforting about conquering dust bunnies and cobwebs.

He'd never had the chance to know what it was like to be a father to understand what Nan and Jayson's mom felt at the loss of their children. As soon as he graduated high school, he'd turned to policing. One thing Nan had insisted on was that he get out from under the Howard curse of the coal mines and choose to do something else with his life. Policing had become his new life, essentially eliminating opportunities for building a family.

The swamping of emotions abated for the moment, Dany stood again, and set to work on the meticulous task of dusting Nan's collectibles distributed along the various shelves in the living room and dining room. He wondered for the next hour or so what he was going to do with himself for the year. Should he take this as an unplanned vacation? He hadn't set any money aside to take one and he had no real desire to go anywhere.

As he set the last knick-knack back on the shelf, his stomach growled.

Well, perhaps the only "anywhere" he should go was into town to get some groceries before the shops closed up for the evening.

Chapter Two

Julia McIntyre ran her hand along the smooth, glassy ebony of her grand piano. This was the closest she'd come to playing it in the last six months as pain would course through the core of her body every time she looked at it. Once her most beloved possession, now it only served as a very real reminder of all she had lost.

First her brother, then her career, then her husband, all at the hands of a madman.

She sat on the piano bench and rested her head on the closed piano lid ledge above the keyboard as tears spilled down her face. Her brother, Michael, had been with her right from the beginning of her career as a musician and performing artist. He'd traveled with her from location to location as her stage manager. Then, in one chaotic moment six months ago, he'd jumped in front of her as she addressed the crowd following a performance in Vancouver, taking the bullet that was meant for her. She remembered thinking in that split second, "What is Michael doing here?" The gunshot was barely audible through the cacophony of the crowd. It wasn't until Michael landed on the stage floor in front of her with blood pouring from his chest, and security personnel descended upon her that she finally understood what was happening. Michael died instantly before she even crouched down to cradle his lifeless body.

She didn't fully register the pandemonium that ensued following Michael's death. All future performances were cancelled and the voice so many people had grown to love – "the voice of an angel" people would say – had been silenced. In the whirlwind of entertainment media, police investigation, and the funeral that followed, she settled into a depression she felt certain would never end.

Her husband, impatient and frustrated with her lack of desire to do anything related to performing, set his sights on a new up-and-coming star. He served the divorce papers on her a few weeks later and she'd signed them without a second thought.

How could she go back on stage? It was that lifestyle which had brought this tragedy upon her and cost her brother's life. No. She sat up and swiped the tears off her cheeks. No. She would never return to that life. Didn't even have any desire to return to it.

But the dilemma remained – what was she going to do with herself now? Teach piano as her mother had for so many years after they'd moved to the London area from Manitoba following the death of her father?

Julia lifted the lid off the keyboard and set her hands on top of the keys. The music that had once flowed so naturally from her fingers never came. It wasn't just her voice that was silenced, but the entire language of music that once flowed from her heart as well. No, she wouldn't teach piano. Didn't even know how to push through the soul-deep pain so music was possible again. She'd always played and sang the music from her soul. Now her soul and heart were broken, and nothing could get through that.

She lowered the lid again and stood.

The phone beckoned from across the room. She groaned at the number on the call display.

"Hello."

"Hello, Mrs. McIntyre. Constable Davis, here."

"Hello, Constable. How are you? I have to commend you for at least keeping me posted on the investigation, although nothing's really happened in the last couple of weeks."

"No, unfortunately not. But we're not giving up. We're committed to seeing this through to the end."

Julia wondered if it had been someone else's brother who had been shot, someone without her public profile, if the police would be as diligent.

"Have you had any more leads?"

"No. Not since last week. The incident was pretty public. It was all over the media. We even did a spot on CrimeStoppers and America's Most Wanted. Someone would have to be living under a rock not to know what happened, so I think it's extremely odd that no one has come forward with anything."

Julia's heart fell. The investigation was really at a standstill. Despite the constable's attempts to reassure her, she doubted her brother's killer would ever be found, and she'd be living in a web of fear for the rest of her life.

"Well, thank you, Constable, for all your efforts. I know you're doing your best."

"Have you heard from P.O. at all? Any more phone calls? Any

more letters?"

Julia shook her head, then said, when she remembered he couldn't see her, "No. Nothing at all. But I know he's still out there."

"Yes, he is."

At his hesitation, Julia guessed what was coming.

"You know, Mrs. McIntyre, we've done all sorts of public exposure on this already, but perhaps if you were to get out more, not performing, but doing something in the public it would draw P.O. out into the open."

"You mean, use myself as bait?"

"In a manner of speaking."

Julia wandered into the kitchen and settled into a white-backed, blue-cushioned chair. Light poured in from open-curtained windows, but no amount of sunlight could brighten the dark cavern in her heart.

"You really think he's watching to see when I go out for groceries?" She hadn't even been out in the last few months to do that. She'd been relying on delivery service from a local grocer. She knew she couldn't hide away forever, but what exactly would she go out to do? She didn't have any children. Her mother had passed away not long after her musical career began. Michael was gone. She really didn't have anybody left to care for but herself. Her traveling schedule had left her with very few close friends, or strictly personal connections. Even the press had eventually drifted away to other more happening news events. She was truly, effectively — aside from Constable Davis' weekly phone calls — completely on her own.

She sensed rather than saw Davis' shrug as something rustled on the other end.

"You know, staying inside really isn't very healthy. I understand your loss. You know I do."

She knew that was true. He probably understood better than anybody.

"I know. And I know you're right, but if he is actually watching me and if you guys really don't have any idea where he is, it doesn't exactly instill me with confidence that I can leave my house without wondering if he's going to try again."

"If he wants to get to you, he won't let the walls of a house come between you and him."

He was right about that too. She really wasn't safe anywhere.

"So, why do you think he hasn't tried again yet?"

"Don't know for sure. I suspect he's pretty disappointed with the fact that he didn't kill you the first time and, like you, hasn't been ready to try again. Though there's no telling if six months is long enough for him to get back on his feet and look for another opportunity. The only way to test that and for us to get any sort of trace on him from witnesses or something is for you to start coming out of your self-imposed shell."

"You're right, of course." Julia sighed and rubbed deep pressure into her thighs as her anxiety about facing the outside world cranked up a few notches.

"Look, it's coming up to Christmas. I know this is going to be a tough time for you, but it's a prime opportunity to get back into life. Decorate your house. Show the press you're trying to get involved in life again after your tragedy. It would be a great feel-good story. Many people are wondering how you're doing ... particularly your stalker."

Julia sighed again. "You're right." The thought of doing Christmas by herself threatened to push her deeper into her pit, but her heart reached out in faith to the God she sang about in her songs. She knew this would be a test of the true meaning of Christmas, of light conquering the darkness. No, she may not have anyone with whom to exchange gifts, but she needed to find a way to get involved in the season. Perhaps she could use her financial resources to help someone else. For the first time in six months, her heart surged with hope -- even it was just a bit. After all, that's what Christ's birth had brought to the world—hope. She knew, regardless of all she had suffered this year, she needed to do something.

"Thank you, Constable."

"You're welcome." His voice hinted at a smile. "I'll be in touch next week. In the meantime, you know where you can reach me. Anytime."

"Thank you," Julia repeated, then hung up.

Chapter Three

"Hey, Dany-boy!"

Dany smiled as his partner, Constable Jackson Kirby, grabbed his hand in a firm handshake and gave him a brief hug. Kirby looked directly at him and placed a hand on his shoulder.

"How are ya?" Jack eyes asked a deeper question.

"I'm doing alright, thanks, Jack."

"I didn't think I'd see you back so soon." Jack returned to his desk set off in a corner of the main floor. Dany was thankful for the seclusion. He'd tried to sneak in without too many people noticing. "What's it been? Two months?"

"About that." Dany nodded.

"Are you back on duty?"

Dany sat in a chair opposite Jack, crossed his legs, and looked at his knees. "No."

"Then what are you doin' here, man?"

Dany glanced up and judged Jack's expression, which was intense and filled with genuine concern. The loyalty of a partner.

"I need you to help me with something."

"Anything. You know that."

Dany smiled. “I know.” He pulled a worn, soda bottle from his jacket pocket and tossed it on the desk. It landed with a solid *thunk* then twirled around and around as if they were playing Spin the Bottle.

Kirby snatched it up.

“What’s this?” He held it up to the light and saw the curled piece of paper inside. Kirby glanced at him, questioning.

Dany nodded. “Go ahead.”

Kirby used a pen to slide the paper through the mouth of the bottle and unrolled it.

“I was cleaning out Nan’s attic when I found this. I remember being with her when she picked it up out of the bay. Had always thought she got rid of it, but obviously not.”

“‘Dear whoever finds this note. This message was written by Julia Connelly from Manitoba on a visit to Toronto. I’m 10 years old and it’s March 2nd, 1986. Our number is (519) 273-9867. Please call if you find this note.’” Kirby stopped reading and examined the note under the light. “That’s a London area code, not a Toronto one. Pretty good penmanship for a 10-year-old. Lots of curls and heart-shaped dots on the i’s.” He tossed the note across the desk. “You don’t want to do what I think you want to do, do you?”

“Well, it’s not like I don’t have the time.”

“That’s certainly true.” Jack stood and walked to one corner of his cubicle so that Dany had to turn and face him. “It just seems kinda … childish.”

“I suppose it does. But perhaps this…” Dany waved the page

"...will help me focus on something else. Just the distraction I need."

Jack nodded. "I see your point." He sat back down and clasped his hands in front of him on the desktop. "So, what do you need me for?"

"Well, you're better at the computer side of things than I am. I need to know where to start digging."

Jack sat back. "You know I can't let you have access to police files while you're on leave. I could probably get in big trouble for even talking to you if you don't have an official reason for being here."

"I know. But I thought you could at least tell me where to start. I mean, I know she's given me lots of information..." Dany skimmed the note again "...I just need to know what to do with it."

Jack's hearty laughter rang through the room.

"What?"

"You really don't know what to do with it, do you?" He chortled as he tapped a few keys on his open laptop. "Do you even know what your cellphone's for?"

Dany scowled. "Of course, I do. It's for making phone calls ... not like I have anyone to call at the moment."

"Well, at least you know how to do that." Jack tapped a few more keys then turned the laptop around so Dany could see. "Let me introduce you to Mr. Google, my friend."

Dany looked up at Jack with a crooked smile. "Thank you."

"Type the information in here." Jack pointed to a blank field in the middle of the screen.

Dany flexed his fingers over the keyboard then started typing in the girl's name and other particulars from the letter. With his hunt-and-peck typing skills, this took a while.

"It's killing me to watch you, you know?"

Dany grunted and replied with a wry smile, "I promise I won't break it."

"My laptop may survive, but not sure my sanity will. Will you hurry up, already? Maybe you should enroll in a typing class while you're off."

Dany hit Enter and within a blink results popped up the first one being Julia McIntyre born Julia Connelly, a performing artist along with a concert photo of her sitting at a piano.

Jack leaned over and scrolled down to skim the other results, most of them news-related articles about Julia McIntyre, and other close results.

"Nope." He scrolled back up. "This one seems the best match." He tapped on one of the pictures and a Wikipedia window popped up with all the details — a bit of family history which matched the basics in young Julia's message, and some more recent details about her musical career.

"Wow. Didn't think I'd find her that fast."

"Neither did I, actually. Lucky for you she appears to be a pretty public figure."

"What's this?" Dany pointed to a few videos on the side of the screen with captions that indicated news reports.

Jack tapped on one of them. The video took a few seconds to buffer and then played through the report of the shooting at one of Julia McIntyre's concerts six months before, killing her brother. Another video was an update telling how Martin McIntyre had been seen with another promising young artist and no future concert dates for Julia had been planned.

Dany sank back against the chair as air whooshed out his mouth. "Wow."

A pregnant silence settled between the two of them.

"You still want to meet her?"

Dany shrugged. "Surprisingly, yes. Finding this out doesn't change that." He shook his head.

Jack sat in a chair opposite Dany. "You could be walking into another unstable situation. Not only do you have your own things to work out, but she's got a swamp load herself. You could be walking from one dangerous situation into another and you may not be ready to deal with something like that yet."

Dany ran a hand over his face. "I know that. But I'm not going there as a police officer to solve a crime."

Jack stared at him, eyebrows joining together. The expression Jack used when he had to play "bad cop." "Now, I've known you long enough to know that being a police officer is in your blood. Even when you're off-duty, in your heart and mind, you're on duty. And now you're thinking about running off to rescue a damsel in distress."

Dany laughed. "Who says I'm off to rescue the damsel in distress? I'd be out of my jurisdiction not to mention still on leave. What could I do that they probably haven't already done?"

"I'm sure you'll think of something."

Dany laughed again. "You do know me well. It is pretty hard to turn off the sense of duty." Dany paused as he considered Jack's comments. Jack was right. Moving from the aftermath of his situation into the aftermath of hers didn't seem like the logical thing to do. But then, the entire idea of trying to find the writer of the message in the bottle under any circumstances wouldn't be considered logical either. He knew in his gut that while he didn't intend on getting involved in the investigation, he probably would end up doing involved in some capacity anyway. He could land himself right in the middle of another situation involving guns. Would he even be able to use a weapon if the occasion called for it? During his psychological evaluation and fitness testing he hadn't been able to pull the trigger.

While finding Julia seemed like the absolute worst thing to do given his situation, from another angle, it might be just what he needed. Not only would it give him a chance to think about someone other than Jayson and his mother, but helping Julia would help him regain his confidence.

Jack was looking at him with a raised eyebrow, clearly wondering what he was thinking about. He decided not to tell Jack everything that had just gone through his head.

"Well, at the very least, it will get me thinking about something else and someone else," he said. "Maybe in its own way, and in a way no one can possibly imagine, it will help me heal too." After a brief moment of quiet, Dany continued, "There's nothing in the terms of my stress leave that says I have to remain in province."

"No, but you know you won't be able to take your service weapon cross-jurisdiction."

Dany glared at Jack. "I know that." He didn't have to tell Jack what he was thinking. Jack already knew. Partners were good like that.

Apparently sensing the end of the discussion and that Dany had made up his mind, Jack stood and offered his hand. "Well, keep me posted and let me know when you're back."

Dany shook his friend's hand. "You can count on it."

Chapter Four

He glared at the television screen. What was she doing there?

He reached for the remote and cranked the volume, as the camera focused on her face.

"…I'm just really thankful I can help out."

Her voice sent heat through his blood, and not the pleasurable kind. The kind that made him want to reach through the screen, put his hands around her neck, and squeeze until there was nothing left and her body lay motionless beneath his.

"This is the first time anyone's seen you since May. Why did you decide to get involved with the Christmas hamper program?"

Her chin dipped to touch her chest and a cloud seemed to settle over her head.

"This has been a very long time of grief and healing, but I thought it was time to get involved in life again, at least for a little bit, to help that process along."

"Do you think at the end of that process you might start performing again?"

She looked like she would burst into tears on screen, but swallowed hard and shook her head.

"No. At least not for the foreseeable future."

The reporter's decision to not pursue that line of questioning intrigued him, as did Julia's answer. She would never perform again. Her voice was still dead. And that had been a bonus outcome of him going to the concert that night.

With that realization, he switched to a sports channel and took a long swallow from the bottle in his hand. All was still right with the world.

Chapter Five

Julia returned to her Christmas hamper registration table. She hadn't expected her presence to draw media attention. She wondered if it was out of genuine concern for her or if they were just desperate for news. The reporter had been nice enough, without the vulture-istic cut-throat tone most reporters had. Perhaps she had once been a fan.

As the next family in line settled in front of her, she knew that, regardless of the risks to her, this had been the right choice. She had no right to sit by with the money from her career and do nothing while these people needed help.

She truly felt the encouragement in the smile she gave the mother with the two-year-old tugging on her arm. The despair of the last six months finally lifted as she concentrated on someone else's needs. Such encounters had a way of readjusting your perception of life and what you had. She would likely learn a whole lot more from these people than they would learn from her in their short interaction.

Dany's plane touched down in the small airport after being air shuttled from the hub in Toronto. The smaller aircraft had bumped around a lot more than the jumbo jet that brought him from Halifax to Toronto, and he was relieved to touch solid ground again.

As he emerged from the disembarking area and waited in front of the luggage carousel with the other passengers, he wondered for the umpteenth time if this was actually going to work. He'd looked up her address, but what were the chances that information was correct? What if he got there and she wasn't home? Her neighbors probably knew all about her story. Would they be ultra protective of her upon seeing a strange man watching the house or appearing on her doorstep? And, if she were there, would she send him away? Perhaps he should have called first. He tossed that idea around and decided that meeting her face-to-face would still be better.

He was taking a risk and he knew it. She was as vulnerable as he was. She may not be ready for someone else to pop into her life so unexpectedly. He had no way of knowing the circumstances behind the bottle. His original thought was that it was just a childhood fun thing, but what if it had been a plea for help? What had her family life been like back then? Would his appearance resurrect painful memories for her?

His experience as a police officer had taught him that nothing was ever like it seemed. You couldn't always judge a person and know precisely what was going on inside their mind or life.

He snatched his satchel off the carousel and headed for the rental car counter to pick up his keys and a map. Those in hand, he slung his bag over his shoulder and walked out to the lot. The weather was certainly milder than Halifax, but then London's weather wasn't affected by the roiling Atlantic Ocean. He had expected to see at least a light dusting of snow, but was relieved it was dry because he didn't want to have to dig out his boots. Finding his assigned vehicle – a black Kia Sorrento – he set his bags on the passenger seat, then rounded the car and got in behind the wheel.

Dany hesitated putting the key in the ignition. This was probably the most impulsive thing he'd ever done. Police officers weren't supposed to be spontaneous. Be able to think on their feet, maybe, and within the rules and expectations of the law, but that was what the job required. Searching out a woman he didn't know completely on a whim because of a message in a bottle found over a decade before would hardly be considered "within the rules." Google had been pretty sure that this was the woman he was looking for, but computers were only as smart as their programmers, right? There was still a chance he was making a huge mistake.

He reached into his satchel, pulled out the bottle, and turned it over and over in his hand. Huge mistake or not, he knew this was something he had to do even if the result ended up being him flying back to Halifax the next day with his tail between his legs. But instinct told him there was something worth pursuing here. He'd known it the second he read the note in Nan's attic, and again when Julia's picture and story popped up on Jack's computer screen. He couldn't quite define it. Perhaps it was an old cop hunch that he was on the right trail.

He set the bottle on the seat next to him, programmed the navigation system with Julia's address, then set out from the parking lot.

Chapter Six

His temper burned hours after her appearance on TV. He'd tried to dismiss her return from the dead as nothing, but reruns of her interview played through the local newsfeeds with the twist that she was a phoenix rising from the ashes of a tragedy.

When her face first filled his TV screen, he'd been satisfied with the thought that Julia McIntyre would never perform again. But, as her story continued to splash across every channel with renewed media speculation about what this would mean for her career even off the stage, he knew he wouldn't be able to sit by and let that happen. She may not actually sing, but guaranteed she'd find another way to spread her drivel.

Julia McIntyre had to die. He had to silence the voice once and for all. Once he'd done that, perhaps the one of the voices inside his head would finally go silent as well.

Chapter Seven

Julia tossed her keys on the table in the front hall, then shrugged off her jacket, and hung it in the closet. Toe-to-heel, she removed her boots and set them below the coat on the mat. It wasn't wet out today, but it did have that certain chill in the air that accompanied Christmastime, and she knew snow would be coming soon.

It had been a long, exhausting day, but soulfully fruitful. She had provided smiles to people who probably rarely smiled themselves simply because she wanted to make them happy for that one small moment in their lives. She smiled again as she recalled the families she had met. She knew many of those families would be helped by her efforts, and experienced the feeling of someone genuinely caring about them. She wished there were more she could do. There was such a focus on charity at Christmas, but all the community spirit stuff seemed to disappear for the rest of the year. In the back of her mind, she knew she could do something about that, but, as she wasn't quite sure just what, she decided to let that idea fester in the back of her mind for a while and focus on making dinner.

She had actually managed to get out to buy her groceries a few days before, so when she opened the fridge there was more to look at than empty shelves and air. She settled on a fresh salmon portion, a small potato, and fresh-frozen broccoli. She set the salmon skin side down on the wavy part of the grill and the potato chunks and broccoli on the flat side with some garlic, black pepper, sliced onions, and then set the lid on to steam.

She wandered into her music room and ran a hand along the smooth piano top. The crippling pang that usually gripped her heart was a lot less than normal. Perhaps the outings were helping. She still had no desire to sing or sit down and play, so there was still a ways to go, but perhaps this was a sign that she'd eventually get that part of herself back on track. She couldn't see herself ever performing publicly again, and truth be told, she didn't even really want to.

Clearly, there was another path set before her. The inertia of her life had certainly changed and she knew there was a reason for it, something she needed to learn though she had no idea what that was. Perhaps it was time for her to look at doing something else with her life. Heaven only knew what that something else would be. She'd liked her life the way it was. She had reached thousands with a message of hope and restoration. Though there were many other ways she could do that on a larger and smaller scale, which were equally as important, she couldn't imagine doing it any other way. She enjoyed performing, interacting with her fans, encouraging those who sought her out, and investing in the lives of those who came to listen. Never in a million years would she have even thought of giving that up.

One of her favorite stories her mother had told her from the Bible when she was little was the one about the gardener, who represented God, trimming off unfruitful parts of a plant so that all the plant's resources can be focused on other areas of the plant. Pruning is a painful but necessary process for a plant to flourish; the metaphor likening a person to the plant the gardener is pruning. Her career had certainly been fruitful both from a spiritual and financial aspect, and yet that appeared to have been pruned off. And to call the death of her brother, and the subsequent loss of her husband and career as painful would be an understatement. She wished whatever lesson she needed to learn could have been started some other way. But behind the pang in her heart, she knew this was an opportunity for her to focus on something else, to change her life's direction, so that she could flourish in ways she couldn't yet see or even imagine. She certainly wouldn't have chosen the journey she was now on for herself, but she only hoped that after she emerged on the other side of it all, she would rediscover a purpose for herself. That's certainly what Michael would have wanted for her, and what her mother had taught her and Michael when they were young.

She walked back to the kitchen to check on the salmon and add some water to the grill to keep the fish from drying out. While the meal finished its thing, Julia headed into the living room to find a Christmas movie on one of the local networks.

As Dany navigated through the city with the help of the GPS, he continued to wonder about Julia's past. Why had she moved to Ontario from Manitoba at that time? Was the message in the bottle meant to be something fun? And what about her life now? Why had a madman tried to kill her? Why hadn't the police been able to find him? How long would it be before he might try again? His mind settled on that part of her story for a moment.

What made a person do what he or she did? The news was filled with stories of people who had committed heinous crimes and, when interviewed, their neighbors and friends often said the criminal seemed like a normal, ordinary person, or quiet and had never been in trouble with the law before. A dead boy's face flashed across his memory and his body convulsed, and he thanked the Lord above he was stopped at a red light. By the time the light turned green, the momentary panic had passed, but remnants of its effects on his body remained – tension in his neck, white knuckles clutching the steering wheel, and heart clenching in his chest.

By the time he pulled to a stop in front of her house, his body had settled back to some semblance of normal, and he felt ready to face her.

He stepped out of the car and into the Christmassy December evening. Lights twinkled up and down the street, and flakes lightly tumbled from the sky. This neighborhood appeared to be a mix – split levels with a couple of high ranches, bungalows, and two-storeys thrown in for good measure – and of the same age. Much more homey than his apartment in Halifax, but then there was no view of the ocean or the intoxicating scent of sea. Although, he had to admit the smell of crisp, snowy, unpolluted winter air had a certain attraction as well.

He turned to look at Julia's house. There was a light on inside, though none over the door. He didn't take that as a sign that she wasn't safety conscious, but that she was likely not expecting any visitors.

She had sprinkled a light coating of ice melter on the walkway so that it was safe for walking. His shoes crunched on the pellets as he neared the front door. The streetlights illuminated the area just enough for him to find the doorbell. He heard chimes resonate from inside and took a step back. How many neighborhood eyes were watching him right now?

The light came on over the door and his heart rate picked up in anticipation. The *thunk* of the deadbolt and a twist of the doorknob and she stood in front of him, looking exactly as she had in her Internet pictures; about 5'5", brown hair that curled naturally just below her ears, and dressed in black jeggings, a comfy-looking sweatshirt, and fluffy, green-striped socks.

Her brow crinkled and he knew she was trying to figure out who he was. He kept his distance on the lower step so she wouldn't feel threatened.

"Hello. Are you Julia?" He knew full well that she was, but didn't want it look like he had the upper hand by letting on he already knew who she was.

"Yes. I'm Julia." She scowled at him. "Are you a reporter?"

"Ah. No. No, I'm not a reporter." Her shoulders dropped a bit, as she appeared to relax at that, though he knew she was still suspicious. He would be too if he were in her position. "I'd like to consider myself an old friend even though we've never met."

She took a step back and pulled the door a little closer to her shoulder. "What do you mean?"

"I'm sorry. I didn't mean to frighten you." He smiled and raised a hand in surrender. "My name is Dany, Daniel Howard. I've come from Halifax to meet you."

She tilted her head back against the inside of the door frame. "You're a fan?"

"Not exactly." He held up the bottle he'd hidden behind him. It only took her a second to recognize it, her eyes widening and her lips forming a shocked "O". She opened the screen door and stepped out onto the landing.

"Is that…?" He let her take it in her hands and watched as she turned it over and over, and then remove the note from inside and unroll it. She looked back up at him and shook her head. "How did you find this?"

"I found it about 20 years ago when I was visiting my grandmother who lived in a house on the Bay of Fundy. She passed on a little while ago, and while I was clearing out some of her belongings, I came across that."

She looked back up at him.

"I just typed in the name and location mentioned on the note into the Internet and your face popped up." He didn't think it was the right time to tell her about his partner's help in this. That would mean having to tell her about how he came to be cleaning out his grandmother's attic, and he didn't really think now was a good time for that. For the moment, he wanted to enjoy this encounter.

"And you came all the way from Halifax to find me?"

Dany shrugged and nodded.

"Without calling first?"

Again, Dany shrugged, then looked at the ground and shook his head. "I thought about it. My gut said meeting in person would be better."

"Your gut?"

Dany nodded.

"You always listen to your gut?"

"Not always, no. But those times I don't, I quickly realize I should have."

Julia smiled at that. "I suppose so." The smile disappeared, and a cloud seemed to settle over her. "Why are you here?"

He had anticipated the question and knew she was still trying to figure out if he was friend or foe. He'd already decided to be completely honest in telling her anything she wanted to know.

"Well, similar to you, I had a tragedy happen in my life recently and found myself needing some time to work through it all, and thought finding you would give me a little bit of fun and closure to a 20-year-old mystery. You are the Julia Connelly who wrote that note?"

She looked down at the bottle and the note in her hand, and nodded, her eyes glazing over in recollection. "It's like looking at a ghost of yourself that was so long ago."

"I'm sorry. I didn't mean to upset you." He turned to go. "I've very much enjoyed meeting you. I guess now that I've solved my mystery I …"

"No! Please, don't go. I didn't mean that. I mean, yes, it reminds me of a past life, but you've also helped solve a mystery for me. After all, what's the point of sending out a message in a bottle without wondering if anyone ever found it."

His broad smile mimicked hers. She surprised him by throwing her arms around him in a hug. He found himself instinctively wrapping his arms around her. Perhaps it was because he knew her story and wanted to protect her. But he couldn't help but notice how her body fit completely, perfectly against his, and a waft of her scent, likely leftovers of whatever shower gel she'd used in the morning caught his senses. He was disappointed when she pulled away.

"Please, come in. You have no idea how happy you've made me. This is the best Christmas present I could have asked for." She opened the screen door and he followed her inside.

Chapter Eight

Someone was in there with her. He had made sure to stick to the shadows. He was pretty sure the man hadn't seen him or sensed he was there. They'd talked for a relatively long time before she hugged him and invited him in.

He muttered a curse under his breath. This was the last thing he'd expected. The guy wasn't one of the local police officers. He knew what they all looked like. Maybe this guy was just a friend, although it did appear she didn't know him at first and she'd been ready to close the door at one point. Although he couldn't tell if she'd been angry or afraid.

He felt it highly unfair for her to apparently be getting back to some form of normal life which would mean complete disruption of his. He'd never wanted to hear her voice again. He'd already silenced the other voices, although their words still rung through his mind. He was just growing accustomed to the silence when she chose to rise from the ashes. Now he'd have to do it again, but this time another way. Killing for her reason for singing hadn't been enough. And, really, he should have seen that coming. If there was any point in the year when she'd try to get back involved in life again, it might be Christmastime.

He'd never had much time for Christmas and all the apparent goodness and peace on earth everyone talked about. He'd never experienced much of it, so perhaps that was why. But while his temper flared that she was emerging from her self-imposed, grief cocoon, it wasn't all that surprising she would try to do something at this time of year.

He watched for another half an hour and, when the guy didn't leave, he decided there was no further point in hanging around. Besides, the longer he stayed there, even in the shadows of the tree, the more chance there was of someone seeing him. The light dusting of snow on the ground would already make it difficult to make a clean getaway.

He swore again under his breath as he walked. Nothing tonight had gone the way he'd hoped. Not that he would have been able to make a second attempt tonight, but his plans for that had definitely taken another turn because of this new arrival in her life. He'd have to keep watching to see how long this guy intended to stay because he would have to time it perfectly so no one else got in the way.

Chapter Nine

"Why don't you have a seat while I tidy up?" Julia picked up her dishes from the coffee table, turned the volume on the television down, then pivoted and headed towards what he assumed was the kitchen.

"I'm sorry. I didn't mean to disturb your dinner." Aside from the dishes she'd just cleared away, the living room was tidy. A red fleece throw draped over the gray, linen sofa where she'd been sitting, and the television in the corner blinked through commercials. A matching gray chair sat opposite the sofa beside the large window covered by closed blinds and deep red, full-length curtains.

"Oh, no. You didn't. I was done." The dishes clattered slightly in the sink. "I was watching *Home Alone 2.*"

"Good movie. One of my favourites. Certainly smells good whatever it was."

"Thank you," she said when she re-emerged. "I'm really not much of a cook. But since I only have myself to feed, I only have myself to blame if I make something I don't like."

She smiled and he couldn't help but chuckle. "I guess so. I tend to order out a lot. I don't trust my cooking at all so you must be better at it than I am."

As if on cue, his stomach growled noisily. He tried to silence it with a hand. "Sorry about that. I didn't plan that, honestly."

Julia chuckled. "Don't worry about it. Can I make you something? You probably didn't get anything too appetizing on the plane."

Maybe it was the unmistakable smell of salmon that reminded him of home, but he was suddenly famished. He'd been so keyed up about the visit, he hadn't eaten much of his airplane meal.

"Actually, I wouldn't mind a little something, if it's not too much trouble."

Julia turned back into the kitchen and waved for him to follow. "Not too much trouble at all. I don't have much, though." A shadow fell over her face. "I only picked up a few things this week. I'm slowly rediscovering what living is like and cooking for one. I'm only just starting to get any sort of appetite back."

"Believe me, I understand." Their gazes met and he knew she saw the pain she felt echoed in his eyes.

"If you found me by looking me up on the Internet, then you know my story."

"It's not just that. I have a story of my own."

Julia looked down at the floor for a moment clearly in thought.

"Hmm." She glanced up at him with a raised eyebrow. "I'm sure you do. But let's not go there right now. You just got here and I'm sure we'll be able to swap stories eventually." She opened the fridge and stuck a hand in. "I did pick up some hummus and crispy naan chips." She took the tub of hummus out and set it on the counter. "This one's garlic and onion and a bunch of other spices."

"Sounds good to me."

"Would you prefer tea or coffee?" She opened a cupboard.

"Tea, particularly at this hour."

"Right." After a curt nod, she brought down two mugs and two bowls, then plugged in the kettle, and took a tablespoon out of a drawer. She scooped out a couple tablespoonfuls of hummus into each bowl, and returned the tub to the fridge.

For someone who claimed not to have much confidence in her ability in the kitchen, she seemed to know exactly what she was doing. Watching her in this more normal situation, her delicate, freckled cheeks, long eyelashes and startling blue eyes highlighted by the overhead light, the wall he'd built up around his heart in the last couple of months melted a bit. He felt completely at ease with her and not like the stranger he actually was. It was as though he belonged there. But he couldn't for the life of him explain why.

"What? What is it?" Julia had stopped her kitchen fussing and was looking at him, concerned.

"I know it's a little early to be saying something like this given that we've just met, but I think you're an amazing woman, Julia."

She long eyelashes bowed to the floor. "Thank you."

"Seriously. Here I am a complete stranger, and you've welcomed me into your house. You're actually much better in the kitchen than I am…" he smiled when she chuckled "…and I don't believe I've ever felt so at ease around someone."

"Thank you. Again. Besides, we're not complete strangers. As you said, you're an old friend, have been for 20 years. The fact we hadn't actually met face-to-face until now doesn't matter. We're joined in a very unique way."

"I guess we are."

She handed him the two bowls of hummus with naan bread chips spread around the edge. "Can you take those into the living room for me? I'll bring the tea out in just a moment. How do you take yours?"

"Oh, black for me, thanks."

He had just set one bowl on the coffee table and settled on the far side of the couch with his bowl when she emerged with two cups of steaming tea. She set one mug on the table in front of him, then sat with hers opposite him on the couch.

For a few moments the only sounds were cracker munching and tea sipping. He couldn't tell what she was thinking, but as it was her house and he was on her territory, Dany thought it only right that she be the first to ask what she needed to know from him. She'd felt secure enough with him based on whatever first impressions she had settled on about him. She had to be curious about him. Mysterious message in a bottle aside, what would have possessed him to hop on a plane and travel 2000 kilometers to meet someone without even emailing first.

"So, tell me, Daniel Howard from Halifax, what brings you to London at this time of year? Why are you sitting in my living room?"

Dany silently shook his head. It was as if she had read his minds.

Her expression was one of curiosity. Perhaps it was the artist inside her that made her very perceptive and see things beyond the surface. Whatever it was, he knew looking into her astonishingly blue eyes that he'd never be able to tell her anything other than the truth. So, he laid it all out for her – a bit of family history, his law enforcement career, the shooting and the personal and professional aftermath, his arriving in his grandmother's house, and then his journey to meet her. To her credit, she didn't interrupt or ask questions, she simply listened, nodding every now and then or mm-hmm-ing.

When he finished, she watched him for a few moments. He hoped her silence was a sign that she was processing everything he'd said rather than contemplating how to kick his crazy butt out onto the street.

"That is quite the story," she said finally, before sipping her tea. She shook her head. "I must admit, I don't entirely know what to say. I appreciate your honesty." She paused. "Besides meeting me and solving your 20-year-old mystery, what do you hope this trip will do for you?"

"To be honest, I don't really know. In one way, it was something to get me away from everything back home. When I discovered the bottle, I'd hoped that tracking down the writer of the note would provide a harmless, fun distraction."

"And when you discovered who I was and read my story?"

He waited until her gaze met his, then shook his head. "That didn't change a thing for me. In fact, if anything, that solidified for me that I had to come. I needed something else to focus on; someone else to focus on."

"You think you can catch him?" She asked with a raised eyebrow. Her eyes darkened and took on a haunted expression.

Dany shook his head, in shock. Again, it was like she could see right through him. He hadn't told her about Jack's comments about rushing off to rescue the damsel in distress. But, solving the mystery of the message in the bottle, wasn't the only reason he had come. Jack knew it. He knew it. She knew it.

"I don't know. I'm really not sure I can be of any help to the investigation or to you. It remains to be seen if I can be involved in that at all. I just knew I had to come whatever was going on here."

"And when it's all done, then what?"

"I really don't know what. We'll just have to play it by ear."

One side of her mouth tipped upward slightly at his comment, but then she fell silent for a long while, the chips, hummus, and tea forgotten. She finally rose and motioned for him to follow. Somewhat surprised and intrigued by her invitation, he followed Julia through the kitchen and then through a set of French doors on the left. A shiny, ebony baby grand piano sat in the middle of the room. The blinds had been closed over the floor-to-ceiling windows. He imagined the room was bright and cheerful when they were open during the day; the ideal place for writing songs and playing music. But she passed the piano with only a casual glance, pain emanating from her in intense waves.

Despite the pain or maybe because of that, she marched stoically to the sitting area across the back of the room, turned on the 40" flatscreen TV mounted on the opposite wall, and selected a DVD from a wooden cabinet beneath the TV. He knew then what she was about to show him.

Despite the fact they'd only just met, he couldn't help putting a hand on her shoulder as she took the DVD from its case. She didn't jump at his touch.

"Julia, you don't have to do this."

"I know. Seems kind of like a formality since there probably aren't too many people who don't already know…" she turned and he was struck by the anguish that distorted and darkened her beautiful face "…but, you've shared your soul; now I feel I need to share mine with you, and it's here, in this room. Also, you need to know what you're up against and who you're looking for."

Her gaze was like ice. So matter of fact, trying to stand bravely in front of all life had done to crush her spirit, while her knees threatened to buckle under the weight and strain.

Not only was she fighting the existence of a killer, but she was also trying to fill the hole left behind by the ghosts of her past. She had listened to his story. He owed her the opportunity to tell him her story in whatever way she felt she needed to. Her pain was so much more personal than his, and rang so much deeper because it involved family and betrayal. Maybe this was the only way she could tell him. The only way he could figure out how to help her.

He moved back and took a seat on the sectional. She put the disc in the machine and turned the television on, then, to his surprise, sat next to him and curled her hand over his. He knew it wasn't a romantic gesture, but her needing support. He didn't pull his hand away.

The screen glowed to life showing a concert in progress. The crowd was swaying and singing along. The audio was clear and in the relative darkness of the room, Dany found the music mesmerizing. He'd never really listened to her music before. Most of his musical tastes were in the more modern Celtic kind of sound of Great Big Sea, the Barra MacNeils and other groups. Hers was a contemporary style of faith-based music, encouraging, uplifting. Her clear voice, the melody and blend of the musicians and instruments drilled right into his soul and he couldn't help but be moved by it, despite knowing what was about to happen.

As the last notes of the song faded, the onscreen Julia rose from the piano and moved to stand in front of it to thank the crowd and segue into the next number. As Julia was talking, there was a commotion to the left of the screen. The onstage Julia didn't seem to notice, likely thinking it was just concert goers getting too excited. But the camera angle changed so the stage lights actually picked up a portion of the man's face as he pushed his way forward. It was clearly a man's face, though that was the only detail Dany could make out. In the next few seconds, the figure and the undulating wave of disruption closed in on the front of the stage. Security had apparently alerted them by this time because Michael appeared at the edge of the curtain about the same time Julia looked down and the figure raised a weapon.

Julia's hand clenched his. Dany placed his other hand over top of hers, offering what security he could.

On the screen, Michael dashed in front of Julia about the same time as the weapon discharged, the bullet hitting Michael square in the chest. The Julia beside him turned her head away, unable to watch as Michael fell to the floor and the whole world erupted into screams and running people. Security advanced onto the stage, but it was impossible to see how close they came to capturing the man or how the he had escaped. Given the panic following the shooting, it probably hadn't been all that difficult for the shooter to slink away. People were likely paying more attention to getting out of there and had created the perfect getaway for the gunman.

Julia pressed stop and the screen went blank, but she didn't sit up or look at him.

"That's it. They never caught him. A week later, I buried my brother. Two months later, my husband and manager left me to hook up with the next big thing. Six months later, here I am trying to rebuild what's left and I have to honestly admit I really have no idea what I'm doing. I spent so much of my life being that Julia…" she waved the remote at the TV "…I really have no idea who I am without her. So I have to completely reinvent my identity. You can't help but be someone completely different when something like this happens."

"That's for sure. Not quite the path either of us would have chosen for our lives, is it? Wish change could happen without that sort of thing."

Julia shook her head. "This way was more like having your soul ripped out and nothing but a big, gaping hole left in the middle of your life. I know that Julia is dead and I'm trying to discover what kind of Julia I'm becoming as the smoke clears from all this, although I can't imagine what was wrong with the old me."

"Maybe there wasn't anything inherently wrong with it. My nan always told me that God's path for us is often different than the path we would choose for ourselves and often to draw our attention to versions of ourselves we never would have considered or developed into otherwise. It's difficult to make sense of it all, though, when you're in the thick of it. It's only in those moments afterwards when we look back on it that we see what we've come through and what we've become because of it. Though we may never really understand why the journey had to happen the way it did."

Julia looked up at him, eyebrows raised. "Your nan sounds like a wise woman. I wondered why you didn't get offended or bent out of shape when I talked about my faith. "

"Nope. Not offended at all. It was one of the things my nan was very strong about even in the midst of her own tragedies."

Julia turned her head forward again and her body tensed. "The officer that's working on the case said I needed to get out of my house, so I spent the last few days helping others and it felt really good to be out doing something."

"I bet it did." What she had left unsaid, but Dany knew from an investigation perspective, was that the investigating officer had also suggested she get out and do something to draw Michael's killer out of hiding.

They sat in silence for a few moments. Dany sensed she wasn't wallowing, but trying to absorb any happiness she could from her community services efforts, and he didn't want to disturb that. He also didn't want to bring to her attention that her hand was still in his.

She looked up at him again. "Thank you for watching it with me and for being here, whatever the reason is that you're here."

"You're welcome." He reluctantly pulled his hand away and wrapped an arm around her shoulder, then kissed her forehead. She didn't pull away and he hoped that was because she knew he meant it as a compassion sort of thing, not a romantic sort of thing. "It was a privilege to hear you. I hadn't heard you before." He gave her a quirky grin. "I'm kinda sheltered, I guess."

She smiled. A ghost of a smile, but still a smile.

"I can see why your soul is in this room, and why it's still here."

The smile ran away from her face as grief once again settled there.

"You do have the voice of an angel," he murmured against her hair. As soon as he said it, he regretted it. He knew it was true, but her expression turned cold and she pulled away from him and stood. He half-expected her to tell him to leave.

"Not anymore. He may not have killed me with that bullet, but he did succeed in killing my soul which pretty much amounts to the same thing."

He stood and approached her, but this time did not touch her. "I know it does. I'm sorry."

The anger left her eyes, then, as she saw the compassion in his and he knew she understood that he knew more than anyone what she was going through.

"Let's get out of here."

He followed her out of the music room, the rest of the house feeling colder. Not so much from them not being together on the sofa – although that was part of it – but because of the spirit in the music room where she had once praised and worshipped and practiced and wrote the music that had encouraged and impacted so many.

"You still have that gift inside you," he said gently. "It isn't gone. Those kinds of gifts don't just turn off, you know. I'm sure you will sing again, when the time is right. As you said, you're still trying to figure out who this new you is. You may not know what your new voice will sound like or what role it will have, but I'm sure it'll come out somehow."

They were in the kitchen now and she turned and looked at him as she leaned against the counter, apparently surprised at his comment.

"At least, that's what I believe."

"You're right. He doesn't. But for now, where does this voiceless angel fit into the rest of the world. Music's been something I've done all my life. It's hard to imagine a world without it there."

"It's still there. It will always be a part of you. It may be quiet at the moment, but it will always be there. Eventually you will discover a purpose for it you might not have imagined before."

"So what about you and your police work? Do you see something like that happening for you?"

She hadn't said it to be mean or judgmental, but as another hurting spirit identifying with the same spirit in someone else. But her statement hit him full in the chest so that he had to lean on the opposite counter, his breath coming out in gasps.

He shook his head. "I don't really know. I can't really see me doing anything else. I suppose in time I'll go back." He was stumbling over his words, squeezing them out against the weight sitting on his chest. "But don't know how.... Every time...." The words stopped as visions flashed through his mind.

He closed his eyes and dropped his chin to his chest.

Her gentle hands landed in the middle of his sweater.

"I'm sorry. I didn't mean..."

"Every night in my dreams I see his face. A child's face with no life in it. I feel the metal of the gun in my hand, my finger on the trigger. I hear the gunshot that killed him. I see the tears on his mother's face. He was somebody's angel. Perhaps made a couple of poor choices, but he was still somebody's angel. And I killed him. I silenced an angel."

She wrapped her arms around his neck and he let her hold his head on her shoulder. His arms settled gently around her waist as the tears flowed between them.

Tears eventually spent, Dany looked up from her shoulder.

"I'm sorry."

"For what?"

"I got your shirt wet."

A smile lit up her face and he silently promised to keep her smiling as much as possible. She chuckled.

"That's okay. I think it'll wash out."

"And, thank you."

"For what?" she asked again.

"For the privilege of hearing you, and for your understanding. I know I have a job to do. Jayson's death doesn't change that. I need to get back to work."

He took a deep breath as he stepped away from her. He swiped away the remnants of tears from his cheeks, squared his shoulders and left the kitchen.

She chased after him. "Where are you going? You're not going back to Halifax, are you? You just got here."

She really didn't want him to leave. He knew it had partly to do with the amazing evening they'd spent sharing each other's pasts. He'd never been so completely vulnerable with someone. She was vulnerable to, in many ways much more vulnerable than he was. And she was terrified. No way he could leave her like that, no matter what had happened to bring him hear.

He turned back to her and smiled. "No." The tension from her shoulders dropped and she let out a deep breath. "I just noticed it's past 11 o'clock and I haven't checked into a hotel yet."

"No need for a hotel." She led him down a hallway to the right, and flipped on a switch. "I have two guest rooms, might as well use them."

"Really? Are you sure?"

"Of course I'm sure. Besides I figure if you were going to kill me you would have done it already."

Dany snickered. "Thanks, I think."

Her face turned serious for a moment, the terror she felt inside very evident in the creases around her eyes. "Besides, I'm pretty sure neither of our stories are finished, yet."

His hand found hers and squeezed reassuringly. "I'll bring my stuff in from the car."

Chapter Ten

A string of expletives erupted from his mouth as he watched Julia's visitor remove his luggage from the rental and head back inside.

No! No! No! This was not supposed to happen. He was not supposed to stay with her. Certainly not in the same house. This would completely interfere with any of his plans. He set his binoculars on the nightstand. It wouldn't do to break those in a fit of temper, and huffed as he paced at the foot of his bed.

What was she thinking, anyhow? She'd only just met him a few hours earlier and now he was staying over. What was she crazy? Crazy or not, she knew he was still after her and she was afraid. If her senses were heightened to him, that would make it even more difficult for him even if he could get her alone. Chances were that with this guy hanging around she likely wouldn't be alone very often.

He couldn't really blame her for asking this guy to stay. If he were her, he probably would have done something similar. But, the question remained – how would he get to her now?

Chapter Eleven

Julia lay in her bed acutely aware of Dany in the room across the hall. Drawers opened and closed for a while and then there was silence. Likely, he'd finished unpacking and was getting ready for bed. She heard him cross the hall to the bathroom and tried to focus her mind on getting to sleep. She knew she was exhausted. It had been an emotional rollercoaster kind of a day. The joy of working with the people and the sense of accomplishment from that, and then Dany arriving on her doorstep bringing with him pain of his own and needing her help as much as she needed his.

Asking him to stay had to have been the craziest and most impulsive thing she'd ever done. She hardly knew him. But, what she had told Dany was true. If he were going to kill her, he would have done so already. He could be playing her up to gain his trust and then kill her? But, he had cried over having killed a boy and she was pretty sure that wasn't an act. His pain was as raw as hers. If all he said about his stress leave were true, though, how much help could he really be? He'd been traumatized by the last time he'd used his service weapon. And he likely hadn't been able to bring his gun with him anyway. If P.O. tried to shoot her again, Dany'd hardly be in a position to offer any type of defense that way, although his experience and cop sense might come in handy in other areas.

Maybe he could think of something the local police hadn't thought of yet, a perspective coming from a fresh pair of eyes – though she couldn't imagine what that could possibly be. They'd watched the footage of the attack thousands of times from many different angles. They'd followed every lead, unfortunately without a good composite or description from her or others at the concert – it had all happened too fast – so it had been difficult to make progress.

He signed the numerous letters he'd sent her with just a simple "P.O." They were always printed from a computer, never handwritten which would have given the police something to use to compare it to others and narrow down the list of suspects. The printer paper and ink turned out to be pretty commonly used and so impossible to track down one specific owner. While his phone messages were left by a landline phone, he never stayed on long enough for the police to trace it, and the number never appeared on the call display. They hadn't recovered a weapon at the concert, only a single bullet casing. They'd traced that, but, like the printer and printer paper, it came from such a common weapon that it was impossible to track down the exact gun and exact owner. All in all, P.O.'d left very few identifiers behind for the police to search with.

The only thing they had to work with really was the gun. For him to own a gun in the first place he would have to be registered for and hold a Possession and Acquisition License. They'd searched the initials P.O. through the registry database and found hundreds of registrants with those initials. They'd followed every single one of those as far as they could go and came up empty, leaving them wondering if perhaps he had obtained the weapon illegally, in which case there wouldn't be a record of registration anywhere. The other possibility was that someone had lied to the police when they interviewed all registered people with those initials. After all, without sufficient motive against any particular individual, all the police could do was ask questions. They wouldn't have been able to search any of the properties without a warrant and they couldn't get a search warrant without having sufficient cause to request one.

Interestingly, one of the people they investigated lived only a few doors down the street from her. It was kind of creepy thinking he could have been that closely watching her, but again, police inquiries had found nothing worth digging deeper into, and the investigation had continued down the list to no avail.

He hadn't left any messages or sent any letters lately, but then she hadn't given him much reason to. Up until the last couple of days when she'd been out in public for the first time in six months, he had probably completely forgotten about her.

She didn't believe Daniel's arrival was a coincidence. During the initial days of the investigation, she had been assigned police protection; but, as time passed and fewer and fewer leads replaced the ones that been discounted, police resources had been redistributed elsewhere. And, unless she could actually go to the police with a report of direct contact with P.O., rather than just suspicions, she knew that getting police protection now would not be likely.

Granted, Dany was a wounded police officer, but P.O. wouldn't know that. It still remained to be seen how the emotional aftermath of the shooting would affect Dany's ability to protect her. Maybe if he were placed in a position where he would have to react purely on instinct to counter the doubt and fear he felt about himself would help him do what she needed him to.

The bedroom door across the hall closed and Julia snuggled into her pillow and comforter, and with one last thought of Dany, smiled and drifted off to sleep.

Dany lay in the guestroom bed, head resting on his hands folded behind him on the pillow.

Of all the reactions and possible outcomes of his quest and visit, he couldn't have possibly imagined being where he was right now – in the spare room, having spent what had to have been the most amazing evening he'd had in a long time.

His cop life and schedule had left him very little time or opportunity for dating. Heaven knew, he now had a lot of time on his hands, and after spending a few brief hours with Julia, he knew there was nowhere else he'd rather be. She had been initially suspicious, but then openly welcoming, accepting, and understanding. Amazingly so. She had also been remarkably vulnerable with him. Perhaps it was the knowledge that he was a cop, and therefore someone she could instinctively trust. Perhaps it was that he was connected to her in a way no one else could have been -- the harmless, innocent childhood mystery of a message in a bottle.

The fact that they had been brought together at this particular time, when they both needed healing and were at the stage in their recovery that they would be open to letting other people into their lives was no coincidence. There was definitely a plan at work here. But whatever came next would see them both step through their respective shadows and work together to solve the one still hanging over her life.

He'd told Jack that he wasn't rushing off to rescue the damsel in distress, which was true. He really hadn't intended to play the role of the dashing knight in armor, but he'd known that was a possibility. He couldn't have known how she would have reacted once he appeared on her doorstep. But the evening had played out far better than he ever imagined and now here he was in the bedroom across the hall wondering what life had in store for him next. Not only had he learned that she needed him, but that he needed her just as much. He knew as well as she did that another attempt on her life was likely coming.

Confrontation would be inevitable and, despite his extreme desire to protect Julia, he wondered if his being here would be more of a hindrance than anything. Regardless of his emotional state, Julia apparently believed that he could help her. Maybe in more ways than one. She was still extremely vulnerable and was just starting to climb out of her grief. She needed someone else who understood that journey to help her through it. It was so much easier doing such things with someone else rather than on one's own. And, heaven knew, he needed someone to believe in him again.

He drifted off to sleep content in that and also vowing to never let anyone hurt her again.

Chapter Twelve

Dany awoke to light streaming through the bedroom window. A glance at his cell on the nightstand showed 10 AM.

He hadn't remembered sleeping so well since the shooting, which was odd considering he was also sleeping in a strange bed. Come to think of it, this was the first night he hadn't had the nightmare. He sat up in realization and tried to recall if he'd dreamed or not. No, no nightmare.

Perhaps that's why he'd slept so long, his body had been catching up on some of the hours he'd lost over the past few months. It was always difficult to settle himself back to sleep after the nightmare, though it wasn't like he slept really well before the dream either. The police psychologist had prescribed a sleep aid for him, but he didn't like to use medication if he could help it. He knew undisrupted sleep was a key factor in his body's ability to physically and emotionally rest and recuperate.

He took a deep breath and let it out, then listened. The house was silent. Maybe Julia wasn't up yet. He padded across to the bathroom to take care of his business and brush his teeth, then dressed and headed down to the kitchen. She wasn't there, but new, used dishes sat in the sink. It appeared she'd been up for quite a while. Rustling noises from elsewhere in the house drew his attention.

"Julia?" Where was she? Had something happened to her while he was sleeping? His heart rate quickened, his senses heightened, and his hand reached for his service weapon on his hip -- which wasn't there. A mild expletive left his mouth. "Julia?!" Still no response. He followed the sound of the rustling through the kitchen, and down a set of stairs opposite the piano room. The rustling grew louder accompanied by a few thumps.

"Julia?!"

He poked his head around the corner into a storage area.

Julia grunted as she lifted a tall rectangular box on top of another. It was clearly heavy, and she was being careful how she shifted the weight, but she was determined. He waited until she'd set the box down again and looked at her efforts with heaving breaths.

"Julia?"

"Huh? What?" She turned. "Oh, hi. You're up." Her eyebrows crooked together as she looked at him. "What's wrong?"

Dany let out the biggest breath he'd ever held, his head nearly swimming with the release of adrenaline so that he had to lean against the wall. It wasn't lost on him how innocent, vulnerable, and enticing she looked in a simple pair of blue jeans and gray Roots brand sweatshirt.

In a moment, she was in front of him touching his chest. "What? What's wrong?"

"When I didn't see you upstairs, and you didn't respond when I called, I…"

"You thought something had happened to me?"

He nodded somewhat sheepishly. He wanted to tell her that it was because of the police officer in him, but he knew it wasn't the only thing that had fueled his fear.

"That's really sweet of you to worry about me, given we've only just met." She smiled then turned and headed back into her boxes. She grunted as she pulled on one. "What's happened to me is that I'm trying to find my Christmas decorations. Every year, I promise myself I'm going to leave them out so they're more accessible, but every year they seem to get buried."

Dany joined her and let out an "Ooof" as she thrust a box at his chest. Something jingled inside.

"Of course, I wasn't the one who put them away last year."

"Well, that explains why you can't find them." He deliberately tried to make light of it to keep her from settling into her pit again. The fact that she was looking for Christmas decorations at all showed she was taking another big step out of her grief and he certainly wanted to help with that. He liked to think her desire to decorate was, in part, related to his visit, and that she'd woken up feeling freer than she had when she woke up the previous morning.

"Yeah, I guess I can blame him and do it right this year." She released a tall, rectangular box with a picture of a tree on it and set it next to the wall, then attempted to move a stack of boxes over. Dany set the box she'd given him on the floor and braced himself to help push. "Thank you," she said when they landed against the opposite wall. "This'll go so much faster with you around."

"Glad to be of service, ma'am." Dany tipped an imaginary hat and did his best to speak with a Southern drawl.

She smiled. "Well, then, if you can slide this pile of boxes over there, I think I will finally be able to get these ones out."

Dany did that, and the moment he stepped back, she shoved two giant plastic blue bins toward him.

"We'll probably need a couple of trips to take all this upstairs." He hoisted the Christmas tree box onto his shoulder. "Where's this going anyway?"

"Living room," Julia grunted as she hefted one of the blue bins off the floor high enough to make it up the stairs.

"You sure you don't want me to come back down for that?"

"Oh no. I'm good."

He led the way up the stairs and through the kitchen, although when he arrived in the living room and set the Christmas tree box just inside the doorway, he realized that Julia wasn't with him. He backtracked through the kitchen and found her standing at the doorway of the music room, the blue bin at her feet.

"Hey," he said gently as his hands squeezed her shoulders. "What's wrong?"

She took a shuddering breath. "I can't explain it. I want to decorate this room too. I used to have a Christmas tree in here and in the living room."

"Then let's do it." It took enormous strength to stare at the room that held the most pain for her and for her to conquer all the memories in it. "I'll be right back." He trotted back downstairs, located a second Christmas tree box, and carried it upstairs. "I think we need to do this room first."

She looked at him, tears bedding her eyes. "I think you're right." Her hand touched his. "I don't think this would be possible if you weren't here."

"I think you still would have thought of it, but might not have gone through with it."

She nodded. "Probably."

"There's a lot of love in this room." He switched on the light. "You-know-who tried to take that away from you. I think inviting and allowing that love back in is the best way to break you-know-who's hold over you."

Julia smiled as the tears streamed down her cheeks and her body shook with sobs not of grief, he sensed, but with release. He set the box down and wrapped his arms around her, her head coming to rest just above his heart. He rubbed her back and let her cry until she was all cried out.

"Thank you," she said when she was done. She reached for a tissue from the box on a side table inside the door. "You're right, of course."

"Just glad to be of service, ma'am." The Southern drawl and tipped hat was back.

She laughed, a tinkling, pleasant sound he knew he would never forget. Her hand touched the center of his chest. He couldn't resist taking it and kissing her palm. She smiled again, this time her cheeks flushed pink, clearly aware of the connection between them and not ashamed of it.

Still, he felt he'd overstepped his bounds, intruded on her trust by reacting so instinctively.

"I'm sorry. I shouldn't have done that."

"Why not?"

He shrugged. "We've only just met. You've invited me into your house. And you and I are both still very vulnerable."

She drew close to him. "I can't think of anyone I'd rather be vulnerable with than you."

Compelled by the same instinct that made him reach for her hand, he touched his lips to hers, gently at first and then a little firmer, his thumb stroking the teary, softness of her cheek.

She shook her head. "I don't know what it is about you being here."

He shrugged again. "I can't explain it either. I had the best sleep I've had in months, no nightmares and I certainly didn't intend for this to happen at all."

She touched his cheek again. "I know you didn't. Neither did I. But perhaps it's the swift kick in the butt we needed to get us back into reality." She grabbed one end of the Christmas tree box, as he grabbed the other, and maneuvered it past the piano to in front of the fireplace about midway between the piano and the sitting area.

"Dany…"

A shiver of pleasure rushed through his body at the sound of her voice virtually singing his name.

"…could you bring up the rest of the boxes?" He looked down at the floor and smiled. That was not entirely what he thought she was going to say.

"Certainly."

By the time, they'd set up the tree, coiled the lights around it, distributed the ornaments and added a few other festive things to other areas of the room it was well after noon.

His stomach growled.

Julia looked at him and brought a hand to her mouth. "Oh my goodness, I'm so sorry. Here I am working you so hard and I haven't even fed you yet."

"That's all right. Why don't we go out and get a break? I'm assuming there's more decorating to be done."

"Yes. The living room and the outside of the house. Have you ever hung lights before?"

Dany nodded. "A long time ago for my nan, but I have an apartment in Halifax. We don't tend to hang Christmas lights when living on the 12th floor."

Julia smiled. "I can see why. It won't be too hard. Mike – We, ah, put up clips one year and it makes the whole light hanging process very easy." Her smile faltered at the mention of her ex-husband, and her face flushed. "I'm sorry. I guess I still talk about him a lot. When you spend so much of your life with someone ... just like P.O., I guess, he just keeps coming up."

"I understand that. That's okay. It's not like he's direct competition or anything."

Julia smiled and took his hand. "Not at all. So, where would you like to go?"

"Well, are there any places that still offer breakfast at this hour?"

"I know just the place."

Chapter Thirteen

"Good-a morning, Miss Julia!"

"Good morning, Sammy." Julia greeted Sammy's broad smile with one of her own as he rounded the counter and with hands on her shoulders, air kissed both cheeks. Her nostrils drank in the intoxicating scents of oregano, garlic and other spices Sammy used in his famous marinara sauce which mingled with the unmistakable aroma of crispy bacon, warm toast, and coffee. Just the therapy she needed.

Sammy's was her only safe haven outside of her home. It wasn't just Sammy's amazing Italian and Canadian food, but also the atmosphere. Sammy's brilliant smile never seemed to fade and was precisely the medicine she needed to keep her going. Sammy never criticized or sent her on her way if he felt she were loitering. He seemed to understand her need for solitude even when she was out of her house, and seemed to take pride in the fact that she found it at his restaurant.

Sammy's was always busy. People rushing in and rushing out on their way to wherever. Couples, singles, families sitting or meeting up. Sammy's had been a stalwart figure of the neighborhood for as long as she, and anyone else, could remember. She was pretty sure it had something to do with his all-day breakfasts, but that couldn't be the only reason. She shuddered inwardly at the thought of what would happen when Sammy decided to retire.

Sammy's eyes widened at the sight of Daniel beside her.

"Anda who is dis wit you?"

"This is Dany. He's a friend from Halifax."

Sammy grabbed Dany's hand, his words punctuated by hearty joviality. "Ah, from Halifax. Whad'ya know! So glad my Julia has a friend." Sammy lowered his voice conspiratorially. "If you ask me, Julia need more than a friend. She been so lonely." His voice brightened again. "But now you come and cheer her up. It been a long-a time since I see Miss Julia this happy."

Julia couldn't stop the heat that rushed to her face.

"Glad to be of service," Dany replied, and took her hand.

"Ah! Wonderful." Sammy clapped his hands as he dashed behind the counter once again. It was astounding how such a rotund man, who obviously loved food, could move so quickly. "What-a can I get-a for you?"

"Two of your famous Sammy's breakfasts, please."

"Ah, you hungry today!"

"We've just been Christmas decorating."

"Ah. I understand. Coming-a right up-a. Jus have a seat. I bring out to you."

"I take it you come here a lot?" Dany asked once they'd settled in a corner booth.

She took the seat with her back to the restaurant, and he sat facing her with a clear view of the rest of the restaurant over her shoulder. He got the feeling she always sat at this table with her back to everything. It was likely the only way she could get out and still have the privacy she needed.

Regardless of whether she intentionally sat there or not, he was glad for it. His cop sense had been on high alert since he entered. Not about Sammy. He was pretty sure Sammy's enthusiasm was genuine and not just an act for his and Julia's benefit, and did not pose a threat. He seemed to genuinely care about Julia.

He hadn't been able to survey the whole diner when they'd first walked in, but now, he had the perfect vantage point from which to scrutinize the other patrons, who were in various stages of eating. The restaurant itself had 60's style formica tables and plastic-coated, red cushioned chairs and faux leather booths. The beige, textured wallpaper had long since lost whatever color it once had and plastic flowers wrapped around the sconces at each wall-side table. Four booths lined the wall and a set of four tables-for-two ran across a wall separating the eating area from the entrance. Two other single tables had been set up on either side of the door, recessed with the front windows.

As for the people, a couple sat at a table for four a few spots down from them. Their dishes had been cleared and they were chatting and sipping away at two steaming cups. They were too far away for him to hear what they were saying. An older lady sat at one of the tables for two along the inside wall, nursing a cup of coffee and reading a *New York Times* bestselling title. Nothing seemed out of the ordinary with those three.

The only other person in the restaurant was a thin man also sitting at a table to the right of the door. He was wearing sunglasses. Kinda strange, but then he was in the window and despite it being early December, the sun was still bright. Maybe he had sensitive eyes. His cop sense though was off-the-chart and he'd learned over the years to trust that instinct. Granted, it was because of the one time that instinct had failed that he was sitting across from Julia now. His heart panged so that he had to white-knuckle the edge of the table, but he disciplined his mind memorizing everything he could about the man in the window.

"Dany?" Julia's sing-song voice and concerned expression brought his attention back to her. Her hand found his free one on the table top and squeezed it. "What's wrong?"

He gave his head a hard shake. "Sorry, my mind was sort of wandering and reminded me how I came to be sitting in front of you."

"You looked like you were deep in thought."

He sat back against the seat, arms crossed and shook his head again. "Silly cop thing. Scoping out the place."

"And that took you back to that night at the store?"

He nodded, not really embarrassed, but upset with himself for letting that memory intrude on the happy time he'd spent with Julia decorating, and the conquering of the ghosts of her music room, which was a huge victory in her recovery journey.

"I know all too well how memories can intrude whenever you least expect them. You don't need to hide them from me."

Dany looked down at the tabletop.

"Guess I'm not as strong as I thought I was. I had a great time decorating with you." He smiled. "Actually, I can't ever remember having so much fun, and thought, just for one day, it wouldn't haunt me."

"Well, you managed to get through one night and most of today. I'd say that was an accomplishment. Every little step or bit of time you spend where you're not completely consumed by what happened is a victory and step toward coming back to life again. Don't be too hard on yourself."

She gently released the fingers of his other hand from their grip on the edge of the table and brought it onto the tabletop. "I believe in you even if you don't quite completely believe in yourself, yet. When the time comes…."

She didn't have to finish her sentence. He knew very well what she was thinking. And the trust in her eyes drove away, at least momentarily, any self-doubt he had about being able to protect her.

Sammy appeared beside them, then, with two steaming plates of sunny side up eggs, Canadian peameal back bacon, crispy, circle-cut "tatoes" tossed with onions and seasoning salt, and perfectly browned, buttered triangle-cut toast slices. He set the plates in front of them.

"I'll-a be-a right back wit your coffees?"

"Yes, please," they said in unison.

"Uno momento."

Sammy bustled back moments later with two coffees. "Enjoy-a, you two!"

He waited by the cash register as Sammy shuffled back from delivering food to the couple in the back corner.

Not just any couple. Her and the apparently new man in her life. He'd almost spit his coffee across the table when they'd walked in. Then Sammy had appeared to welcome *him* as a friend, like it was a good thing. What may have been a good thing for her was bound to be a bad thing for him. Dany apparently was his name according to her introduction to Sammy.

He'd also overheard that they'd been decorating for Christmas. She was getting stronger and looked happier than he'd ever seen her, except perhaps when she had been performing. After six months of misery, how had she managed to make such strides as to appear in public the way she had? And how was it if she'd been to Sammy's since the shooting, he'd never met up with her until now. Anyway, now that she appeared to be getting out of her house more, there was more of a chance that he'd bump into her again. She still had no idea who he really was and that would make hunting her all the more fun, though a part of him still wished she were hiding away. It would have made his life so much simpler. One less voice in his head.

Even in the brief time *he'd* been in her life, it was obvious that her visitor played a part in her transformation. Now, instead of her huddling back in her hole after the press coverage, she was growing more confident.

He didn't hear Sammy's prattle as he rang up the total for his meal.

"You have a lovely day-a, Peck."

He forced a smile to his face. He had sensed Dany's eyes on him earlier, and it wouldn't do him any good to make a scene and give Julia's guest any reason to suspect him further.

"Thanks, Sammy. I'll see ya later."

With a wave, he walked out, the bell above the door jangling behind him.

Dany watched the figure go, his face hidden behind the sunglasses and body covered by a long black wool coat appropriate for the cold weather. The only description Dany could get was Caucasian, about 5' 8", slim build given how the coat billowed around him as he moved, and clean shaven. He walked with a confident gait, no hesitation, no limp or scuffing. Not much to go on, but better than nothing. Of course, all he had was his suspicion though. He couldn't go to the local police with a hunch, despite Julia's faith in him. The tricky thing was going to be trying to find out who this guy was and whether he in fact had any connection with Julia's brother's death.

Julia turned and looked in the same direction he was.

"What is it?"

"Oh, nothing." Dany mentally cursed himself for watching too long. He was supposed to be working to divert her from any anxiety, to help her come back into life and enjoy the little things again.

"You were staring over there for a long time. Did you see somebody you knew?"

"Oh no." Dany waved a hand. He didn't want her to worry about anything else but Christmas decorating. "Just another old cop thing. Can't turn it off."

"Do you think he was here?"

Damn! Why did she have to be so insightful? He met her gaze.

"Oh, I don't know. I'm suspicious of everybody. I probably don't know the people here like you do, so I don't really trust anybody around you."

Her smile sent shivers down his spine.

"That's very sweet of you given I've only known you for less than 24 hours."

Dany shrugged and one side of his mouth tipped up. "I'm a long-time friend. And yet you're the one who invited me to stay."

This time, Julia shrugged and shook her head. "I really don't know why I did that."

Dany settled back against the booth and slid into law enforcement mode. "Yes, you do. Despite the obvious connection between us, you know your life is still in danger and you're terrified, and I would be too if I were in your shoes."

Julia looked down at the table. So much for trying to keep her distracted. No matter what he did, this shadow would always be hanging over her. She may learn to do other things and gradually come more and more out of her depression-imposed isolation, but it would always be there, unless....

Dany sat forward again and took her hand and kissed it. He wished the table weren't between them so that he could hold her and so she could draw strength from him, but holding her hand would have to do.

"You and I both know he's still out there. And since no one has a description of him, he could be anyone."

Julia nodded, eyes still on the tabletop.

"He's kept you in a prison of grief since his attempt to keep you locked in a prison of fear failed. I have a feeling I've gotten in the way of any plan he might have come up with to start stalking you again. He very well may be doing that already, but he never counted on me being here, and I think that has thrown him off his game, flustered him."

"You really do think he was here."

Dany shrugged again. "I don't know, Julia. It really is just a kind of sixth sense. I have nothing to go on. It was a gut reaction and I've learned to trust my gut."

She shivered.

"Hey." He waited until her gaze met his. "You know I'll protect you the best I can. I don't intend to let anything happen to you."

"I know."

With the earlier setting winter sun, the sky was already growing dark and sunlight would be gone in another couple hours.

"But, for now, I'll settle for fueling up with this amazing meal, and then hanging some Christmas lights."

Julia smiled. "Sounds like a plan."

Chapter Fourteen

Julia sat back against the arm of the sofa, a steaming cup of gingerbread tea warming her hands. Lights twinkled on the Christmas tree they'd just finished decorating, bright-colored bulbs bubbled around the living room window, and icicle lights glowed around the eavestroughing.

Despite what had happened at Sammy's, she'd thoroughly enjoyed her evening with Dany. As anticipated, the already mounted all-season hooks let them put up the outdoor lights in less than an hour. And now, at 10:30, they were relaxing and admiring their handiwork and the cheerfulness the lights gave the whole house. It seemed to almost completely dispel the reality of her situation. It could change at any time, but for the moment, her world was at peace.

She let out an exhausted, but satisfied sigh.

"What was that for?" Came Dany's voice from behind her. He sat in a chair also nursing a cup of gingerbread tea.

"I don't know what it is about Christmas lights. It's one of those things I think we should do all year round. They're cheerful and bright and, for whatever reason, peaceful. I don't even know if it's really their association with Christmas that does it. I find it somewhat odd that it's okay to turn them on for the few short weeks leading up to Christmas, but try leaving them on at other times and people say, 'What do you have your Christmas lights on for?'"

"Hmm. I know what you mean." They settled into another moment of silence.

"I think we did a pretty good job." Julia sipped her tea and let the heat seep through her body until she thought she might fall asleep.

"I would have to agree. Not bad for a day's work."

Julia's mind played over the day including their meal at Sammy's and Dany's possibly having seen P.O. at the diner. Dany wouldn't have had any clue what he looked like, no one did. But she had no doubt it was him. And, although today's almost encounter had been entirely coincidental, she could pretty much guarantee that not many other P.O. appearances would be. She also knew that meant Dany would become very deeply embroiled in the investigation with Constable Davis. Since the rest of her week was filled with volunteer hours, that would at least give Dany something to do.

She sat up and set her tea on the coffee table.

"I have to get something from my car."

Dany sat up quickly. He looked ready to protest her going.

"What do you have to get?"

"Constable Davis' card. I expect you'll want to talk to him about the investigation." She stood.

Dany jumped up and placed a halting hand on her arm.

"Do you have to do that right now?"

"I want to do it before I forget. I'm volunteering tomorrow and in the rush of getting out and getting there, I know I'll forget to give it to you."

Dany was clearly weighing his concern for her over the possibility that he might be overreacting to such a simple thing. "All right. I'll watch you from the window."

She slipped on a jacket and headed out under the glow of the blinking red, green and white lights. On their return from the diner, she'd parked her car half-way up the driveway so they could get around with the ladder and the lights. Dany's rental was still parked on the street. She pressed the unlock button on the FOB as she approached.

Julia had just stepped down from the porch onto the walkway, when her cell phone on the side table rang. Dany silently cursed the annoyance. Answering the phone would mean having to take his eyes off her for a few moments and he didn't want to risk that. But as the ringing phone nagged at him, he finally succumbed and picked it up, wondering for a split second why her voicemail hadn't picked up.

"Dany speaking, Julia's phone. She's not here right now. Can I take a message?"

"Sure. You can tell her I think you did a bang up job with the lights. So cheerful and everything. Reminding the world of the light of Christmas."

The voice was breathy and tauntingly angry. This person was obviously not a friend with every word being spat in sarcasm and disgust.

Dany's blood pressure sky-rocketed and he rushed back to the window. Julia was almost at the car door.

"Who is this?"

"Oh, my name's not important. What is important is the problem with the lights."

Dany knew he had no choice, but to play along. If he kept whoever it was talking long enough perhaps he would give up information he could provide the police.

"What's that?"

"They're not quite bright enough for me. But, like I said, a *bang* up job."

Dany caught the emphasis on the word "bang". Julia's hand was on the door latch. He dropped the phone and charged out the front door.

"Julia! Stop!"

She was about to lift the latch, but she turned.

"But, I…."

Damn that she parked the car so far away, and even with the presence of ice melter, the wintery conditions made it dangerous for him to run as fast as he needed to. He watched helplessly as she turned back to the door and everything happened in slow motion.

"No! Don't open that door."

"But, I…."

He finally reached her as she lifted the latch and pulled the door open. He grabbed her by the waist and launched them both onto the snow-dusted lawn as Julia's car exploded into a ball of flames.

Despite the heat of the house, Julia sat on the sofa, her gingerbread tea long forgotten, shivering under a wool blanket while the police poured over the scene outside. The charred remains of her car had been taken away for further investigation, and the neighborhood crowd that had initially gathered had dispersed since the initial excitement was over.

She was barely aware of Constable Davis in uniform blues sitting in the chair where Dany had sat only a couple hours before, staring at her and talking to her. Shock had fogged her senses. Shock that *he* had gotten to her. Shock that *he* had planned it all – from planting the device on her car without them seeing, which meant he'd been planning and waiting for the opportune moment, and then calling her cell, knowing full well Dany would answer. Shock that he was so obviously still watching her. She hadn't said a word, leaving Dany to tell the story, but everything gelled together on a subconscious level, despite her emotional cocoon.

Dany watched the tidy up and scene-containment efforts from the living room window. The whole incident replaying in his mind along with thoughts of what it would have done to him if *he* had succeeded in killing her.

"He was watching that's for sure," he muttered. "He knew the moment she stepped out the door. He had to have been watching to know when he could plant the device without us seeing him." Dany turned and faced Constable Davis who rose from the chair. "I also don't think he really intended to kill her. If he had, he wouldn't have called her cell phone to tell me at the risk of me being able to stop her in time. I think it was a scare tactic to get her to back into her little hole."

"Hmm." Constable Davis smiled despite the situation. "Very keen observations. I can't lie to you, Senior Constable Howard…"

Dany raised a hand. "Dany, please. I'm off-duty."

"Dany," Davis conceded, "I won't lie to you. We have done everything possible, gone over every piece of information we have, video recordings, audio recordings, every tip that was phoned in, but P.O. has very successfully kept us in the dark." Davis turned and walked to the head of the sofa. "How long do you plan to stay in London?"

"Until he's caught."

Davis smiled again.

"And I want to assure you that Julia asked me to stay with her. I didn't ask. But it was obvious to me that she anticipated something like this happening. I couldn't say no."

Davis nodded. "I understand that. And, in truth, I'm glad for your presence here. Up until this attempt on her life, I wouldn't have been able to assign any officers to her protection and, with you here, I don't have to worry about that so much, and I can focus on seeing if this bomb can provide us any new information."

"I would like to do more than just stand in as a bodyguard, Constable Davis--"

"Clint, please."

Dany smiled this time. "Clint. I would like, if you don't mind, to go over the evidence you've got already and the results of your investigation. Not that I think anything was done poorly or improperly. I'm sure you've been very thorough. But, I'd like to be a fresh set of eyes on that information."

Clint nodded again. "That's probably not a bad idea given that this appears to be starting back up again." Clint scratched his head. "I've combed over everything in my mind wondering what I've missed. Was there something, something so obvious — you almost become too familiar with things and may miss a little snippet of conversation or whatever? A fresh pair of eyes would be welcome where I have very limited resources right now."

"Well, I've already given you my description of the man I saw at the diner, and that I overheard Sammy call him by his name, although I was too far away to hear what it was. It might be a place to start." Dany looked down at the floor. "I should also tell you that I'm currently on stress leave for mental health reasons and so wouldn't have any right or jurisdiction to participate in anything else. I don't even have my service weapon with me since I had to turn it in."

Clint rubbed a hand across his chin. "Hmm. You were the one involved in that shooting of a kid a few months back."

Dany nodded and turned his head to one side. "Yeah."

"Believe me, I understand."

Dany looked up again. "Thanks."

"Whatever your status, we need you here. She needs you here." Clint bobbed his head at Julia sitting motionless on the couch, knees clutched to her chest beneath the blanket. "I would like you to accompany me when I go interview Sammy tomorrow. And I will see what I can do about getting a temporary transfer for you. Your leave isn't for disciplinary reasons, so I should be able to temporarily reinstate you."

"Won't I have to go through psychiatric evaluation or something to prove I'm fit for duty? It's not that I'm unable to help in an investigation, but to be able to handle a weapon again...?"

Clint nodded knowingly. "Well, we can probably get you working with the resources we have here. I'm going to ask that we temporarily reinstate you with proviso that you work with our psychiatric staff." He lowered his voice and leaned forward conspiratorially. "You know as well as I do where this situation is potentially heading. You've already shown that your head is in the game. I really don't think it's going to take long for the rest to follow."

Dany glanced at Julia. Whatever had happened in the past, Julia needed him. It wasn't coincidence that they were brought together at this time. He didn't believe in coincidence. His nan would have said it was a "God-cidence". Not only did they need the companionship, but she also needed personal protection that the local police couldn't provide. He couldn't imagine what it had been like for her to step out her door alone with the obvious threat hanging over her. He wondered if she'd ever imagined her next encounter with her brother's killer would have been her car exploding.

"You put her up to it, didn't you? Getting out again, I mean."

Clint looked down at the floor. "Yes. The trail had gone cold. Even though she wasn't physically dead, she might as well have been and we would never be able to catch him. I honestly didn't think he'd react so quickly." Clint turned and looked at Julia, then moved to sit next to her on the couch. "Julia, look at me."

Her head turned, but she didn't say a word, her body quivering under the blanket. Dany stood at the arm of the couch. He wanted to do nothing more than to hold her and tell her that she was safe, but he knew that wasn't true, and something told him that she likely wouldn't accept physical contact right now, so he just crouched beside her. Perhaps she would take some solace and strength from him being near.

"Julia, I wanted you to know I think you're doing the right thing. Regardless of what he does, you deserve to have a life and to not live in fear of what he's going to do. He's made you a prisoner. You need to rediscover the Julia that persevered and performed anyway despite his threatening letters and messages. You didn't let that stop you."

"No. And my brother is dead now because I didn't stop."

Her words were like a knife through his heart.

"No," Clint said emphatically. "Your brother died because we were unable to catch him in time. You getting out in public again will draw him out, and he'll make a mistake. We've already got new information we didn't have before that will put us on his scent. This time we will catch him."

Julia didn't say anything, but stared straight ahead again. All Dany could see was her sliding back into her little shell and he would give anything to keep her where she'd been earlier today digging out Christmas decorations, eating out and engaging with other people, and hanging Christmas lights. Would she be able to come back from this?

"Well, I'd better go see how things are going outside." Clint stood. "Go to sleep, Julia, if you can. That will help." When she didn't respond, he walked to the door, Dany followed him.

"Thank you for what you've done here tonight," Clint said as he offered his hand.

Dany shook it. "I didn't really do anything special."

"It may not seem like it now."

"No, it seems on a certain level I've contributed to the problem rather than help."

"I know. But if we're ever going to be able to catch him, this needed to happen. I'm just glad she isn't alone. I will get back to you about the transfer. Come and see me in the morning."

"Will do."

Dany stared at Julia from the doorway for a moment before approaching and sitting where Constable Davis had been.

"Julia? Please let me hold you."

She nodded and leaned against him, as his arm curled around her shoulder, her body warm and quaking next to his. He rubbed her arms and kissed the top of her head.

"You can't sit out here all night. You really need to get to bed. That's the best recipe for shock. You have volunteer time in the morning." Hopefully reminding her of made plans would coax her off the couch and into her bed. But she didn't move. After a few moments, the quaking subsided and Julia's breaths fell into a regular, deep rhythm.

Without loosening his hold on her, he settled himself against the arm of the sofa at his back, laid his head against the cushioned corner, and drifted off.

Chapter Fifteen

His hands rested behind his head as he gazed at the living room ceiling drunk in the soul-satisfying thrill of the hunt. A contented sigh escaped his lips.

Everything had gone perfectly. He really didn't think he'd succeed this first time. It was meant more as a reminder to her that he was still watching her – not like she'd ever forgotten. But the blast that rocked the neighborhood had been glorious. He hadn't intended on any collateral damage. It was lucky she'd parked her car away from the house.

It had been pretty simple to plant the device on her car once they'd gone inside. As far as he could tell, they were so caught up in their decorating they never even noticed him watching them from a couple lampposts away. He'd been careful to change his clothes after the encounter with Dany in the diner.

Later, in the aftermath of the blast, he'd stood outside the police barricade with the other nosy neighbors watching the clean up.

Yep, everything had gone more perfectly than he'd imagined. And they still had no idea who he was. Dany had pegged him at the diner, true, but hadn't seen his face, and clothes were easily changed. He knew the cops were waiting for him to make a mistake so they could pick up his trail, but he settled to sleep secure in the knowledge that he hadn't made any today.

Chapter Sixteen

Dany awoke to a cold spot where Julia had been, the intoxicating aroma of freshly brewed coffee, and soft-rain patter of the shower. He inhaled deeply as he sat up, disappointed he'd woken up alone, but thankful Julia was up doing normal things. That told him she was fighting back against P.O.'s attack on her yesterday, which was a good sign.

He stretched the kinks out of his body as he stood, his legs and back protesting. He'd been remiss in his fitness routine since his leave. Since it appeared he would be staying here a while, it would be worth getting back to at least some jogging. That would serve two purposes, keep him fit and give him a chance to scope out the neighborhood.

A glance at his watch told him it wasn't quite 7 o'clock, which correlated with the relative morning darkness of Eastern Standard Time, with the sun peeking over the horizon. He had just poured his coffee when his cell phone rang.

"Dany? Clint, here. How'd you guys make out last night?"

Dany was tempted to say, "Actually we didn't," but resisted.

"She drifted off to sleep not long after you left," he said instead. "Seemed to have slept well. No disturbances. She's up now having a shower. I know she's scheduled to volunteer again this morning."

"I'm assuming you're going with her?"

"Of course. Wouldn't think of letting her go alone. Besides mine's the only vehicle at the moment."

"Good. I'd like to interview Sammy after the early breakfast crowd, say, around 9?"

"That should be fine. That would give me time to drop her off, go for a run and then get cleaned up."

"Great. I'll meet you over there about 8:45 and we can go in together?"

"Sounds good. But, how…?"

"I've already been in touch with Halifax, this morning, since they're an hour ahead of us. I should have the paperwork in by the time we meet."

Wow. Certainly didn't waste any time. This was happening a lot faster than he ever thought and he relished the surge of adrenaline that often came with the thrill of the hunt of a criminal. It was one of the things he enjoyed most about police work. When done right, nothing could match the sense of achievement and pride in seeing the outcome of hard work. When done wrong …. He shook those thoughts from his mind. No time to be dwelling on the past and the self-deprecating thoughts that lingered there. It was time for him to take control of himself again, doing what he loved doing, and protecting someone he cared very deeply for.

"Sounds good," he said again. "I'll meet you at Sammy's at 8:45."

The shower shut off moments later just as his phone rang again. He dropped a sliced, multigrain bagel in the toaster, then set four eggs to boil on the stove, as he cradled the phone with his shoulder to his ear.

"Y'ello."

"Dany-boy! How are ya?"

"Jack! Gosh, it feels like ages." Dany leaned against the doorframe of the music room.

"It hasn't even been a week."

"I know."

"How are things?"

Dany sighed.

"That good, huh?"

Dany smiled. "You know what you said about the damsel in distress?"

"I hate to say I told ya so."

Dany laughed. "No, you don't. You love telling me that."

Jack's hearty laughter rang through his ears. He knew Julia would likely appear in the kitchen at any moment, and though she was well aware of his involvement in the case, he really didn't want that to be their first point of conversation for the day.

"Listen, I won't keep you long because I know you've got things to do today. I wanted to tell you that we've received the request for temporary transfer from the London Police. Clint Davis has assured us that their mental health services will be keeping an eye on you, and the powers that be, here, appear to be satisfied with that. Actually," Jack lowered his voice, "I think they're pulling for you to get back in the saddle and are relieved to see you get involved in something."

Dany raised an eyebrow. Oh, he was getting involved in something alright.

"Anyway, I gotta go. Don't be a stranger, eh? I've been your partner for ten years and you just kinda dropped me like a hot potato."

Dany chuckled. "Sorry. I'll keep you posted."

"You'd better."

Just as Jack hung up, Julia appeared behind him with a plate of toasted bagel with strawberry cream cheese and two peeled, perfectly hard-boiled eggs. She wore a pair of black pants with a poinsettia-colored blouse that flared at the hip, and her hair pulled back neatly with a clip so that the length of it flowed down around her shoulders. And when she drew closer, he caught a whiff of her freshly showered scent. The sight and smell of her rendered him practically speechless. When she got close enough, he wrapped an arm around her waist and kissed the top of her head so he could inhale as much of her as he could. What was this effect she had on him?

She blushed when he let go. "Is that what I get for bringing you your breakfast? Hmm, maybe I should do that more often."

"Sorry." He followed her back to the kitchen table where they took opposite chairs. "Couldn't help myself. You're the most beautiful thing I've ever seen."

She blushed again. "Thank you. I know volunteering may not seem like an occasion to get dressed up, but these people need a little happiness in their lives. For so many of them, this is the only ounce of happiness they may have during the year."

"You're the most amazing woman I've ever met. Even in the light of your own troubles, you find room for compassion for others."

"That's the most important reason to do it. To make sure P.O. doesn't win and *He* does." Julia pointed to the ceiling, but Dany knew she was pointing to the heavens. "The whole Christmas season is about light shining in the darkness; even a tiny one, the size of a child, can make a world of difference. I'm pretty sure that's the main reason P.O. has targeted me. My music sings out that message, and for some reason, his life has had so much darkness in it, that the light is more of a threat than a relief."

Dany considered that as he munched on his bagel.

"D'you really think that's why?"

"Don't you?"

Dany shrugged and bobbed his head to the side. "Probably. So many of the criminals I've come across have a story, something hidden. A teacher who says the wrong thing, or some complete stranger passes them on the street and does something that makes them question everything. It could be something major or something so minor it leaves you shaking your head as to how such a little thing could have such an impact."

"True. I've wondered that from the very beginning of this whole thing. Why has he done all this to me? What has happened in his life that has caused him to hate me so directly? Perhaps it's just a misunderstanding. So many people can't grasp the concept of the loving, heavenly Father I sing about with so much badness going on in the world. I'm not sure I could ever explain it myself. But until someone feels the impact of faith, meets Christ on a very personal level, the world is a very dark place. I'd often hoped if I just had a chance to talk to him, I might be able to give him the hope and peace he's desperately seeking. I believe that's at the root of any kind of crime like this. People don't know what to do with the hurt in their lives and react in kind of a kill-or-be-killed way."

Dany shook his head.

"What?"

"D'you really think you would--could do that? Convince him to give it up, I mean?"

"I know I should feel angry with him. People might consider me crazy for not feeling that way. But, I just know there's so much more going on in P.O.'s mind and I know that whatever it is, if I could show him how to let all that go and turn whatever he's experienced into a way to make a change that could make sure it doesn't happen to anybody else.... I know it would set him free, even though the change of heart won't keep him from going to jail."

Dany watched her from an angle as his head tilted to one side in amazement. "I honestly don't know if I'd be able to do the same if it were me, but I understand why you need to try. My nan would probably agree with you." With a lopsided smile, he popped the last of his egg in his mouth. "So, what time do you need to be there? I assumed 8 o'clock."

Julia nodded through a mouthful of egg. "Yes, and I'm there until 4. I'm sorry to leave you alone all day. I didn't plan to have a visitor when I booked my hours."

Dany waved a hand. "Don't worry. I'll keep busy enough."

"You're going to help Constable Davis today, aren't you?"

Dany nodded. "Appears so."

"I think that'll be good for you."

"My partner appears to agree with you."

"Was that who you were talking to when I walked in?"

"Yes."

"Checking up on you, was he?"

"Yeah. He can't seem to help it." Dany's mouth curled into a smile. "He's been my best friend for ten years, I guess he can't really let it go."

"So, how are we going to work this?" Julia turned serious for a moment and he almost ran around to the other side of the table to shake her back into the happier Julia he'd just been speaking to.

"I'm assuming you mean transportation and protection for you?" Again, he slid seemingly seamlessly into his police mode. It was coming easier. He pushed his finished plate aside, perched his elbows on the table and intertwined his fingers. "I'll drop you off and pick you up. I don't want you going anywhere without someone with you, preferably me. And don't be afraid to call me for any reason." He dictated his cell phone number to her which she programmed into hers. "You know as well as I do that he's watching and can appear anywhere when you least expect it. I don't want you to be so frightened and hyper-aware of where he might be that you don't enjoy engaging with the people, but given last night, I imagine your senses will be on alert anyway.

"He showed last night that he views me as a threat, a barrier for him getting to you. He knows he has to separate you from me for him to get able to you. He has to take me out of the picture."

Julia gasped. "You don't think he'd…?"

"Literally take me out of the picture?" Dany shrugged. "That may be a possibility, but that's my job, Julia, keeping you safe, even if it means my life for yours."

She stood and wandered into the kitchen, shoulders hunched, her back to him.

"Julia?"

"That's what Michael did."

He stood and followed her. "I know."

"The same thing could happen to you." She hung her head and a tear fell from her cheek.

"I know." He hoped his gentle, but matter-of-fact tone would help her accept that something like that might happen. For him, it would all be in the line of duty.

"You would really give your life for mine?"

"That's my job, but that's not the only reason I'd do it. That's what love does, Julia. Love protects. Yes, Michael died trying to protect you because he loved you. And, I can't explain it, how our hearts seem to have connected the way they have, but I would give my life if that's what it takes to save yours."

When she didn't say anything he continued.

"One of nan's favorite verses was the passage that says there is no greater love than to lay down one's life for one's friends?"

Julia turned, every inch of her beautiful face wrenched with anguish. "Then you should go back to Halifax."

Stunned, he took a step back and shook his head. "What?! Surely you don't mean that."

"I do. Really, you should go back. Job or not. I couldn't..." a sob escaped her throat "...I've already been responsible for one person's death and that's going to haunt me for the rest of my life." She shook her head as tears spilled down her cheeks. Her words broken by sobs. "I couldn't bear it if I were responsible for yours too."

He folded her into his arms. "Now, now don't start. You won't bring happiness to all the people you see today if you show up with red, poofy eyes." He felt her chuckle more than heard it even through her tears. He wished he could promise her that he would do his best to stay alive, but that was one of those piecrust promises – easily made, easily broken. The confrontation they both dreaded was coming, and there was no way to predict when or how it would happen – or what the ultimate outcome would be.

But there was one thing he could say.

He rubbed her back and kissed the top of her head again. "You're not responsible for what P.O. does or did. You're not responsible for Michael's death or the choice he made to jump in front of that bullet to protect you." He tilted her head up so her gaze met his. "You're not responsible for any of this. P.O. took that control away from you and you're starting to take some of that power back, and he's feeling threatened. I honestly don't know what's going to happen, but if anything does happen to me, I don't want you feeling responsible for it. You haven't done anything wrong. It's P.O.'s choice and his only. And you know what?"

Julia shook her head.

"I knew as soon as I read your story that I had to come. Jack warned me about rushing off to rescue the damsel in distress, but I knew that's exactly what I was doing. I chose to come anyway, knowing the risks. Although, I have to admit, I really didn't plan on this." He slanted his mouth over hers, her body surrendering into his for a few blissful moments. "You're not going to get rid of me now. What's coming is not going to be easy, that's for sure. But I wouldn't dream of letting you go through it by yourself."

Julia's body molded to his as if she were trying to absorb strength from him to assuage her fears.

"I guess there's no sense in trying to talk you out of it?" she asked as she looked up at him again.

He shook his head. "Not a chance. You're stuck with me."

"Well, I suppose you ought to get cleaned up while I take care of the breakfast dishes. I have to be there in fifteen minutes and I assume there's probably media people waiting for me outside."

Dany nodded. "Right. Give me five."

When they emerged precisely six minutes later, they were greeted by the crater in the driveway asphalt, Dany and Julia-sized outlines in the front lawn snow, and a handful of reporters.

Julia looked up at Dany. Even though it was a relatively small group, she felt as if she were facing the Spanish Inquisition.

"You don't have to talk to them if you don't want to."

"Well, it's not about wanting to. We don't really have time this morning."

She tried to use their presence to distract her from the evidence of the attempt on her life, but had it not been for Dany standing beside her, she might have turned and run back inside. His strength was driving hers right now.

"Sorry, guys, I don't have much time to comment. I have to be somewhere in ten minutes."

"Just one question," one reporter asked, the same reporter who had interviewed her at the volunteer center a couple days before.

"Yes, Mariah."

Julia didn't think she'd ever get used to having a camera pointed at her. She certainly wasn't afraid of standing and speaking in front of an audience, but the camera seemed so … impersonal.

"We all know that there's been another attempt on your life…"

Julia nodded. She reached behind her for Dany's hand to keep panic from spiralling through her body at the reminder and flash of memories.

"…we just want to know if you have a message for your attacker?"

She looked up at Dany and saw his determination and love for her. It was enough to strengthen her soul to say what she wanted to and mean it.

"I do." Julia turned and looked right into the camera. "I know you're watching this. And I know you're watching me. I have no idea why you have targeted me, and why you keep doing such things, but no matter what you do to me, you will not win. There is so much more to life than the hate you've obviously been living with, and today I am renewing my choice to not let you take over my life, and rule over me in fear."

Julia looked back at the reporter who looked like she was about to hug her.

Instead, with a broad smile Mariah said, "Thank you."

With that, the mini-media circus parted, and they reached Dany's car without any further interruptions.

Julia let out a breath she didn't know she'd been holding. She was used to addressing thousands of people in concerts and other events, why was her body shaking and heart racing? Perhaps it was because she'd finally confronted P.O. directly. It may not have been face-to-face, but it may as well have been because oddly enough, it felt like he were standing right there. She took deep breaths in through her nose and out through her mouth to try to dispel the panic.

Dany glanced around as he waited for Julia to get in, and then again as he walked around to the driver's side.

He had a feeling they were being watched, and not just by the media. *He* was there.

Julia'd been so focused on responding to the press she probably couldn't sense *him*. While she was talking, he'd scanned every square inch of the neighborhood, as far as his vantage point would allow him. There wasn't anyone particularly obvious, but then it was highly unlikely P.O. would make himself stand out from the crowd now.

With one last glance at the media vans parked around the neighborhood, Dany slid into the driver's seat.

"I thought you did awesome," he said, as he put the key in the ignition and the engine fired to life.

"Thank you. The press aren't really hostile to me around here. Everyone knows the story." She looked down at her lap, her hands folding and unfolding themselves. "Do you think he was watching?"

Damn! She did it again. Completely catching him off guard. He didn't know if she meant if P.O. had been watching from the neighborhood, or watching on television. But, again, he knew he couldn't lie to her.

"Yes. I think he was."

Julia surprised him again when she took a deep breath, smiled and then nodded.

"Good. Let's go."

Peck peaked out from behind the Channel 22 van across the street which had served as his watching post. He couldn't hear what she had said, but he'd set his PVR to record it while he was out. Given how the reporters had reacted – or not – and were now heading his way, it was clear that this was no longer newsworthy, and they were off in search of other local stories.

He knew Dany had been alerted to his presence. Dany had been looking in every direction, and would have picked him up if he hadn't ducked back behind the van at just the right time. The next time he peeked out to look at the house, he'd made sure he blended in with the group of reporter heads. He had no idea how Dany had even known he was there. It was an instinct, a kind of ESP he'd only seen with … cops. That was it! But if he was supposed to be protecting her, he wasn't packing a weapon, so he wasn't on duty. And the Kia was obviously a rental and not department issue.

His mind churned with it all so that he almost didn't notice a reporter and her cameraman approach the van until it was nearly too late. He pulled his hoodie up, turned around the side of the van, and headed toward his house. He had somewhere else he needed to be anyway. He was a car length or two away when he heard the sliding door of the van open.

Now that the report was done and the camera off, Mariah Colverton tugged the knit turtleneck higher up under her chin, then flipped the lined hood of her beige jacket over her head and clamped her hands over her ears as she and Craig headed back to the van.

She hadn't been out that long, maybe about an hour waiting for Julia to emerge, and it wasn't that far below zero, but an hour had been long enough for her ears to get frost nip.

"Where to next, boss?"

"Don't know y-yet."

A hunched, hooded figure ducked behind the other side of the van. When she reached that corner, she peeked around to see the back of a man who was attempting to slink away. He was trying to make it look like he was casually walking, but he kept a brisk pace that belied the fact that she and Craig had almost caught him watching them. Her trained reporter's eye knew he was trying to look like a young person in the hoodie, but his pants weren't dangling around his knees and his shirt was still tucked into the waistband. One thing was for sure, he had been watching the crowd in front of the house. That wasn't unusual in and of itself, but then why had he been hiding behind their van and not standing out in the open? She'd seen him poking his head around their van as they walked back. Then a thought had occurred to her that perhaps it was *him*. Coming back to admire his handiwork. He wouldn't have been able to hear Julia's statement from that distance, but that wouldn't necessarily have kept him from watching her. That's what stalkers did.

Her cameraman was about to pack up the gear when she set a hand on the top of the lens case.

"Craig?"

"Huh?"

"Don't put that away yet."

"Huh? Why?"

"Shh! I want you to get him." She pointed. "Can you film him without making it look like you're filming him?"

Craig's smile gave her the answer she needed, and he sat himself on the curb with the camera on his shoulder, using the van ahead of them as cover. Mariah stood over him, peering around the corner of the neighboring van, until he disappeared. But he didn't just disappear, he turned into a yard about six or seven houses away about where the street curved.

Mariah nearly clapped with glee. "Did you get him?"

"Mm-hm," Craig said as he hopped up off the curb. "And, I can probably give you a pretty good idea of which house is his, too."

Mariah beamed. "Craig, I could kiss you!"

He laughed as he returned to the open side door and placed his camera in its case. "That won't be necessary."

Chapter Seventeen

Dany pulled the car up to the staff entrance of the Community Housing and Social Services building. He surprised her by unbuckling his seatbelt.

"This is a no parking zone, you know?"

"I know. Wait. Don't get out. Wait for me."

Julia wrestled with her temper. She didn't want to be angry with Dany. He was doing his job. But even when she was touring she never liked people and things interfering in how and what she liked to do. She had meant what she said to the reporter that she wasn't going to let P.O. dictate how she should live her life, and yet Dany was doing everything based on the fact that P.O. was around.

She scowled as she stepped out once he'd opened the door.

"What?"

"Is this really necessary?"

His gaze held hers, his intensity and confident authority sent her simmering temper cowering.

"Do you trust me to protect you?"

"Yes."

"Then, yes, it's necessary."

"It's just this extra cautiousness and protectiveness just kinda rubs it in what's going on and what he's trying to do and what I'm trying not to let him do."

Dany pushed a lock of her hair aside. "I know. But, it has to be this way. There's no way of knowing what he's got planned next. I have to be sure before I leave you." His lips came down gently on hers and the building swirled around her. She was breathless when he stopped. "You have to trust me 'cause I would never forgive myself if something happened to you."

She tried to respond, but her voice wouldn't come, so she just nodded.

"You go in first, but not too quickly. I want you to stay where I can see you."

It sounded almost like her mother's instructions as she headed out to play when she was little, in the days when they lived by the Red River in Winnipeg. By the time they'd moved to London when she was 10 following the death of her father, she'd far outgrown her mother's instructions. She shook her head of those memories, very keenly aware of Dany's imposing 6'2", 230lb presence and people's stares as she greeted the other volunteers. She couldn't tell if they were only curious about Dany's appearance in her life since they'd seen her the day before, or if they were concerned with the news reports about the car bombing. Perhaps it was both.

"Good morning, Martha." Julia hugged the older, curly-haired lady as they met in the hall. She had fallen in love with Martha's bubbly personality the instant they met, and Julia realized just how much she needed that bubbliness. Martha was one of those workers whose compassion and unmitigated love for children had won over the hearts of many adopted children and grandchildren and great-grandchildren. When Martha wasn't working with the Christmas Hamper program, she was in the libraries and schools reading to children and visiting children in hospitals. Martha's joy shone like a lone candle in a dark room, which was the only world many people who came to the Community Housing and Social Services knew. They all needed a reminder and escape from that darkness even for a few minutes, and that's what Martha was to them.

"How are you doing, sweetie?" Martha's gaze held such concern that Julia knew wasn't just asking about her health.

"I'm doing fine, thank you, Martha. Really."

"Really? You wouldn't be lying to me now, would you? He tried to hurt you again."

"No, I wouldn't dream of lying to you." Julia slid her cell into her pocket and turned into the small staff kitchen where she secured her purse in a locker and took stock of what was left in the two bags of child-appeasing toys and stuffies she kept there. Dany waited at the door, looking up and down the hall, seemingly content that there was no immediate threat in the kitchen.

"You've brought a young man with you this time."

"You don't miss anything do you, Miss Martha?"

She wore a broad smile as she shook her head. "No. Nothing. Besides, how could I miss this?"

Dany turned then, took Martha's hand and kissed the back of it, looking like Rhett Butler in *Gone with the Wind*.

"Dany Howard, ma'am. I'm visiting from Halifax."

"Halifax, eh? You here to protect our Julia?"

Julia gasped.

Dany nodded, completely good-natured. "That's my job, ma'am."

"Good. She needs a good man in her life, not like that husband of hers that just up and left her after the tragedy with her brother. So sad." Martha shook her head.

Dany's gaze met hers over Martha's head, so intense that she felt heat rush to her cheeks, and she was thankful Martha was still looking at Dany.

"I don't plan on going anywhere."

Martha nodded in approval. "Glad to hear it. Well, I'm going to go get set up at my table. I'm surprised we aren't swarmed already this morning."

"I better get out there, too."

"Just a minute." Dany held up a hand.

"But, I ..."

"I want to check the place out first before I let you go."

Julia, with great effort, dowsed her temper. "Right."

The Social Services Christmas Toy and Food Hamper registration room was actually a gymnasium with several tables set up around the perimeter, each one labelled with different alphabet letter pairings. The tables were set against the wall so each volunteer faced the middle of the room. With this set up, there wasn't any place for P.O. or anyone else, for that matter, to hide.

"Can I go now?"

"Yes, it looks good."

Julia headed to a table labelled M-P set against the wall adjacent to the door so that a person had to turn as he or she entered the room, and those supervising the tables wouldn't immediately see who was coming through the door.

"You sure you want this table?"

Julia scowled. "I can't change everything because of him. I refuse to second-guess myself."

Dany nodded. "Okay. I'd much rather you be at a table that would allow you see the door."

Julia's face relaxed. "I can understand why. But it's not like I would recognize him anyway. I've never actually met him."

Dany leaned over the table so he was almost nose-to-nose with her, and kept his voice level, but laced with authority so there would be no doubt in her mind what he was getting at. "You may not know who he is, but he knows who you are."

She raised a finger to his mouth. "I know. But I'm not going to focus on that. These people need my help. He's not going to stop me from doing that."

He couldn't resist kissing her finger that lingered over his lips. "I wouldn't dream of stopping you from doing that, but you need to be careful." He knew it was time for him to go. He had to do his run, and meet Clint at Sammy's. Still, he had to nearly drag himself away from her.

She seemed to sense his reluctance because she took his hand and squeezed it. "I'll be fine. Really. There's a key hidden under the step plate at the front door. It's slightly loose and will lift up."

She really was trying to get rid of him. "Call me. Text me. Anytime. And don't leave here alone. I will come in and meet you at 4."

At her agreement, he headed out to his car. A disgruntled driver was waiting for him.

"What you doing parking there?! This no park zone?! I call the police!"

"I am the police," Dany tossed over his shoulder, as he slid into the driver's seat, then maneuvered the vehicle out of the parking lot and steered back to Julia's house.

Ten minutes later, he'd changed into running gear and set out on a half-kilometer path to the right, wandering through a couple side streets and then back again. It was only a fraction of his normal run, but it was all he could do with the half-hour window he had and he would need time to shower before going to Sammy's. He normally had music driving his tempo, but this morning he had so many things on his mind he decided to forego the music. Julia, P.O., the car bomb, and theories and fears over where this entire investigation would take them both. There was no real way to predict what P.O. would do next. He knew Julia didn't like the idea of watching around every corner, and was annoyed he was doing it on her behalf.

She was trying very hard not to be a prisoner in her own house, in her own community, in her own life, but P.O. was making her attempt at regaining her freedom very difficult, and, if he had his way, her freedom could be the last thing she achieved. He wondered for the umpteenth time since he'd learned who Julia McIntyre was why P.O. had targeted her. Why does any stalker target anyone? Someone does something, perhaps taking a public stand on a particular issue. The most obvious thing about Julia was her music. Perhaps it had something to do with her music, her faith, even a particular song. It wasn't unusual in the current offended-about-everything-and-anything society for someone to take issue with a faith message of any sort.

"A bit cold for a jog, this morning, in't?"

Dany raised his head and shook thoughts of Julia and her stalker out of it. He was approaching a man about his age dressed in ratty jeans and an old, well-worn green polar fleece with a Green Bay Packer logo on it. Dany slowed his pace a bit as he processed the man's appearance and that of the property he was leaving. The clothing didn't quite match the apparent meticulousness of the two-storey Colonial. The windows were clean, the siding lacked the layers of grime that most other houses in the neighborhood had, the driveway and walkway didn't have a speck of ice on them, and the shrubs encircling the living room window were covered with a protective tarp. Someone who paid that much attention to outdoor detail wouldn't leave the house in such scruffy clothes.

Dany smiled, while alarm bells rang in his head. "Yeah, a bit. But I'm usually out in all kinds of weather."

The man grinned then turned and headed toward his garage. "That's right persistent of ya. You must be heartier 'n me." The man rubbed his arms with his hands.

An eastern Canadian accent. But hard to tell if it was his natural voice or a put on simply for Dany's benefit. Dany pegged the man to be in his late 20s.

" 'ave a good day, sir."

"You too." Dany waved a hand and jogged on. But, instead of continuing along the sidewalk, Dany stepped onto the road on a diagonal track towards Julia's house. When he got there, he turned and looked back over the path he'd come. That man's house was on a direct line of sight with Julia's. Dany bet a large sum of money, far more than his police officers salary, that he would have a perfect vantage point from from the second storey to watch Julia's comings and goings.

But suspicion alone wouldn't be sufficient reason to get him a warrant to search it. Julia had mentioned something on the drive over to the community center that morning about one of the previous leads being someone just down the street and how that lead had gone cold. He was going to need more information.

Fifteen minutes later, showered and clean, Dany arrived at Sammy's. Clint was already waiting for him, and greeted him with a firm handshake.

"Good morning, Dany."

"Good morning."

"I have something for you." Clint reached into his unmarked cruiser and withdrew a bulletproof vest, a service weapon, and a holster. "I'm assuming you still have your badge?"

Dany patted his front pocket.

"Don't know if you're going to need this stuff with Sammy, but you never know."

Dany tossed his jacket on the passenger seat of his car while he strapped on the vest.

"How was she, this morning?"

"Determined to be strong and not let P.O. get in the way of what she wants to do."

"I expected as much. That was a pretty feisty statement she gave to the media this morning."

Vest in place, Dany donned his jacket again, then pulled the weapon out of the holster and inspected it. "Are you sure it was a good idea putting her up to making herself bait for him?"

Clint shrugged. "I don't know about it being a good idea, but his trail had gone completely cold. It was either that or he remain at large. You know as well as I do he would have remained in hiding so long as she did."

"Yes, I know."

"Her doing that was the only way to draw him out into the open. He obviously feels threatened by her, and with her completely off his radar there's no reason for him to target her anymore. I didn't tell her when or how to do it; she decided that on her own. I certainly had no idea he would do what he did last night. That's not how I envisioned his re-emergence at all."

"How did you imagine it?"

Clint shrugged. "I really don't know. I thought he'd start off with notes and phone calls again. I didn't think he'd go right to attempted murder. I get the feeling he likes the build up to the event as much as the event itself."

The bell above Sammy's door jangled as Dany pushed through the door.

"Ah, good-a morning-a! Mr. Dany and Officer Clint. How are you? What-a can I get-a for you?"

"Some information from you, Sammy." Clint leaned on the corner of the counter and lowered his voice. While the main breakfast rush was over, there were still a few customers and he didn't want them to overhear or think Sammy was being investigated for something. "Do you have a couple minutes? It won't take long."

"Of course, follow me." Sammy waved a hand and led them behind the counter to a little office just before the kitchen which smelled of an interesting combination of breakfast, burgers, tomato sauce, and oregano. Sammy closed the door. "Now, what-a do you need to know?"

At Clint's glance, Dany asked, "Remember when I was in here with Julia yesterday?"

"Of course-a. How-a could I have forgotten you and-a Miss Julia?"

"Do you also remember the man that was sitting by the window with the long black coat and the sunglasses?"

Sammy's eyes dowsed of their usual joviality. "Yes. He no say much. His name is Peck. Dat's all I know. He started coming as a little boy, been about twenty-some years, I think."

That was intriguing. "Peck? No, last name?"

Sammy shook his head.

Damn! But now they at least had one initial figured out.

"Do you know if that was a nickname or his real name?" Clint asked.

"Don' know." Sammy shook his head. "I only ask one time what-a his name and dat's all he said. An' not very friendly-like either."

"Has he been here when Julia was?"

"He usually arrive after Julia, every time, at least when she wasn't touring, and always sit in front of the window."

"Have you ever seen him without the sunglasses on?"

"Most-a da time he wears those sunglasses. The only time he took dem off was not long after Julia's brother were shot, he came in and she wasn't here."

"Would you be able to describe him?"

"Brown eyes. Pointy nose. That's all he show. He always covered with hood up. Didn't seem to have much to 'im, needs some hearty Sammy cookin', en."

Dany smiled in spite of himself. The remedy for everything was either a good British cup of tea, or hearty Italian food. "Anything else you remember about him?"

Sammy shook his head. "You think he done dat to Julia's car?" Sammy's face flushed red at the thought.

Dany looked at Clint, then back to Sammy, and shrugged. "Just a hunch, nothing really concrete, yet."

Clint leaned in. "Sammy, I hope I don't have to tell you not to let on to him that we've been asking questions about him."

"Officer Clint, if he done something to hurt Julia, you have my promise dat I won't say a thing to him."

"Thank you." Dany followed Clint's lead and stood to leave. "We'll let you get back to your customers."

"It my pleasure." Sammy led them out to the front of the restaurant again.

Outside, Dany could hardly contain himself over the information Sammy'd given them.

"Well, that was certainly more than we had before," Clint said, snowflakes forming a small teepee on the crown of his head.

"I have more...." Dany told him about the man he'd met while jogging and his observations.

"You think P.O. – Peck – and that guy ...?

Dany cocked his head to one side. "Hard to say for sure. I didn't get a close enough look at him to know if he had brown eyes. He was wearing baggy clothes, so I don't know that I could definitively say he matched the body type of the guy Sammy calls Peck."

"Still, it's worth a look through our evidence files."

Dany smiled. "I thought you'd never ask."

Chapter Eighteen

Julia wound her way through the lines of hopeful, stressed parents, squalling babies – with at least one needing a diaper change – and fussy children to her table, greeting all with whom she made eye contact with a smile and a good morning. A little girl with blond pigtails looked up at her with the biggest, most startling hazel eyes she'd ever seen.

Julia crouched down with a cup of hot apple cider in one hand.

"Hi, there."

The little girl shuffled behind her mother's leg and peeked out.

"Have you been a good little girl for mommy today?" Julia cast a glance up at mom who didn't seem too sure.

The little girl nodded.

"Are you sure?"

The girl nodded again, this time a little more emphatically.

"What's your name?"

"Mia."

It was barely a whisper, so Julia had to lean in to hear her.

"Well, since you've been such a good girl waiting with mommy, I have something for you." Mia's eyes widened and Julia felt them on her as she returned to her table. She had also drawn the attention of the other children in line. She set her cider on the table and picked up two bags, one full of dolls and other stuffies, and one full of cars, trains and trucks.

She returned to the line. Mia was bouncing on her toes, barely able to contain her excitement.

"Mia, because you've been such a good girl, you can pick one toy from either of these bags."

Mia looked up at her mother, who nodded with a smile. Julia didn't know if the smile was out of thankfulness for Mia getting a little toy, or for the fact that she was keeping the girl occupied for a few moments.

Mia reached into the doll and stuffy bag and pulled out a small Raggedy Ann doll. Her eyes lit up and she hugged the doll tight. Then, without warning, Mia flung her arms around Julia's neck, nearly knocking her over.

Julia hugged back. "You're welcome, Mia."

Other children started crowding around.

Julia set Mia back at her mother's feet. "You have a wonderful Christmas, Mia, with your new doll. I have to help these other children now, okay?"

Mia nodded, and her mother smiled a thank you.

After handing out the toys to the other children waiting in Mia's and other lines, Julia returned to her table, her cider no longer steaming, but still warm enough to soothe. Just the aroma of the cinnamon sent chills of relaxation through her body. She'd read somewhere that inhaling cinnamon increased a person's mental capabilities. She certainly hoped that were true. She needed that boost to get through the rest of her day. She could feel her energy draining fast, despite her lunch break.

Her first couple hours had been pretty busy with a steady stream of people making their way over. She had cleared her Christmas food hamper and toy registration line by 11:30 and had decided to take a quick break before the next onslaught. It wasn't the plight of the people coming to her for help that consumed her mind and energy, although some of their stories left her thinking how it was sad that all this focus on helping the poor only happened at Christmas time, leaving families to struggle through the rest of the year. In actuality, the constant stream of people early on – and Mia and the other children – helped her forget, temporarily at least, her own personal situation and P.O.'s attempt on her life, though it simmered in the background.

She'd hardly thought about it all morning. But, now that the crowd had ebbed at least around her table, her mind turned to the evening before. It didn't even wander before ending up there; it just sort of pounced there, as if the memory had been waiting in the wings for the just the right moment of mental inactivity to re-impose itself on her life.

She didn't know if the car bomb was P.O. reminding her that he was still watching her, as Dany and Constable Davis seemed to think. She thought it equally likely that it was an act of protest against her getting out to do more things, trying to get out of the prison of fear he'd had her living under, or because of Dany's presence in her life. Even if P.O. didn't know Dany was a cop, the fact he had shown up on her doorstep and within a few hours had become a semi-permanent fixture in her house meant Dany presented an extra obstacle for P.O. to get around to get to her. Perhaps he had been frustrated by that and had planted the bomb.

All she remembered about the bomb going off was Dany's arms around her and her face full of snow while fire burned behind her. She vaguely remembered Dany carrying her into the house, checking her over for any injuries and then setting her on the couch with a blanket, all the while talking to the 9-1-1 operator. Constable Davis had arrived on scene at one point, as she kind of suspected he would, though she couldn't say exactly how long it took him to get there, how long he stayed or when he left. The next thing she remembered was the house was quiet and Dany's arms were around her and his body was next to hers, and that's when she'd surrendered to sleep.

When she'd awakened, her head resting on Dany's chest, his heart thumping softly beneath her ear, he'd looked so peaceful. His strong cheek bones, stubbly face, full lips … she'd been tempted to kiss him, but she was sensitive enough to him to notice he hadn't had any nightmares again that night, and decided to let him sleep. Instead, she'd taken his other hand, which had slid off the couch, and examined it. She gasped when she saw the cuts, singed hair and burn lesions on his strong fingers and back of his hand. She'd sat there for a few moments with tears streaming down her cheeks at the reminder that Dany had put himself at risk to protect her. After a few more moments, she knew she needed to get a shower if she were to make it to the community services on time, so she kissed the injured areas, and then gently laid his hand across his stomach.

Instinct had told her Dany was bound to get involved in the investigation, not only because he was a police officer, but because everybody wanted to see P.O. caught, and Dany just happened to have experience the police needed. She was so lost in thought that it took her a second to notice the man in jeans, a green polar fleece, and hood pulled up waiting at her table. She was struck by his chocolate brown eyes.

"Oh! I'm sorry. My mind was completely wandering away." Julia quickly smiled and gratefully shook further thoughts of P.O. away as she focused on the man in front of her. "What can I do for you?"

"I'd like to register for a Christmas hamper, please. I haven't had much work. Luckily, I don't have a family to provide for, it's just me, but I don't have much left."

Julia nodded. "Absolutely. Have a seat and we'll get this sorted out." The man sat and she took down his information. Anthony Oberman. Age 45. Unemployed. Address: 4809 Nightingale Rd., London.

Julia recognized that this was not far from her house, but kept that realization to herself. While she needed to be friendly with registrants, she couldn't get too familiar with them and let them know too much about herself. It didn't seem that many of them recognized her, and that was actually okay with her.

"All right, Mr. Oberman. That's all the information I need. Please sign right there." He signed it, then handed the card back. She set it aside, handed him a green sheet of paper and verbally reviewed with him the instructions on it about when and where to pick up his Christmas hamper.

"Thank you," he said, green sheet in hand.

"You're very welcome. Have a great Christmas." She watched until he'd vanished behind the crowd of people waiting in line at the table next to hers.

As Julia picked up the signed information card to file with the others, she noticed a small Christmas-card sized envelope. Perhaps it was a thank you card. It wasn't unusual for some registrants to do it. She opened the flap, slid the card out and opened it, and her breath stuck in her throat. The note wasn't handwritten. It was done with letters cut-out of newspapers and magazines.

You are Always on my Mind.

P.O.

Chapter Nineteen

"Julia?"

Dany? Why could she hear him but not see him?

"Julia? Come on. Wake up."

Wake up? What was he talking about?

"Is she going to be alright?" Martha asked.

"I think so." Dany again.

What did Martha mean? They were talking about her. Why wouldn't she be alright?

"Come on, Julia. Open your eyes."

Her eyes popped open to see Dany's face above her, and Martha's and others beyond him. She realized there was a weight on her chest, and found it was Dany's hand holding hers.

"Wha--?" She tried to sit up, but the world spun.

"Easy." Dany's free hand on her shoulder helped her get upright.

"Wha- what happened? What're you doing here?"

"You fainted, honey," Martha said.

"Fainted?" She thought back to what she'd been doing. She'd been at her table. The man. The card. In her hand. Her eyes widened and panic crushed her chest as she clenched Dany's hand and showed him the card crumpled in her other hand.

Dany's expression turned from one of concern to one of anger. "I'm taking her home."

"Of course," Martha said. "She's been through so much."

"You take her home. I'll go out with you, but will have things to take care of here." Constable Davis was there too.

Minutes later, after giving her a chance to grab her purse from her locker, Dany plunked her in the passenger seat of his car and strapped her in, muttering a torrent of mild expletives. Constable Davis hovered over Dany's shoulder.

"He was there, wasn't he?" Dany asked as he squatted in the open car door.

Julia nodded. She still couldn't get her voice through the pressure in her chest. She managed to unclench her hand to show him the card. Dany twisted out of the way as Constable Davis reached for it with a gloved hand.

"Did you get a good look at him? Did you find out anything about him?"

Julia nodded again.

"Did you get a name?"

Julia widened her eyes and nodded. She tried to get the name out, but all she managed was, "A."

"Adam?"

Julia shook her head.

"Andrew?"

Head shake.

"Anthony."

Julia nodded enthusiastically.

Dany smiled. "Good girl."

"I'll check your registry box when I go back in. I'll let you get going now." Constable Davis stood. "I'll come around your house later and let you know how far we get."

Dany stood too and closed the door, leaving her in the cocoon of the vehicle. She rubbed her arms with her hands, but felt very little of their warmth. Her mind felt frozen – not cold, but as if in a fog, paralyzed, unable to move or think. After talking for a few more minutes, although she couldn't make out what they were saying, Dany opened the driver's side door and slid inside.

Though he wasn't outwardly raging or anything with his temper, she could sense it. It vibrated through him, and she wished she could break through the haze around her to let him know she didn't blame him and that, despite what had just happened, she was alright. All she could do was look at him and try to make sure he saw the message in her eyes. Instead of fear and timidity, she forced resolve and tenacity to her face in stark contrast to what her insides felt. Perhaps this appearance and attempt at strength was as much for him as it was for her. It was all she could do until her body started cooperating again.

Dany restrained the urge take out his temper on the steering wheel. Instead of pounding it to pieces, which was what he was tempted to do, he wrung his hands around it until he was sure it would come apart in his hands.

How could he have been so stupid as to have left her there all by herself? His lack of sense had put her directly in an opportunity for P.O. to get to her. Maybe she was right. Maybe he should go back to Halifax. Fat lot of good he was doing here. He opened his mouth to tell her and then turned and met her gaze. Instead of defeat and surrender to the fear, he saw determination and defiance in the midst of it. He knew she had to be terrified and what he saw on her face was probably more for his benefit because she knew he felt responsible. Still he felt a confession was needed.

"I'm sorry, Julia, for leaving you. I should never have done that."

Julia shook her head, as she still struggled with words.

He took her hand, squeezed it, and kissed it. "I put you in danger today. Now, I know I could never protect you. I'll take you home, and head back to Halifax. You were right. I should go back."

Julia shook her head more frantically this time.

"I – I was wrong." Her voice cracked, barely a whisper. "You're not to blame for what he did. I need you here."

She echoed the very words he had used with her earlier to reassure him that he wasn't to blame. Logic agreed with her, but he still felt like he'd failed her.

A car horn from behind jarred them both, and Dany got the car moving.

What was she doing here?

Peck stared at the well-dressed woman standing on his front step as he pulled into his driveway. She didn't look like the JWs or Mormons that occasionally campaigned up and down the street. What could she possibly want? Instead of parking his car in the garage as he normally would have, he stopped in front of it and got out instead, anxious to send his visitor away. He wanted to relish his afternoon's accomplishment and watch the news coverage he'd PVR-ed that morning.

"Can I help you?" He called as he rounded the car. She smiled and followed the walkway down to him. He recognized her as she got closer. Mariah Colverton. Channel 22. But she was alone. Apparently, she'd left her cameraman at home.

"I hope so. Mariah Colverton, Channel 22."

"Yes, I know who you are."

"You were watching us this morning at Julia McIntyre's house."

"There were a lot of people watching."

"I don't mean on TV, Mr. …?" When he didn't offer his name she continued, "I meant from across the street, from behind our van specifically. Why would you do that?"

"Why did you think it was me?"

"We saw you slinking away and my cameraman was able to figure out which house was yours."

Damn! This was an unexpected complication. First that Dany showed up, and now this nosy reporter. He had to get her inside before neighbors noticed.

He smiled. "You and your cameraman are very astute." He looked around for her vehicle. "How'd you get here?"

"My car's parked just down the way. I didn't think you'd like coming home to see a strange car in your driveway."

He gave her a thin smile. "Certainly not." His mind churned with how to get rid of it, a diversion for the police when they eventually showed up, but first he had to take care of her.

"All right, Ms. Colverton. Come along."

He led her through the garage to the side door. It wouldn't do to have her come in the front door where someone might see her.

"You have a lot of courage coming here on your own." Courage. Hardly. If she really suspected who he was, she had to be the stupidest person on the planet.

She smiled back. "I figured you'd feel uncomfortable with a camera here. I thought it would be better just you and me."

"Hmm." Better for me anyway. He unlocked the door then pushed it open and swept a hand inside. "After you."

"Thank you."

Mariah's heart leapt into her throat and threatened to choke her, but there was no turning back now. Perhaps she should have allowed Craig to come with her. She just hoped the recorder in her purse was picking up the whole exchange.

She stepped into what appeared to be a mudroom with a small dining area off to one side, and a kitchen on the other. The kitchen was tidy and clean, but the dining area – or at least what used to be a dining area – was full of pictures, newspaper clippings stapled, thumbtacked and pushpinned to every square inch of space of the walls and ceiling. They were all of …

Mariah gasped and raised a hand to her mouth, then whirled to face him. "It is you!"

His slanted, sly smile sent shudders of terror and revulsion down her spine. She needed to get out, but he stood between her and the door. The front door. If she could get through the kitchen, but just as the thought formed in her mind, he stepped close enough to grab her wrist and twist so that bones snapped. She screamed in pain and her knees crumpled, but he held on and met her nose-to-nose.

"Yes, me." He dragged her down the set of stairs next to the side door and she now knew why he had come in this way. Going through the front door would have been too public. Heaven only knew what was waiting for her down below.

He didn't turn on a light as they descended so she could only see shadows of boxes and other things through the fireworks of pain in her eyes from her broken wrist. It was damp, gauging by the musty smell which deepened as they walked farther away from the stairs, and the ground beneath her feet was soft and rolling, rather than hard and flat like concrete.

"You know you won't be able to hold me forever. My cameraman knows where I am. He knows I came here."

"I won't need to hold you forever. Just long enough."

He stopped, opened a door that creaked on its hinges, and tossed her inside. Her cry of pain was silenced as her head hit something hard, and everything around her swirled and went black.

Dany parked the car on the street and led her around the crater in her driveway, careful to make sure he stood between her and the hole, minimizing her view of it. She was grateful for his thoughtfulness. Despite her attempt to be strong for him in the car, she really was just holding on by a thread.

Unfortunately, the first thing she saw as he stepped aside to let her in was her music room. That melted what little of her resolve remained and she dropped to her knees and sobbed. Dany's strong arms curled her into him as he maneuvered himself between her and her line of sight to the music room, and he just sat there with her until her tears were spent. When she was done, she rested her head against his chest and relished his proximity and sense of maleness.

"I'm sorry." His voice rumbled inside his chest.

"For what?" She turned her tear-streaked face up to look at him.

"I was trying to protect you from the scene outside, I didn't think that, that--" he waved a hand behind him "--would be the first thing you saw coming in this way."

She shook her head, as she swiped her hand across her cheeks and sniffed. "It's not your fault. No matter what you do, he's always going to be there. Nothing can change what he's done."

"No, I suppose not. At least you're talking now." He hugged her one last time, then stood and reached down a hand to help her up.

She missed the feel of his body next to hers immediately, but took his hand and let him lead her to the living room.

"I'm dying to know more about what happened," Dany said as she sat on the couch and snuggled her back into a corner, "but I think it's best to wait until Clint gets here so you don't have to tell it more than once. In the meantime, I'll turn these on." He reached down and plugged in the Christmas tree lights, then stopped and looked out the window, his chin dropped to his chest, and his back moved as if he were breathing deeply to stop from crying.

"Dany?" She pried herself off the couch onto her feet. The adrenaline that caused her fainting spell still coursed through her body and she could barely stand, but he needed her. She wrapped her arms around his waist and leaned her head against his back. "What is it?"

"I could have lost you today."

"No, I really don't think so. He didn't go there for that. I don't think he's ready yet."

"I could have lost you today," he repeated. "And it would have been my fault."

She withdrew her hands from around his waist and set them firmly on his shoulders. When he turned, the anger on his face relieved her. He had been trying to rein in his temper, but he was directing the fury at himself. She drew strength from that and steadied her voice.

"No, it wouldn't have been your fault. It would have been his. You're the one who told me that I wasn't responsible for *his* choices. You're not responsible for them either. He's not exactly the most predictable type. How were you to know that he would show up?" Her mind flashed back to P.O.'s face as he had stood in front of her. She swallowed the panic that threatened to swarm over her again. Dany just looked at her for a moment. "Who called you anyway?"

"Martha. From your cell phone."

Good ol' Martha.

"The children?"

"I don't know how much they saw, at least not him. Seeing you on the floor would have been plenty scary enough for them."

Julia nodded. "I guess it would be. Do you think I should go back?" His police officer persona slipped on again. That's good. That's the mode she needed from him right now. She needed to keep him focused on the job he was doing, rather than her.

"My overprotective instinct says, no. But, I think it's highly unlikely that he will risk going there again. He took an enormous risk already doing what he did."

Julia headed for the kitchen as her stomach growled. "Why do you think he did that anyway, besides the obvious?"

"Maybe he doesn't realize the things we've already pieced together and didn't think he'd provide anything really helpful." Dany's voice was behind her as she brought bread and margarine out of the fridge, then a knife out of a drawer.

"What do you mean?"

The doorbell interrupted his pending explanation. "Let me get that."

Constable Davis' voice joined Dany's as she finished preparing the sandwiches. When she emerged with a plateful, she found the two of them in the living room.

"So, what have you found? Dany was about to tell me what you were working on today." She offered Constable Davis the sandwich plate and he took two triangles.

"First thing's first," he mumbled around a mouthful. He set his sandwiches on the side table and withdrew his notebook from a pocket inside his uniform. "What did he look like?"

Dany perched himself on the window ledge beside Constable Davis. She knew she shouldn't feel like she were being interrogated, but in their official capacities they were both very intimidating. She noticed for the first time the bulkiness under Dany's jacket and when he unzipped it, the butt of his weapon poked out from under his left arm. A shiver of fear ran through her as it seemed Dany being in more official police garb made her circumstances feel all the more serious. Not like she didn't know her life was in danger before, but the situation suddenly became that much more real to her.

She closed her eyes, took a big breath, and recalled the moment she had looked him in the face, several times, in fact, while they completed the registration card. "Pointy nose, brown eyes, black hoodie pulled up, with only a tuft of dark hair peeking out over his forehead. Couldn't tell if it was black or brown hair. He wore a pair of scruffy jeans, and a green Green Bay Packers polar fleece."

Dany stood up straight so abruptly that Julia cowered back against the couch even though she knew she needn't be afraid of him. He looked as if he were about to break through the front window.

"You're sure he was wearing a green Green Bay Packers fleece?"

"Y-yes."

Dany looked at Constable Davis. "It's like he wants to get caught. What the hell is he doing?"

"He can't possibly know the information we already have. If he knew he likely wouldn't have gone so public with this."

"But going right to her table, knowing that she'd be able to see his face? Wearing something so noticeable?"

"She'd been frightened into a hole once before. Maybe that's what he was hoping to do this time. To shock her into silence again."

"Why would he give her his address? He had to know we would connect the dots."

"Does he know who you are?"

"No. When I jogged by him this morning…"

"Wait. What? You saw him?" Julia cringed inwardly at the squeak in her voice, as her mind ping-ponged from Constable Davis to Dany and back.

Dany turned to her, eyes intense, like an animal honing in on its prey. Dany knew they were on P.O.'s scent, and it was only a matter of time now before he got 'im.

"I went for a jog after I dropped you off. He was just coming out of his house, dressed in a pair of jeans and a Green Bay Packers polar fleece."

"And … the address of the house?"

"4809 Nightingale."

The world started to sway and Julia brought a hand to her chest as she forced air into her lungs.

"Julia?"

She raised a hand and shook her head. "I'm … I'm okay. H-he's b-been here all this time?"

"Looks like it."

"But we don't have enough to connect him yet," Constable Davis said.

"What?"

"We have a suspicion that he's involved, but we still have to prove that P.O. and this Anthony Oberman are the same guy, that would give us a pretty strong case to take to a judge for a search warrant otherwise an argument could be made that it's a son or other relative or even someone renting the house from him."

"But … I-I know it's him. Dany saw the same guy…"

"I know that, you know that…" Constable Davis waved a finger at her, "…but we need more than that to convince a judge."

Julia worked to dispel the panic rising through her body that was already exhausted from the earlier fainting spell, but she knew she was losing. Too much had happened. He'd gotten too close.

Constable Davis appeared to pick up on that because he tucked the notebook into his uniform again, then stood. "Would you be able to come down and help us come up with a composite? Do you have volunteer time planned tomorrow?"

Julia shook her head.

"You want to do it now while you remember?"

Constable Davis took a couple steps back when she looked up at him. "I could never forget."

"No, I don't suppose you could," he said rather sheepishly.

"I'm sorry. I shouldn't have been so curt."

He raised a hand. "Don't apologize. Get some sleep. I'll see you tomorrow." He turned to Dany. "You'll bring her by in the morning?"

Dany nodded.

"Good. We'll also need to lay out our plan for getting that search warrant." Constable Davis took his half-eaten sandwiches and grabbed a handful from the plate, then stepped toward the door. He held a hand up at Dany when he moved to follow. "No, you stay here. He's not going anywhere anyway. I know I don't have to tell you to set the security system before you go to bed."

Julia shook her head.

Without another word, Constable Davis let himself out and a pregnant silence settled upon the living room.

Because of Eastern Standard Time, darkness had swallowed up the daylight already, and it felt like it had been night time for hours, yet it was barely supper time.

"So, what do we do now?" She asked.

Dany shrugged. "I really don't know."

"I feel kind of like a deflated balloon, now that all the adrenaline of the day has gone out of me, I'm just withered and stretched out of shape."

Dany picked up the plate of uneaten sandwiches. "How about starting with something to eat? Even if you don't feel hungry you should eat something."

Julia nodded and took one. "You're right." Silence fell again as they ate, but Julia couldn't sit. Earlier, she could hardly keep her legs from collapsing under her, now she paced the living room more out of anxiety than restlessness, spiders tiptoeing over her nerve endings.

"You're going to wear a path into the floor," Dany said after a while.

"I just feel like a caged animal. Trapped in my own house. I don't feel safe here. It's like he's around me everywhere – outside, inside…" she waved a hand in the direction of the front door and music room. "And if the guy down the street really is him, then he's probably watching my every move. But I don't really have any other place to go."

Dany smiled and his eyes lit up with a sense of play – at least, it looked like a sense of play to her.

"What? What are you thinking?"

"Let me put these away." He nodded toward the remaining sandwiches. "I know just the place."

Chapter Twenty

Body wracked with shivers, Mariah worked to clear the cobwebs from her mind. Where was she? Her eyes were open she was sure of it.

Pain shot through her right arm as she tried to feel around her, and with that her whole ordeal flashed through her memory. The man. The door in the garage. The house. The pictures. His face in hers. The snapping of her wrist. The stairs. The door. The darkness. The cold.

As she tried to sit up straight, her head swam with the effort and she threatened to blackout again. A few deep breaths brought her the scent of mildew and weathered wood, along with a hint of fresh air that carried the aroma of snow, winter-evening crispness, and burning wood from a neighbor's hearth. It wasn't much, but it was enough to steady her senses. She touched a hand to the back of her head. The spot was dry – so no blood – but tender.

Once she was on her feet, her back leaning against what she assumed to be the door he'd flung her through, a muffled, single, short tone, sounded, so faint that at first she wasn't sure she'd actually heard anything. It chimed a second and third time before she realized it was her cell.

She used the fingers of the broken wrist to push the phone enough out of her pocket so her other hand could reach, its yellow notification light providing the only illumination in the room. She unlocked the keypad with a swipe and her touchscreen code, then groaned as the screen confirmed the meaning of the yellow indicator light – she had about 10% of her battery left. Her other problem was that, despite being in high-traffic Wi-Fi area, the thickness of the walls around her had left her with only two bars of signal strength. Even if she could type a message, it was doubtful it would reach the recipient.

She tapped her texting icon, but the decreased signal strength meant that even that took time to load, the increased buffering time consuming precious battery power. Typing the message also took longer because she had to do it one-handed. By the time, she tapped "send," her battery power had fallen to 2%. She wouldn't be able to get another message out if this one failed, and there was no guarantee that this one would ever make it through the walls. The only thing she could do with the phone now with its last ounce of life was use it to get a better idea of her surroundings.

She switched to her flashlight app and with a few sweeps confirmed her hunch that she was in an old cold storage room, and surrounded by three cinder-block walls with three rows of well-worn, long-abandoned wooden shelves each. There was a grate above the uppermost shelf and a thick wooden door at her back with an old skeleton key kind of lock. Too bad she had chosen an elastic tie-back for her hair today, instead of a clip.

There was no way she could beat her way through the door, or try to dig her way out around or under it. The only other possible way for her to draw attention to herself was to try to open the vent grate above the shelf.

As her cell phone finally died, pitch blackness swarmed in around her, all she could do was follow her nose, her memory, and the trail of her one good hand. From her flashlight survey of the room, she recalled that there was a shelf at hip height, another about nose height, and another just a couple inches above her head. The more she looked up, the stronger the fresh-air scent became. She ran her good hand along the flatness of the shelf, and discovered deep grooves. Would there be sufficient shelf left for her to do what she needed to do? As she pushed up and down on it, it felt well supported and sturdy.

She balanced her hip on the first board and, after testing her weight against it, brought her foot up in front of her, then pushed up towards the next board steadying herself with the elbow of her right arm. It was a precarious balancing act, particularly with only one hand and one elbow available, but the brackets beneath the shelves held and after a long while she reached the top shelf.

She brought her knees under her and bit by bit shifted her weight on the shelf and it held. The ceiling stopped her from being able to straighten all the way up, but she was at least level now with the air, and her good hand discovered the slats of the air intake grate. She tried to get her fingers in between the wall and the grate, but despite the obvious age of the room, it was well-attached to the stone.

She let out a disappointed sigh. She lowered herself so she could sit on the board. It wouldn't last long under her full weight, but it would be very difficult for her to climb up again, and she didn't want to waste this opportunity to use the vent.

She may not be able to see anything, but maybe she'd be able to hear – and maybe someone would be able to hear her. It was a neighborhood street after all. Sound carried farther in colder, wintery air – though that also meant that there would likely be very few people roaming about the side of their house. They'd more likely be cozy inside.

She heard a soft *thomp* outside, then a second, then a third. She quickly, but gently got back to her knees and leaned her ear against the grate. Several more *thomp*s, and then boot-sized footsteps. Multiple sets. Car doors. Multiple footsteps in close proximity to each other. Perhaps it was the police? With her luck it was probably carollers, but regardless, those sounds meant people. She started shouting and whacking the metal grate with the butt of her dead cell phone.

Peck watched the recording again and again. Her face filling the screen at one point looking off to the side likely in the direction of a reporter's question – probably that annoying Mariah woman now stowed away in his cold storage – and the next minute looking into the camera and directly at him, defiant. Shivers of rage raked through his body every time he replayed her words.

How dare she come out! How dare she challenge him! Did she not know that she would only increase his need to silence her and make him go to more drastic measures to do it?

He couldn't stand to be on the couch anymore and took out his rage on his coffee table until it lay smashed to splinters beneath the living room window. He was still seething with temper when the doorbell rang.

Who the hell could that be?

It took every ounce of self-control to rein in his temper to bring his breathing down to a normal rate. Deep breaths. In through the nose, out through the mouth.

"I'll be right there!" It would be useless not to answer the door since the blinking light of the television would have been clearly noticeable to someone looking at his house from the street, since he had neglected to close the heavy drapes earlier.

He ran a hand through his hair, hoping the action would tame it rather than make him look as disheveled as he felt.

As he reached for the doorknob, he had one small comfort in that whoever was at the door wouldn't be able to see the destroyed coffee table, his shrine behind the kitchen, or his one small consolation prize hidden away downstairs. There was no way they could know who he was.

He switched on the front landing light, then unlocked the door, opening it just enough that he could poke his head through – enough that he could see them, but that they couldn't get a good look at him in the shadow. He swallowed several expletives when he saw the gaggle of police officers imposing on his front step.

"Good evening, sir."

He recognized the front-most police officer as the one who had come around the neighborhood six months earlier after his failed attempt on Julia McIntyre had killed her brother instead -- at least that's how the papers had described it. He'd managed to send them away last time by convincing them he was a renter. It wouldn't do for him to lose his cool now. They couldn't connect him with anything so long as he played this smart.

"Good evenin', officer. What can I do ya for? Forgive me for not openin' the door more, I don' want fer the cat to git out."

The officer smiled and waved a hand. "That's alright, sir. As I'm sure you know, your neighbor's car was blown up last night. We're canvassing the neighborhood to see if anyone saw anything suspicious or has remembered something they neglected to tell us, last night?"

"I remember that, awright. Quite a blast. Shook me windows. All o' us were concerned. No one hurt, was there?"

"Luckily, no."

"Ach, well, I was in my house when it 'appened. As I said, shook me windows. Only came out to see what all the fuss was about. Not much to see at that point, particularly when we was kept across the street. Sorry, I can't be much help. Sure hope you catch the guy though." That last line was a stroke of genius.

The officer nodded. "That's alright, sir. I just have one more thing to ask you."

He muttered a curse under his breath, his temper threatened to boil over. The more questions they asked, the longer he had to keep up the accent and charade, and the more suspicious the police were likely to get.

"Sure." He hoped he sounded more good-natured than he felt.

"Where were you between 12 and 2 this afternoon?"

Why would they ask him a question like that unless….

How the hell had they found him?! She couldn't possibly have recognized him from around the neighborhood. He'd been very careful not to actually meet her face-to-face before today. The officer's expression changed from professional curiosity to that of focused suspicion and he knew he'd waited too long to respond and he hoped that the shock of having been asked that question hadn't registered on his face.

"A man wearing a faded green, Green Bay Packers fleece sweater appeared at the community center and caused one of the workers some severe distress. Before that, a passer-by saw someone from this address wearing a similar sweater."

The only one who had seen him this morning was that Dany guy. It wouldn't have taken much to connect him with the encounter at the community center. But they weren't demanding for him to let them in. They mustn't have had sufficient evidence yet to get a search warrant. He planted a smile on his face, satisfied they were only following up on a lead and hadn't figured everything out yet.

"I was out doin' some Christmas shopping." He nearly spat the word. He hated the very idea, but it was the only thing he could think of and it was an alibi that would be virtually impossible to corroborate. The stores were packed at this time of year. No one would be able to recall if they saw him or not amongst the thousands of other faces they'd seen. "It'll be 'ere 'fore you know it. 'Sides, I can't be the only Green Bay Packers fan. Can't arrest me for that, can ya?"

The officer smiled. "I'm a Bills fan, so you never know. You the homeowner, sir?"

"Nah, just rentin'. I coulda got my own place, but I like da neighborhood."

Peck sighed when the officer stepped back from the door.

"Thank you, sir. I'll leave you to the rest of your evening." He offered a business card, and not wanting to appear rude, Peck reached through the door opening for it. "Please be sure to call me if you recall anything, anything at all. You never know what little piece of information might actually crack our case wide open."

Peck tipped the card off his forehead. "Fer sure, officer. Good luck to ya."

"Oh, what happened to your hand?"

Peck looked down. An inch-long gash across the back of his hand was bleeding, probably from his battle with the coffee table.

"I-I don' know. Must-a been when I was hangin' lights earlier." As if to emphasize the point, Peck flipped a second switch and white lights came on around and above them.

"Ah, well. You should get that looked at. Wouldn't want that to get infected."

"No, certainly not, sir. I'll do that."

He waited until the troop had stepped off the porch front step before closing the door. Didn't want it to look like he was too anxious for them to leave by closing it when they'd barely turned away. He leaned against the closed door, and heaved a huge breath of relief.

They were *this* close.

Clint looked back at the house from the middle of the front walk, drinking in every detail he could about it. He turned and looked down the street toward Julia's house, and, as Dany had told him, while naked trees obscured his view from the ground, the trees were short enough that the windows from the upper story would provide a clear view.

And, despite Anthony's attempt to hide in the shadows, he'd gotten a pretty good look at him when he reached out to take the contact card – pointy nose, chocolate brown eyes, which appeared darker in the night. And this time he wasn't wearing a hoodie so that his full head of brown-black hair was clearly visible, and all sticky-uppy. It was certainly more information than what he had when he arrived, and only helped confirm Julia's and Sammy's descriptions.

He knew he would be able to find the green polar fleece if he could only get into the house, but he couldn't do that without a warrant, and they still didn't have enough evidence for that.

He looked at Julia's house as he drove by. Dany's rental wasn't parked out front. Surely, he wouldn't have left her alone?!

He punched his hands-free button and voice dialled Dany's number.

Damn! They weren't going to the other houses.

He watched the police disperse into their various vehicles through the living room window from behind his drapes where they wouldn't notice him. They weren't canvassing the other houses. Of course, there was always the chance that his house had been last on their list, but he didn't give that possibility more than a passing thought.

That would mean they'd come to question him with a purpose – to connect him with the incident at the community center.

He cussed like a sailor and railed against the remnants of his coffee table. They were getting too close. He'd thrown them a bit of a curveball already, but that wouldn't hold for much longer. He hadn't exactly lied when he said he was renting the house, but that wasn't the whole truth either, and that was the only thing that was going to keep them off his tail long enough for him to do what he needed and that was to get Julia away from here. There was only one place left he could go.

"No! No!"

The words died in the small, dank room.

The footsteps tromped away, followed by slamming car doors, and engine start-ups. No one had appeared to hear her.

Her throat burned from screaming, and only pieces of her cellphone remained in her hand. She sat down on the shelf, then gently slid herself off. With no light, she couldn't see the floor coming up to meet her until her feet slammed into it, the impact knocking her on her backside and the air from her lungs. She leaned back against the door and cradled her wrist against her belly as she gasped. She tossed the remnants of the cell phone on the floor towards the wall. Useless. She didn't even have any way of knowing if Craig had received her text.

Assuming he didn't, his next step would be to go to the police if he didn't hear from her by 10 PM. He had promised, and given how upset he'd been at her insistence that she go alone, she figured he would do it the moment the clock turned over.

Craig had been more than upset. He'd been furious when she insisted that she confront the guy alone, but she just knew she wouldn't have gotten any answers at all with a camera shoved in his face. She certainly wouldn't have found out so definitively that *he* was Julia McIntyre's stalker and the one responsible for her brother's death. And, she wouldn't be sitting in a freezing cold room with a dead cell phone waiting for a rescue, with no guarantee she would leave this house alive.

She had definitely thrown off this guy's plan though, and Heaven only knew what he planned to do with her now. Would he try to kill her? Would he keep her here? And for how long? He had to know that it wouldn't take long for someone to notice she was missing. Assuming that he did know, it was reasonable to also assume he would step up any plan he might have had to try to kill Julia again. By getting in his way, she may have become an unwitting participant in his obsession to do away with Julia, and no one really knew why. And no one, except her, even knew who he was.

Chapter Twenty-One

Julia was just about to putt for birdie on the 5th hole when Dany's cell phone rang out *Star Wars*.

"Yo, Clint. What's up?" Dany cradled the phone against his ear with his shoulder, tucked the putter under one arm and plugged his other ear with a finger. It was far from crowded, but perhaps the cell signal wasn't very good. At the mention of Constable Davis' name, Julia left her ball, two-inches from the hole and tried to listen over his shoulder. "Yeah, no, we're fine. Don't worry … You did what?!" From Dany's wide-eyed glance at her, they must have done something big.

"What? What is it?" she whispered with a shrug of her shoulders.

Dany shook his head and waved a hand.

"Okay. We'll meet you there at nine."

"What? What happened? Did they find out something new?" she asked as he slid the phone back into his pocket.

"They went to his house."

"They did what?!" For a few moments she couldn't think of anything to say as she let that news set in. "Did the constable tell you he was going to do that?"

"No, but it makes sense that he would. He would have to follow up on the information we had about a guy from that address giving you that note."

Julia nodded. "What did they find out?"

"We have a better description of his hair now because he answered the door without his hoodie on, and Clint said he got a pretty good look at his face."

Julia shuffled back over to her waiting ball and, after a measured tap, it bobbled into the cup. She held up a hand as Dany was about to say more.

"Let's not talk about that anymore. He's been part of my life virtually 24/7 for the better part of a year, if not longer if you count to the build up to all this. Going indoor mini-putting was a great idea. Let's not ruin it by bringing him in here."

Dany smiled and nodded. "If that's the way you want it."

"I do. It's your putt." She twirled the putter on the green while she waited. His ball rolled over the hole and back out. "This really isn't your sport, is it?"

Dany sighed. "I guess not." He lined up his last shot, then retrieved his ball after it fell into the cup.

"Hmm. That's double-bogie for you." Julia marked the scorecard.

"Hey, what fun is it if you're keeping score?"

Julia laughed and skipped out of the way as he reached for the pencil and card. "Lots of fun!"

"Well, just remember who's paying for your fun – in more ways than one."

"Actually, it would be a whole lot more fun if you weren't still wearing official police gear. It kinda goes against the whole 'casual, fun outing' persona." She crooked two fingers in the air.

"I know. But I feel naked without it, particularly while you're still in danger. He could be anywhere."

Julia had been studying the next hole when she looked back at him with a scowl.

"You sure know how to kill a mood. No more talking about him."

Dany held up his hands in surrender. "Okay. I'm sorry. That'll be the last time, I promise."

Julia dropped her ball on the worn out tee-off line. This one was trickier. She had to get the ball through one of three holes along the front of the barn to reach the other side where the green turf then curved to a round space with the hole on the far right side.

"Gee, who thought of this one?"

"Ha ha, Ms. LPGA! Let's see how you do now?"

She cast a squinted eye and a turned up mouth at him. "Like you're going to do any better."

"Don't be so sure. Your confidence may be your downfall."

"We'll see about that."

At her first swing, the ball bounced off the barn wall between two of the holes with a *pop* and rolled back to the tee-off line.

"I don't think confidence has anything to do with it. More like some golf geek's concept of absurdity."

After two more tries with same amount of success, they dissolved into laughter until they cried.

"I-I think you may have a chance to catch up here," Julia said between gasps.

"I'm going to do my best," Dany replied, still trying to regain his breath. The remainder of the laughter died in his throat and his eyes turned cloudy, as if he were staring off into space.

"Dany?"

He stumbled then fell to the ground.

"Dany!" She dropped her putter, and took his face in her hands. He wasn't responding to her, but his eyes were open and moving as if in REM sleep, like he was dreaming.

The shot sound from her golf ball rebounding ricocheted through his mind, and the mini-putt world around him kaleidoscoped. He reached for something to lean on, but there was nothing, and he landed unceremoniously on his behind as a storm of memories claimed his mind and every ounce of his consciousness. He was aware of Julia's voice somewhere in the distance, but all he saw, in eerie slow motion was the masked figure running from the store, the flash of his weapon discharging, the figure falling, and the face of the fifteen-year-old mingling with that of his grief-stricken mother. The tornado of faces, clashed with his promise to protect Julia, seeing her passed out at the community center and the visions of what possible confrontations would come with P.O.

"Dany."

Julia? The maelstrom of faces steadied to a gentler eddy.

"Focus on my voice. Come on, Dany. Focus. Come back to me. You're alright. You're safe. I'm safe."

Julia. Her voice was stronger now, slowly breaking through. One by one the faces cleared from his mind until all that remained was Julia, and finally his eyes cleared and she materialized in front of him. He gasped for breath from the mental exertion, and realized he was lying on the ground. He raised a hand to his forehead.

"Hey." He sat up.

"Hey, yourself."

Thank goodness there was no one else around to witness his indignity. He mentally chastised himself. Julia didn't look upset or embarrassed, just concerned.

"Gosh, I'm sorry about that. I really don't know where that came from."

"You don't have to apologize to me." She looked around. "Let's go over here." She pointed to a bench off to the side of the course.

Once he was seated, Dany leaned forward so his elbows rested on his knees and covered his face with his hands. "Gosh, I'm so sorry. This was supposed to be a relaxing night for you. And I let this…." He shook his head and let out a heavy breath.

Her arms wrapped around his shoulders, and her voice sounded in his ear, its rich, singy quality countering the tension in his crunched up muscles.

"I told you, you don't have to apologize."

"But, I'm supposed to be the strong one. I'm supposed to be

protecting you."

"You're not Superman, you know?"

"I know that." It came out as a growl. Couldn't she understand the monumental responsibility on his shoulders?

"Do you also know that I don't want Superman?"

"No?"

"No. I think you're expecting too much of yourself."

"You do, do you?" He couldn't stop the annoyed edge to his tone.

Her eyes widened in surprise. "Yes... Dany… I … ."

He stood and walked a few steps away, stomping back and forth in front of her. "People expect police officers to be invincible. People expect police officers not to make mistakes. And then when an officer does make one…" he waved a hand at her "…they seem to assume that you did it on purpose. What most people don't realize as they're angrily calling me a murderer is that we're just as human as everyone else, just as prone to making mistakes as everyone else. They don't understand that our responsibility puts us in greater danger than people can possibly fathom. Every time we report for duty, we know that there's a very good chance we may not return home that night. And we are hyper aware of the costliness of any mistakes we might make in a split-second decision -- let someone shoot at us and injure or kill someone else, or prevent other people from getting hurt.

"Those same people who think I'm the most horrible person on the planet, don't realize that I actually do feel like the most horrible person on the planet. Their judgment assumes that I don't feel anything. They somehow think that we're out for blood and in some way enjoy the power that we have by having a gun, when the truth is far from that. And that that boy's face will haunt me for the rest of my life. I'll likely never have the public's trust again.

"Not only have I destroyed Jayson and his family's life, but that one mistake has also destroyed mine, and likely yours as well." He turned to look at her. "I really have no right getting involved in this investigation, in getting you to trust me to protect you. It's unfair of me to do that."

"No…" Julia shook her head, but he couldn't let the faith in her blue eyes sway him. She needed someone stronger than he knew he could ever be.

"It is. You deserve someone better. Someone who's not going to fail you at just the time you need them most." He looked up at the ceiling. "Gosh, I've done it again. This was supposed to be a fun, stress-free night and I've ruined it." He flopped back down on the bench.

"Dany … I-I don't really know what I can say." She sat next to him, took his hand and started turning it over as if she were examining it, rubbing her hands over the palm and the back, her magical, musical fingers releasing the stress from his body. "We're both dealing with tragedies. You're right when you say I didn't cause Michael's death, but you're dealing with the reality that someone – a child – has died as a direct result of something you've done. You were in a position of responsibility to protect the lives of others.

"I may not know what it's like to be a police officer, but I know what it's like to have everyone watching me, watching my every move with big expectations every time I step on stage, every time I speak, every time I sing, and in those moments when I'm not 'officially' on duty and just want to be myself. People expect me to be a perfect Christian every moment. Being a Christian really has nothing to do with being perfect. We don't stop making mistakes. But that's what people expect. I'm sure there are people out there who are thinking I must have done something pretty terrible to have such horrible things happen to me. That I must have deserved it for whatever monumental sin I must have done.

She shook her head. "It's an enormous burden to know that every action or inaction, decision or indecision impacts people's lives, and we really have no way of knowing whose lives we're impacting for the good or bad."

Julia stood this time and turned her back, her shoulders hunched under the weight of the burden she currently carried as justified as his own.

"I have no idea what I've done to deserve to have P.O. or Anthony – or whatever his name is – hate me so much that he wants me dead." She turned around, her royal blue eyes deepening to azure. "You may not feel like you can do this…" she knelt on the ground at his feet and looked up at him "…but I believe in you. I know it may not make much sense, but I don't need you to be perfect. You're expecting too much of yourself. You may have failed once, and you may fail again. But that doesn't mean you're not the right person to be here for this moment in time."

She laid a hand on his heart and he couldn't stop his sharp intake of breath at her feathery touch. "I know you don't feel like you're any good at doing your job and you're afraid of failing me. But I know the real you is in here still. The you that does know what he's doing, and who I know will not fail when the moment comes. You will be able to do what you need to do. What *I* will need you to do. You were brought into my life for a reason. I don't believe this is at all coincidence. You needed to be here. And I needed you here. I've come to learn that we are created with what we need to fulfill our ultimate purpose in life. God's already equipped you for what he's got planned. If you can't trust yourself, or trust my faith in you, trust His."

She was so close and, maybe it was the language that only musicians knew, the language that could reached into the soul so that even without the piano or angelic voice, she could still move a man's heart, but at that precise moment, he knew he would move heaven and earth itself for her.

He stroked her cheek with the forefinger of his free hand until it rested beneath her chin and tilted it up. He drank in every inch of her startling blue eyes, long eyelashes, feminine cheekbones, perfectly proportioned nose, and partially parted lips, then brought his mouth down on hers.

"I guess I said the right thing," she said when he stopped, her mouth millimeters from his.

"I guess you did." He kissed her again, more deeply this time and probing with his tongue, and was slightly surprised at her ardent response. He smiled when he reluctantly let her mouth go. "You've got to be the most amazing woman I've ever met."

"Thank you." Her face flushed red. "But I have to warn you,

flattery will get you nowhere. And don't think that kiss has disarmed me, mister."

"Huh?"

Julia stood and wandered back over to the sixth hole with a smile. "We still have to conquer this hole, and this place closes in two hours."

"Well, let's get back to it, then." He lined up his ball and whacked it through first try. "By the way…" He turned and smiled.

"What?"

"Thank you." He stroked her cheek again, and planted a quick but gentle kiss on her mouth.

Her electric smile sent shivers through him. "You're welcome."

As the clock looking down on them from above the snack shack tick-tocked closer to closing time, Julia munched on a nacho heaped high with salsa and melted cheese.

"So, you were living in Winnipeg when your father died, froze to death ice fishing. You moved to London not long after that. Your mother was a piano teacher."

"Right."

"Why London?"

Julia shrugged. "I don't really know. I don't recall my grandparents at all. Mother never told us why she had decided to move here. Maybe she was just tired of prairie winters.

"So, tell me about the message in the bottle then?"

"Well, we couldn't afford much by way of a family vacation in those days, but that year, 1986, my mother decided to take us down along the waterfront in Toronto. I said I wanted to put a message in a bottle. So, she bought a bottle of Coke from a corner store with the last pennies she had, and we all shared the drink until the bottle was empty, and that's what we did. I wrote the message, put it in the bottle and filled the top with clay, and tossed it in Lake Ontario and I think that's where your story comes in."

Dany grinned as he munched. "I guess it does. It's not a very happy story either. I was visiting my grandmother's house in a little village of St. Martin's, New Brunswick, on the Bay of Fundy just after my father died. There wasn't much there at the time, but St. Martin's has a rich shipbuilding history. Shipbuilding was gone when my grandfather was living there. He inherited the house from a great-uncle or something who had been part of that industry, but my grandfather actually worked and died in the Springfield mine. Much to my grandmother's chagrin, my father took to mining too, and he died in the Westray Mine disaster. She was quite relieved when I chose policing over mining, though it's not like that didn't come with its own set of risks.

"She didn't live long after dad passed. I guess the grief of losing Grandpa and Dad was too much for her."

"I can't imagine what it would be like to bury your own child, even if he were an adult. Children are supposed to outlive their parents."

Dany nodded, the light of storytelling left his eyes and Julia wondered if he were about to slip away on her again. "Yeah, they are." He took a few deep, steadying breaths and reached for her hand. "Guess I can't completely avoid it, can I?"

His pained expression grabbed her heart, and Julia gasped, then raised a hand to her mouth. "No. I'm so sorry. I said it without thinking."

Dany shook his head. "Don't be sorry. I guess I will always think about Jayson when someone says that."

"Probably. Completely understandable. And I wouldn't want you to avoid it. It's better to let the feelings out rather than keeping them penned up inside. I'm not afraid of them."

Dany's eyes lightened again. "Have I said lately that you're amazing?"

Heat rushed to her cheeks. "I think you said that earlier."

"I meant it, you know?"

Julia nodded, bashfully. "So, after your father died...."

"Yes." His posture straightened and his gaze held the intensity of recounting memories. "My mother died about the same time, so I was the only family member left and inherited the house. I love it. It's a great old house, and I had many awesome summers there as a kid, but police life hasn't left much room for downtime. It was easier to stay in Halifax. So, I've only been back there a few times over the years until this October when I needed to get out of Halifax, to escape all that life had brought down upon me.

"It needed a good cleaning and one day I had assigned myself the attic, to see what was up there more than anything, and found the message in the bottle. Yeah, I found it first when I was visiting Nan. I guess I was about 20. There's a beautiful beach there, and a covered bridge that you have to cross to reach most of it. When the tide goes out, you can walk right out on the ocean bottom, and into these caves along the shore. The bottle had settled behind a couple of rocks when the tide went out."

"Why didn't you look for me then?" She swallowed the last chip and took a few long pulls on the straw in her ginger ale.

"Well, I did open it as soon as I got home, obviously, but we didn't have the Internet back then, and with mom's passing, and then Nan ... I guess it kind of got lost in the shuffle. I don't even know how it got in the attic." He shook his head.

Julia caught the glare of the server behind the counter.

"I think they're about to kick us out."

Dany turned towards the counter. "I think you're right. Don't want tonight to get any messier, given the shellacking I took on the greens today."

Julia gathered their finished dishes and carried them to the counter.

"Thanks so much, Jenny. Sorry, we kept you so long."

"It's okay, Ms. McIntyre. Thanks for coming by."

"Actually, if I could trouble you for one more thing. I'd like that case of six Cokes, please."

"Certainly. They're the vintage style bottles with polar bears. This is our last set."

Julia paid for them, then pulled two out of the container, and used the bottle cap opener attached to the wall to open one, which she gave to Dany, and then opened the second.

"Thanks so much. Have a good night."

"Feeling a bit nostalgic?" Dany asked as they retrieved their jackets and boots from the cloak room.

"About the bottles? I guess so. I don't normally buy soda at all. I prefer water. But I've always thought the polar bears were cute."

"I keep forgetting," Dany said as they stepped out into the cold.

"Forgetting what?" The words coming out in a breath cloud.

"That I'm with someone famous. So many people know who you are. You must get starstruck-ness all the time even from people you don't know."

"Yeah, it took some getting used to when I started performing, and then again when I dropped off the face of the musical earth, but no one's been rude about it. The thing I find neat is that I know my style of music isn't for everyone and yet no one seems to mind." Dany's car beeped as he unlocked it with the fob. She shivered as she reached for the door handle. "I'd usually be singing Christmas carols about this time of year," she continued once they were seated inside, and shook her head. "I used to love singing Christmas carols."

"Used to?"

"Used to. I don't have the heart for it anymore. And when I don't have the heart, it shows in my voice."

"Have you tried?"

"What, singing?"

Dany nodded.

"No. There have been times when I thought I could, but I wasn't even able to take a breath. After all, I've been doing this for 20 years. It should just come automatically, right? But I have no desire to sing anymore."

"That's a shame."

"I guess I'm just not ready yet. When I can't even sing *Silent Night*, and the sight of my piano still completely cripples me." She shook her head again. "My heart's just not ready. I'm not even sure I could do it, anyway. As you said before, it's probably not gone. Just need to wait for the right moment and see what God's next role for me is."

Dany set his soda bottle in a cup holder, then turned the car on.

"Oh, I know there's still the voice of an angel in there somewhere. You'll sing again."

"Just the thought hurts too much."

"Because of Michael?"

Julia shook her head. "I'm not so sure it's only about that. It was my whole world for 15 years. Now, none of that world remains and I'm trying to rediscover the inspiration to do it. I don't just get up there to sing for myself. My songs all have a message. A very personal message for everyone who listens … or at least that's the intent when I write, play, and sing them. Now, there's nothing left in me to put my voice into those messages. It's not that God's not there anymore, but … I don't know." She shook her head again and looked at her hands in her lap. "I'm just not connected in the same way I was then, so many things have happened that have tried to sever that connection I once had, and I'm still trying to find my way back. I don't want to be an angel anymore. I don't want to be on stage anymore. I have no music left to give."

"Hey." When he didn't continue, she turned and looked at him, and everything around her faded into nothingness. "You will sing again." In that instant, she believed him, and a spark peeked out of the darkness of her life-trampled heart. "It may not be to thousands of people. But there will be a purpose for it. Perhaps a purpose that you never thought or imagined."

Tears that spilled over and trailed down her cheeks. "Thank you. And thank you for this evening. I've had a great time."

"You're welcome." Dany gently swiped away her tears with this thumb, then glanced at the dashboard. "Oh, gosh. Nearly 11:30. Clint is expecting us at the station at nine."

"Yeah," Julia said through a long, deep yawn. "Guess we'd better get home then."

Chapter Twenty-Two

Craig paced back and forth through Mariah's small apartment living room. She had promised to be in contact by 10. It was now nearly midnight. He'd had to fight his gut instinct to not call the police at 9:59. Maybe she was editing her recordings or something. But she'd never been this late, at least not without having been in touch.

He couldn't stand it any longer and pulled out his cell.

"Constable Davis, please," he said when his call was answered.

"What is it regarding, sir?"

He stifled a sigh of exasperation. "My name is Craig Sanders. I'm a cameraman for Channel 22 with Mariah Colverton. I have reason to believe something bad has happened to her and it relates to Julia McIntyre's stalker."

"One moment, please." There was a click, and Craig thought for a moment that the dispatcher might have hung up on him, but about 30 seconds later another voice came on the line.

"Davis."

"Constable Davis?"

"Yes. Craig, is it?"

"Yes."

"The dispatcher's given me the basics. What have you got for me?"

Craig laid it all out for him, from having seen a suspicious man skulking away from in front of Julia's house earlier that day, to capturing him on camera, to his review of the film to find out which house the guy had gone in, and to his and Mariah's agreement for her to talk to the guy alone. Craig could almost see Davis salivating over the mention of the recording.

"So, you think he's got her?"

"All I know is that's where she went, and she hasn't contacted me."

"And you let her go alone."

Craig hung his head. "I know it was stupid. I knew it was stupid then, and let her convince me to let her go on her own. She said it would make for a more candid interview."

"You've tried calling her."

"Of course. But I just keep getting her voicemail."

"And, where are you now?"

"In her apartment."

"Obviously, she's not there."

"No."

"Would she have gone to your apartment instead or to the station?"

"I called the station and security said she hadn't checked in, and no, we'd agreed that I would wait here for her. I only have a cell phone for her to get in touch with me anyway, so it wouldn't matter where I was. I haven't heard from her in over five hours."

"Have you notified your boss?"

"I was hesitant to. If a missing persons story about her is plastered all over the TV world, what's *he* going to do to her? But she's due to report at 6:00 tomorrow morning."

"You'd better call your station manager and tell him what's happened. I'm assuming because she was so secretive about it that she didn't get his approval before going ahead with confronting him?"

"No. She wanted it to be an exclusive and it would have given her the prime opportunity most journalists only dream of."

"How soon can you get down here?"

"Thought you'd never ask."

Mariah couldn't stop the shivers. Roll after roll they claimed her body and she wondered how much longer she would be able to endure the cold before they stopped altogether. The only good part about the cold was she could no longer feel her broken wrist. She had no idea what time it was. She only hoped it was late enough that Craig had notified the police. All she had to do was hang on 'til morning.

Julia awoke to the sun glowing through her blinded bedroom window. She silenced the alarm on her bedside table which blinked 7:30 at her. She lay back on her pillow, as she waited for both her mind and her body to arrive at the same level of awareness. No sounds yet from Dany's room across the hall. He must still be asleep. Given the hour they'd returned from mini-putting, they didn't say a long goodnight when they got home. There hadn't seemed to be any lasting ill-effects from his anxiety attack, but she wasn't naïve enough to assume there wouldn't be more. The emotional challenges of both their traumas would last for a while, but for the moment at least, she had helped to calm him and bring him back to where he needed to be. To where she needed him to be.

P.O.'s face flashed through her memory. The face she'd have to describe to Constable Davis this morning. The last thing she wanted to spend her day doing was virtually staring at P.O.'s—Anthony's—whoever's face, but this was their chance to catch him for murdering Michael and terrorizing her for so long. Only when he was caught, would she truly be free from the prison he'd created for her.

She mentally kicked herself in the butt and sat up on the edge of the bed. She longed to stay snuggled under her purple striped comforter, but she had a full day ahead. Plus, she wanted to see Dany.

It had seemed so natural to see him standing in her kitchen the previous morning. Like he belonged there. Strange that they'd become so attached to each other in the extremely short time they'd known each other. She remembered reading somewhere that people involved in a crisis together often drew closer. The experience of working to survive bonded people together in some unique way that calmer situations just didn't. No one really knew why.

Regardless, she'd need his strength again today. Just being with him was enough and gave her strength she didn't know she had. But, if she was going to be of any use to anyone, she needed to get moving.

After taking care of her bathroom duties, she headed down to the kitchen for some breakfast and coffee. In front of the coffee maker she found a note:

Good morning, Beautiful...

Got a break in the case and had to go in last night, didn't want to wake you.

Will see you at 8:30.

Julia shivered, not from cold, but from the idea that she was alone in the house. Even with the alarm set, the house felt empty, unsafe, vulnerable without Dany in it. How would she would ever go back to life without Dany once the case was over?

Michael's death, the demise of her musical career, and the divorce from Martin had left her in emotional ruins that she never thought she'd come out of. She never imagined she'd ever fall in love again. The way they had talked the night before, enjoying just being together had been one of the nicest nights she'd ever known. True, Dany still had issues of his own to resolve, but didn't everyone? No one entered into any kind of relationship without some sort of influence from their life experience up to that point. Part of growing together meant helping each other through those things and establishing a new sense of trust and understanding, and overall new memories to cherish.

It had been so nice to talk about normal things, families and jobs and homes, rather than stalkers and profiles and protection. Even before Michael was shot, having a stalker meant that security along with the touring schedule was all she, Michael, Martin, and everyone else talked about. There was actually very little downtime when she was touring or doing church events. When she wasn't writing, singing, or practicing, she was answering fan mail or planning or organizing something for the next event. This gave her more personal contact with her fans, so Martin had been left to manage the other things. Martin and Michael had both tried to convince her to surrender some of the PR stuff, but she'd refused.

That's how she'd come across the first letter, just after her concert in Winnipeg at the MTS Centre in May 2012, dated and signed P.O. Another had followed, then another, then another -- always after a concert. Those plus the messages left on her voicemail led her to report it to the police, and her life had never been the same since. Everywhere she went, security went with her to the point where there wasn't even much privacy in a women's restroom. She'd basically become a prisoner in her own life, not free to do anything for fear that P.O. would find her when someone wasn't looking and do whatever his disturbed mind wanted to do to her.

None of the letters or messages ever said why he was angry with her. They were more along the lines of "Stop singing or else" kind of things, with the occasional song lyric thrown in as if driving home the point that he was watching her, like the message he'd given her at the community center.

The community center. That had completely thrown her off guard. Dany too. She didn't blame him for not thinking that P.O. would show up there. To her knowledge, she'd never seen him in person, although, given that she had no idea who he was, he could have stood in line at an autograph session and she would never have known.

She recalled seeing Dany's face as she'd come around after fainting the day before.

Hm, Dany. Somehow her thoughts always seemed to come back to him. How was it someone could so quickly become a fixture in her life? Perhaps over time, as things settled, her heart had become more open to letting someone into it. Although, Dany wasn't just anyone. He was exactly what she needed. Her personal circumstances had obviously played a major role in her acceptance of him in her life. If she hadn't already started stepping out in public again with the knowledge that P.O. would pick up on her scent, would she have even asked Dany to stay in the house? Likely not. She had a feeling given what had happened in Dany's life at that time, that he likely would have appeared in her life anyway. But would he have taken up the role of her protector? Again, likely not. She probably would have let him check himself into a hotel. It was their respective levels of vulnerability and them being thrown into crisis mode almost at the outset of their meeting that had fueled their current relationship.

His strength and company, even while he was sorting out things in his own life, had definitely been instrumental in strengthening her attitude and resolve. In fact, if it hadn't been for Dany, she very likely wouldn't be here now. She would have been incinerated or at the very least severely injured in the car blast.

That was another thing about this whole situation. How could someone she never met and didn't know hate her so much that he wanted her dead? She had voiced that question to Dany the night before. She was not entirely sure she would ever know the answer to that question. P.O. was quite obviously not in his right mind. How could anyone explain what was going on in a mind like his?

But it did appear that she and Dany were both healing. Aside from Dany's apparent anxiety attack, the rest of the evening had gone uneventfully. She had beaten him soundly on the scorecard. And the gray cloud that had hung over both their heads had eased off revealing the sunlight between them and the realization that she didn't want to wake up without him in her life.

His had been the first face she'd seen the morning after the car bomb, and then again after the incident in the community center. She didn't know how much she'd been looking forward to seeing him until she found his note this morning and discovered that he wasn't here.

She glanced at the kitchen clock. Half an hour. He would be here in half an hour.

She turned on the television in the living room and sat down on the sofa with a couple slices of rye toast with peanut butter and a bowl of fresh-frozen strawberries.

She was just in time for the 8 o'clock news. They were just getting to the weather when her cell went off.

Who would be calling at this hour? Maybe Dany, checking up on her and reminding her that he'd be there shortly. Her heart cartwheeled.

"Good morning, honey girl."

The food in her mouth turned to sand and she was barely able to swallow. Definitely not Dany.

"You showed some guts yesterday morning on TV."

"I'm glad you thought so, Anthony." Good. Just enough bravado, but not overconfident.

He chuckled. A sound that made him sound like a deranged Harley Davidson, and her stomach churn. "Anthony, huh? You really think that's my real name?"

She nearly choked on her own saliva. Not his real name? What other information had he given her that was not right and that had wasted considerable time for Dany and Constable Davis?

"Wh-What do you mean?"

"Oh, that's for me to know and Dany-boy to chase his tail for a little while longer."

Anger pushed the usual terror she felt at the sound of his voice down to the furthest part of her stomach.

"Why are you calling me?"

"I know Dany-boy's not with you this morning."

"So, you're just calling to keep me company, is that it?"

"Ooh. Feisty. Nice try, honey girl, but no. I'm calling to tell you about an unexpected visitor I had last night who is now keeping me company."

If she hadn't already been sitting down, she would have fallen. Fear, dread, heartache, and anger all nearly suffocated her.

Dany. He had been called in last night while she was sleeping. Had he gone on his own to confront P.O.? Had he decided to follow-up on whatever tip Constable Davis had been working on when he called them at the mini-putt?

Tears bedded her eyes, but she kept her voice level and lethal. "What have you done to him?"

The Harley Davidson chuckle returned. "Nothing … yet."

Julia sighed. P.O. hadn't killed him. Not yet. He was probably only using Dany for one purpose – to lure her to him. There was no guarantee that if she surrendered to him he would let Dany go, or that he'd even spare Dany's life. She had no way of trusting anything P.O. said.

"Let me talk to him."

"I can't do that."

"Then how do I even know you're telling me the truth?"

"Do you really want to test me?"

She didn't, but she also knew she couldn't just sit in her house and do nothing.

"Don't you hurt him. I'll come if you promise me you won't hurt him."

She couldn't decipher the next sound that came through the phone. Was it glee? Victory?

"I promise."

"If I come to you, you will let him go?"

"Yes. If you come to me, I will let him go. Completely unharmed."

Her body raged with the war between her mind screaming that something wasn't right and her heart knowing that if she didn't respond and something actually did happen to Dany as a result of her inaction, she would never forgive herself. She would never be able to live with that guilt. The guilt of knowing she hadn't done everything possible to save him.

"Then, I'll come."

It was quiet on the line for a few moments. P.O. was probably celebrating.

"I'll look forward to it," he finally said.

Julia sat in shock for a few moments after P.O. hung up. This was it. The confrontation she'd been dreading. He'd finally succeeded in getting her. Of course, that was assuming that he actually did let Dany go, and Dany actually left after she surrendered. Dany wouldn't be happy that she offered to sacrifice herself for him, but she also knew that him being free was the key to eventually getting her out of the whole predicament.

She was dressed and ready to go in ten minutes, her breakfast forgotten on the table. There was one more thing she needed to do.

She dialed Dany's cell. It was entirely possible that P.O. didn't have Dany at all. When she got his voicemail she hung up. There could be many reasons why he didn't answer the call. His phone could be dead. He could be involved in some sort of aspect of the investigation that he couldn't pull himself away from. If part of that work had meant confronting P.O., he could be unconscious.

Her next call was to Constable Davis and only got his voicemail, too. Maybe already working on getting Dany back.

Oh, well. A message would be better than nothing.

"Constable Davis, it's Julia McIntyre calling. I received a phone call from P.O. He's got Dany. He's promised to let Dany go if I go over there. So that's what I'm going to do. I tried Dany's cell and he didn't answer. May not be able to answer. I'll be in touch when and if I can."

She hung up and slipped the phone in her pocket. On a whim, she put the two empty Coke bottles and the remaining four loose in her satchel, and headed out the door.

Chapter Twenty-Three

Five minutes later, she stood at the end of the walkway to his house. It didn't look like the house of a stalker or murderer. It looked like an ordinary one that a family would live in. It was a pretty large residence for only a single guy. When this house had been investigated in the follow-up to Michael's death, P.O. had told police he was renting it. It seemed like that might actually be the case.

She tentatively walked up the path, and the steps to the landing. Just as she was about to ring the doorbell, he opened the door and there he stood in front of her – beady, brown eyes, with overgrown eyebrows that almost met in the middle, pointy nose, front teeth that jutted out just a bit too far. The very man who had destroyed her life, and threatened the little bit of happiness life had brought to her since. She resisted the urge to turn and run.

She took a deep breath and steadied her nerves.

"Where is he? I want to see him. I want to know that he's alive."

"Come in, honey girl."

It was one thing hearing him say that name on the phone, it was another to hear him say it in person. Creepy crawlies scurried up and down her body and she shuddered.

As he closed the door behind her, she walked far enough in to see his living room. The remnants of a coffee table lay strewn all over the floor. What had happened here? His reaction to her media statement perhaps? Aside from that, the house was clean, she had to give him that. Afraid to go any further, she turned to face him.

"Where is he?"

Harley Davidson chuckle. "Oh, he's not here."

Her stomach plummeted to her toes and she braced herself against the wall with an outstretched hand. He stood between her and the front door. He had already succeeded in trapping her inside her own life, and now, if what he said were true, he had trapped her literally. She had nowhere to go.

"Wh-What do you mean?"

He towered over her until, back against the wall and unable to go any further, she was forced to look at him. She said a silent but ardent prayer that it wouldn't be long until the constable received her message.

"He's not here," he repeated, exaggeratingly enunciating each word. "Pretty clever, don't you think?"

"What do you mean, he's not here? Where is he?"

P.O.'s eyebrows crooked down over his nose making him look like the villains in the Saturday morning cartoons she used to watch as a child.

"Not. With. Me."

She really believed him. Dany wasn't here. He had tricked her.

"But you said you had an unexpected visitor, last night."

"That I did, but it wasn't Dany. Although it would have made for a much more interesting evening, I'm sure."

She caught a whiff of his stale breath and coached herself to breathe not actually smell or, given the adrenaline coursing through her veins, it might be sufficient enough to make her faint.

"Th-then who was it?" She took deep, steadying breaths to keep the room from spinning and the looming darkness at bay.

"Come along. I'll introduce you." He led her down the hall and to the left. He didn't turn on any lights as he went. The only source of light came from the big bay window in the living room, and the dangling bulbs in a room at the end of the hallway across from the kitchen. She gasped and all but collapsed against the kitchen wall.

"My ode to you. Don't you like it?" She jumped at his voice in her ear. She quite honestly didn't know what to say. It wasn't a shrine of admiration like most fans who might have posters and signed CD covers and greatest hits montages. This was a testament to his obsession with and hatred of her. How could anything she had said, done, sang, or written drive someone to hate her this much? And she began to wonder if anything she might say would actually have any impact at all on his hardened heart.

"Now, now, we'll have time for questions later. Come. There's someone waiting to see you."

While it went against all the brain cells screaming at her not to go down, she didn't see that she had much choice. Even if he had lied about Dany, he had obviously captured someone, and whoever that was needed whatever help she might be able to offer.

He stepped aside to let her go down first, then he followed her down into the musty blackness. She hated creepy basements. Even as a child, she avoided them. She relished the idea of finished basements and furnaces that didn't look like they were going to eat you alive the moment you set foot on the floor. P.O. pushed past her and led her across the room. She focused on his silhouette until he stopped in front of a wall. After a moment, a door opened and he grabbed her arm and tossed her inside, her knees scraping along the floor. Before she could get to her feet, he slammed the door behind her with a, "I'll be back for you later."

With the door closed, the only light came from above her. She appeared to be in a cold storage compartment given the temperature, and the cooler air blowing in from the vent above her which let in slivers of sunlight. It was probably covered by the thin layer of snow, which was why the light had more of a soft glow to it than pure, bright sunshine.

Julia turned and saw the outline of a woman on the floor. She knelt down and touched the woman's face.

Mariah Colverton! She was ice cold. Her breaths very shallow and far apart. Hypothermia? At any rate, she needed to get Mariah warm and quickly.

"Mariah. Mariah! Can you hear me?" Her head moved. "Mariah." Julia removed her coat and wrapped it around the woman front ways, then settled herself between Mariah's back and the wall, and pulled the coat around them both.

Finally – she had no idea how much time had passed – Mariah started to stir, her face appeared more of a flushed pink than white-ish.

"Mariah?"

A grunt.

We're making progress.

She left Mariah in the coat against the wall and moved around on her knees so that Mariah could see her.

"Mariah. It's me, Julia."

Mariah's eyes fluttered open. "Julia?"

"Yes."

"Am I ever glad to see you." Mariah reached an arm around outside the coat and hugged her before tucking herself back inside the warmth. "What are you doing here?"

Julia related the story of P.O.'s lie to her about Dany to lure her over. "What are you doing here? Trying to get an inside scoop?"

Mariah looked at the ground sheepishly as she snuggled into the coat and replied through the shivers: "Yeah. Pretty foolish of me, huh? Craig, my cameraman, was not very happy when I insisted I come alone. I assume he's gone to the police by now. He was supposed to last night when I didn't return and didn't call him. I tried to text him when I was thrown in here, but not sure the signal even made it past the walls. And then my phone died."

"If he did notify the police that's probably the break in the case that Dany mentioned. I called Constable Davis before I came here and left a message that I was coming here looking for Dany. No idea when he's going to get it though."

"What do you think he plans to do with us?"

Julia shook her head. "I don't know. I think the ultimate target was always me. Now that he's finally got me, I don't know what he'll do next. Hold us hostage? Standoff with the police? Kill us outright … or at least kill me outright. He tried to do it before and failed. I wouldn't be surprised if he tried it again now that I'm close enough for him not to make a mistake."

Mariah shifted under the coat and gasped in pain.

"What? What is it?"

Mariah brought out her awkwardly hanging wrist.

"Oh my gosh! Did he do that?"

Mariah nodded.

"Well, let's see what I can do for that." She took the scarf from around her neck, tied it around Mariah's to create a sling. "Not much, but at least it has some support now."

"That'll be fine. I couldn't do much with it last night because I hit my head when he threw me in here and blacked out and when I came to it was pitch black. You don't happen to have anything to eat or drink in that satchel do you?"

"As a matter of fact, I do." Julia pulled out a snack size bag of chips, two protein bars, two bottles of Coke, a bottle of Tylenol, and a pack of gum.

Mariah raised an eyebrow. "Wow, you came prepared."

Julia shrugged. "I didn't mean to. I always have a few snacks on hand since when I'm performing … er … had when I was performing. I never knew where I'd be that I'd need a snack. These…" she waved the Coke bottles "…I picked up last night when I was out mini-putting with Dany. No real reason. Just a gut thing really."

"Always listen to your gut," Mariah chuckled.

She opened a protein bar and popped the soda bottle cap on the corner of a shelf, and handed them to Mariah.

"You might want to take these first." Julia handed her two pills out of the Tylenol bottle. Mariah nodded, and swished them down with the Coke.

"So, how does he fit into all this?" Mariah asked with a contented sigh, around a mouthful of bar.

"Who, Dany?"

Mariah nodded. Julia relayed the story of the message in a bottle, Dany's history as a police officer in Halifax, how they came to meet and his involvement in the investigation.

"Do you think they'll find us?" Mariah asked when she'd finished the story.

Julia shrugged again. "I don't know. They may, but whether or not it's before he gets to do anything to either of us, I don't know. I don't even think he's worried about being caught. He didn't take my satchel from me or ask me for my cell. Heaven knows, we could dig our way out of here with something and he'd never know it."

Mariah sat up. "Do you have something in there that could help us get out?"

Julia shuffled through it. "No. Just the bottles, my wallet, female products."

"We could break one of the bottles and use the pieces to dig our way out."

Julia considered that and then looked up at the vent. "Even if we did, I'm not sure it would be the effective against the concrete. We could dig out around the vent, but that would mean letting the winter in full blast. It would take a while before it was big enough for one of us to fit through, plus we'd have to do it rather precariously on those shelves."

"Well, we need to try something. Whatever he's got planned for either of us can't be good. I'd rather take on the Great Canadian Winter than sit around waiting to see what happens next."

"You have a point." She took one of the used soda bottles out of her satchel and walked over to a corner where shards of glass wouldn't get under foot, and smashed it. She picked up the bigger pieces and carried them back.

"Okay, great." Mariah took one piece. "And if we can stack the boards on top of each other we may be able to stand on them to reach the vent, rather than having to climb up."

Julia tried to lift one of the shelves up, but they were securely fastened. "They're screwed into their brackets, and I know I don't have anything that we could use as a screwdriver, and even if I did, these are probably so rusted they wouldn't turn."

"Well, then I guess we're going to have to kick them or something."

"Hmmm. I don't know how that's going to work for the higher ones."

"We can use the ones we kick down to lever up the others."

"Sounds like a plan."

By the time they'd broken down all the shelves, both were out of breath and sat down for another Coke.

"Not bad work," Julia said after a few swigs, her chest heaving.

Mariah shook her head. "Not bad at all." Then, after a few quiet moments, "Julia? Why is he doing this? I've been following this story ever since it broke about two years ago. I was at the concert when Michael was shot. Even with all my and the police digging, we've never been able to find anything about him. He's hidden his tracks pretty well. Has he ever told you?"

This time, Julia shook her head. "He's never said. Singing the kind of music I do – er, did – it's bound to ruffle some feathers. No one likes being told what to do or that every choice they appear to have made has been wrong, even if you're trying to point out the forgiveness and grace that's available once we've come to the realization of the errors of our choices. So much of what our society now says is right or okay directly goes against what the Bible says is right and wrong. He certainly wasn't the only person who expressed disagreement or displeasure with my message."

"No, I don't imagine so. Still, you think he would have given you a hint."

"You'd think. But, up until yesterday, I didn't even know what he looked like."

Mariah's eyes widened. "Really? You're serious?"

"Dead serious."

"How'd you find out what he looked like?"

"He showed up at the community center while I was volunteering."

Julia relayed the story.

"Wow." Mariah handed the now-empty bottle back to her. Julia stowed it back in her satchel. "What's up with this guy? From all accounts he was so careful at keeping himself out of the limelight. The police didn't have a clue who he was and now he does this."

"I don't know." Having finished her snack, Julia stood with the shard of bottle glass in her hand and stepped up to one side of the vent. "It doesn't make much sense to me. But then how much logic is there in the mind of a person who only seeks to destroy someone else's life?"

"True." Mariah stood on the other side of the vent with her shard. "Well, let's get out of here before he has a chance to finish what he started."

P.O. examined the items in his trunk--or rather, his brother's trunk--satisfied that he had what he needed. A few duffels full of clothes. The contents of his cupboards in reusable grocery bags. A smaller black bag full of tools he'd collected over the years. A pair of knee-high winter boots and a thicker parka. A pair of traction treads, a foldable shovel, thermal blankets, and a coil of thick rope. Never knew what the roads would be like and it wouldn't do to get stuck in a ditch or something without the proper tools. Where they were going, there would be no mobile reception or 9-1-1 service, and it would be very unlikely anyone would happen by and offer to help a fellow driver in trouble.

He slammed the trunk shut. It was time to go.

With that nosy reporter and now, finally, Julia in his basement, the police would be breaking down his door any moment, even though they still didn't know who he was. They only thought they did. But, even then it was only a matter of time before they figured it all out, and he couldn't do what he needed to here.

He entered the house via the side door. Too bad he wouldn't be able to do it here, as had been his plan all along once he'd discovered who she really was and had decided she needed to die. He didn't remember the precise moment he had come to hate Julia McIntyre or when he'd decided to kill her. It had been a complete shock to find out their connection, the price he paid for snooping through his brother's house.

He had to admit though, Dad had never treated him differently, and Anthony had always treated him like a brother. And his mother, the only mother he remembered had always treated him like he were her own son – but that hadn't been enough. Although he looked enough like Anthony for people to know they were brothers and often mistook the two for twins, he never really felt like a true member of the family. Something was always off. Like, he was skinny while his father and brother were well-built and strong. He had brown hair, while his father and brother had pitch black hair.

Not only were there differences in appearance, but also in intellect and interests. He'd always been considered more of a geek in school and demonstrated a talent for music, while his father and brother were both well-known athletes and had since become a construction foreman and a superintendent for an oil company. He had loved music, still did. It wasn't Julia's music that made him hate her. It really had nothing to do with that. It had to do with …

What difference did it make what it had to do with. The fact was he'd been waiting for this moment for two years, and she was finally right under his nose. He had a chance to get this right, but as soon as that reporter had shown up, he knew he wouldn't be able to do it at the house. There were too many people around. At first everyone was completely unaware of him, as they all had been while he was growing up. But with Mariah Colverton's arrival at his door, and that Davis cop piecing together the chance encounter with Dany-boy and his appearance at the community center, everyone was now watching him.

He couldn't focus under all the scrutiny. He needed just a little more time. Time that living in the city couldn't provide him. That's why he needed to get out. That's why it was time to go.

"She wasn't there!"

Dany burst through the door of conference room where Clint, Craig, and a few other officers had gathered to piece together what they needed for a warrant. Fear and anger churned through his body, he was barely restraining his temper. He couldn't afford to give in now. His temper would fuel his desire to get to her, but he needed his mind clear and logical to do things right. He couldn't afford another screw up.

Clint turned, straightened to his full height, and ushered everyone, but Craig out of the room.

"What do you mean she wasn't there?" He said when the room was clear.

"She wasn't in the house. Her breakfast was left on the table. Her satchel's gone."

"My God. She really did go there, didn't she?" Clint set his hands on his hips and looked down at the floor with a shake of his head.

"He used me to get to her."

Clint glanced up at him. "It certainly appears that way, but it may have just given us the edge we need to get that warrant." Clint brought his head all the way up again. "We have reason to believe two crimes have been committed. We can't claim it's a hostage situation because we haven't received any communications for ransom from him, but we do know that the last evidence of Mariah's and Julia's whereabouts was at this guy's house who is part of an ongoing investigation and was seen at the community center interacting with Julia the day before."

"Whatever we do, we have to do it fast. For all we know he could have killed her already."

Clint nodded. "I will add this new information to our filing for the warrant." He turned to Craig. "In the meantime, I would like you to go public with your recordings of him from yesterday morning. Just mention that he's wanted for questioning by police, nothing else. We don't want to spook him or someone else to spook him and him to jackrabbit. We just need to pick up his scent, and make it hard for him to hide. We need to do this right."

"Yes, sir. Right on it." Craig dashed from the room, the door slamming after him.

Clint returned to his desk where he sat and typed for several agonizing minutes. Dany wandered past the desk to stand in front of the window.

"Did you ever think he would take her?" Dany asked, wistfully looking out the window at the wintery scene outside--slushy, wet streets, cheery Christmas baskets lining the downtown street lamps, people--shoppers and workers--huddled against the cold inside their coats, and someone walking their dog.

"No. I didn't think so. Though it was hard to tell. He didn't have a history of personally interacting with her. It was more through notes and phone messages. So far as we know, the only time he personally made himself known to her was when he shot Michael, and yesterday when he appeared at the community center." More clicking of the computer keys. "This was not what I imagined at all."

Dany turned and leaned his back against the wall. "I shouldn't'a left her." He shook his head.

"There was no way you could have anticipated what he would do with you not there."

"Because that's what people like him do. He was waiting for the precise moment I left her because that meant she was vulnerable to him. An open target."

"You can't blame yourself for that." Clint stopped typing and stared at the screen in front of him, clearly reviewing what he'd typed, before tapping a couple more keys and a ream of papers appeared on the printer next to him. "It may not be precisely what I expected, but I think you and I both know that he would have had to get her away from you somehow. You were a threat to him."

"Yeah." In the seclusion of Clint's office, Dany allowed himself a moment of heartache. It would be a virtual marathon from here on in, with little time for emotion. His shoulders hunched as air caught in his lungs. "I'll never forgive myself if something happened to her. I knew the moment I found out who she was that I would become part of this. Jack told me I was rushing off to rescue the damsel in distress. In essence, that's exactly what I was doing and I knew it. I never imagined I would actually fall for her." He looked at Clint. "That just adds a whole new element to this case."

"And what's that?"

"Before I was just content to help with the investigation. I was still on stress leave and not sure I would be able to offer anything else. Now, I am determined to nail the bastard with my bare hands if we get close enough."

Clint smiled. "Good." He waved the sheaf of papers at him. "Then let's go get 'im."

Chapter Twenty-Four

Keys jangled on the other side of the door.

"Mariah, stop!" Julia whisper-shouted. "He's here."

Mariah dropped to the floor from her perch on top of the stack of wooden shelves, just as P.O. poked his head in the door.

"Ah, nice to see you ladies both up and about." He grabbed Julia's arm. "You're coming with me, honey girl."

"What do you mean? Where are we going?" She nearly choked on the words. How would Dany find her if she weren't here?

"Tsk. Tsk. Spoilers. Don't want to ruin the surprise, but let's just say it's away from prying eyes and out from under Dany-boy's grasp."

Julia looked at Mariah as he yanked on her arm.

"What about me?"

"Sorry, missy. This is just for me and Julia. I've waited a long time for this."

"But I'll freeze here."

"Not my problem."

"Wait. I'll come with you. Just let me bring my bag." He looked about to refuse. "It's that time of the month."

He rolled his eyes. "Fine! Better than getting a mess in my brother's car."

She hoisted the bag over her shoulder careful not to let the bottles clink and handed her jacket to Mariah. Hopefully it would keep her warm until the police showed up. It was all she could do to help now. She cast one last glance over her shoulder at Mariah before he closed the door between them.

P.O. tugged her up the steps and out into the garage. About the only thing she dreaded more than being locked in the cold storage or leaving Mariah behind was getting in a car with him. Heaven only knew what he had in mind.

He dragged her around to the trunk and opened it. "You're getting in here."

She glared at him. "You've got to be kidding me."

He stepped up to her until he was nose to nose with her, the abject hatred in his eyes blowing away her bit of resolve like the winter wind outside. "Do I look like I'm kidding?"

She shook her head, then climbed inside so that she was curled in a c-shape space he'd made among the bags. Wherever he was taking her, he obviously planned to be there a while. Perhaps anticipating that he wouldn't be able to come back to the house for several days. With one last smirk of victory, he closed the trunk lid. A few moments later, the car rumbled to life, and then started rolling.

Time stood still with no way for her to tell where he was taking her, but she was far from helpless.

She took her mobile from her pocket which told her it was just after noon. The phone also provided enough light for her to see. She dug through her satchel for a piece of paper and found a few receipts in her wallet. She found a pen and wrote, "VOAA" on six of them, then rolled one up and shoved it inside one of the empty pop bottles. When the car rolled to a halt, probably a stop light or stop sign, she popped the trunk lid slightly using the emergency release latches, just enough to squeeze the bottle out, and listened to it roll away.

Then she turned on her mapping program. Finding her location within 300 m wouldn't provide an exact location for Dany, but it would at least help with the trail she was creating. She hit SEND LOCATION then selected TEXT mode. Before the link that appeared, she typed, "I'm here" then hit SEND.

Next thing she had to do was keep warm. Without her jacket and with the trunk not being heated, it wouldn't take long for the cold to set in. The bags behind her were soft and squishy. Clothes, probably. There was something heavier, crinkly on the outside but soft sitting on top of the bags. A parka? She smiled in the darkness and maneuvered herself into it, then wriggled the bags out of the way so that her back was up against the back seat. Just as she was about to drift off to sleep from the cocoon around her and the soothing rhythm of the car, she slipped another note into another bottle. She left the trunk lid ajar for a bit longer to refresh the air, then sent another text message before succumbing to the darkness.

"I can't believe it took that long!"

Dany trotted down the steps of the court house hot on Clint's heels, seething.

"Three hours. She could be dead by now and we would never know it."

"I know. All we can do now is hightail it over there." Back in the cruiser, Clint barked orders into his mobile. "They were already on standby anyway just waiting for the go ahead from us." He pushed the button for the lights and siren and peeled away from the curb.

A few blocks out, he turned the siren off, and then parked the cruiser when they were a few houses away, behind a white Toyota. He reported their arrival to the dispatcher. Clint turned to his onboard computer and typed in the license number.

"Just have one of those hunches," he said when Dany glanced at him.

A few second later, "A-ha. Just as I thought. That's Mariah Colverton's car. She's here."

Dany stepped out of the vehicle and unholstered his weapon as he followed Clint across the street and pulled up behind him at the property line of shrubbery. The shrubs didn't provide that much cover at this time of year, but it was a sufficient distance from which to start an approach once backup arrived. An agonizing two minutes later, more cruisers arrived, essentially blocking off the street, and Clint started giving out instructions.

Thomp!

Thomp! Thomp!

Mariah sat up as much as her shivering would allow. Even Julia's coat, which was extra on top of hers, was no longer warm enough against the unrelenting cold. She had managed to dig out enough around the air vent to remove it, and some of the snow around the opening. While removing the snow made it easier for her to see, and would mean an easier time getting out should the hole ever be big enough for her to attempt it, it also removed the insulation the snow provided between her and the outside. As her fingers had slowly stopped moving from the cold, she knew that she had no hope of making a Mariah-sized hole.

But that had sounded like doors slamming. And, yes, those were footsteps. They were heading towards her. Maybe help was coming. She slipped off Julia's red scarf and tied it to the end of one of the shelves and shoved it out the opening, the exertion sending her backwards onto her bottom into a corner, spent and weary, as an army of footsteps stomped over her head.

"Upstairs is clear," one of the officers reported over the radio.

"Main floor is clear," came the call from someone else.

"That leaves the basement," Dany said, as he followed the flow between the kitchen and shrine that he vowed to come back and examine later.

"And there's so far no sign of Mariah either," Clint countered.

Footsteps stormed down the stairs, flashlights and weapons at the ready.

"We found a door, sir."

"Is it clear?"

"Floor's clear, sir, aside from whatever may be behind this door."

Dany followed Clint down. Where could she be?

Clint tried the doorknob, but it was locked.

"Is anybody in there? Mariah? Julia?"

"It's a pretty thick door. Not sure they'd hear. Looks like an old cold storage. We could try to pick the lock," Dany suggested.

"Kennel, see if you can get this open. We're going outside." Dany followed Clint back up the stairs and out the side door into the garage. "Empty. Too bad we don't have a description of his car."

"Could this mean he's taken Julia and Mariah somewhere?"

Clint shrugged. "It's possible. Anyway, let's check out the side of the house where that cold storage is."

Dany found the button for the garage door and in a minute or two was able to duck through the opening. Checking around corners along the way, Dany trotted around the side of the house, Clint following. As they rounded the garage, he saw something red against the snow near the side of the house. They drew closer and discovered a scarf attached to an old board sticking out of a hole in the wall.

Dany pulled it out. "Is anyone down there? Mariah? Julia?"

The hole was too small for him to stick his head into.

"Kennel. Any luck with that lock?" Clint called into his radio.

"Working on it, sir."

"Let's finish scoping out the area. Team 2 meet us out back behind the garage." When a scouring of the backyard yielded nothing, they all headed back inside and down to the basement. Dany noticed a sledgehammer in the garage and brought it with him.

"Think this might help?"

Clint set a hand on the hammer. "He could have it rigged to blow."

"He could. But someone's in there."

"Maybe not. As you said, he could have taken them in the car."

"I got it, sir," Kennel said as the door popped open.

Inch by inch, Clint nudged it open, Dany ready to yank him out of there if something sounded off.

"Room's clear," Clint said after a sweep of his flashlight around the room and behind the door. "But we're going to need paramedics."

Dany ran in and helped check for vitals. "That's Mariah, but that's Julia's coat. She's ice cold. Pulse is very faint. Dare we move her?"

Clint looked around. "As much as I would love to get her out of this environment, we have no idea what kind of injuries she could have sustained. Better to wait for the paramedics. In the meantime, we can try to warm her up. Kennel?!"

The officer's head popped in through the door. "Yes, sir."

"Bring in a few of the thermal blankets you've got in your car and your first aid kit."

"Yes, sir."

"Let's stay on either side of her. It may not be much, but we can at least block the cold air coming in until Kennel gets back."

"I'm desperate to go through that shrine on the main floor."

Clint met Dany's gaze. "I know you are. I am too."

"Do you know what this means?"

"You mean, that we only found Mariah?"

Dany gave a curt nod. "That she's alone with him. Somewhere. Anywhere. We have no idea where they've gone." Panic started swirling within him, and he reached a stabilizing hand to the wall beside him as the world kaleidoscoped. Clint's voice brought him back.

"Dany. Listen to me." Dany mentally kicked himself and took a few steadying breaths. "I need you to focus. She needs you. It's not going to do her any good if you slip away now."

Dany closed his eyes and took one more deep inhale through his nose and let it out slowly through pursed lips. His mind cleared until all he could see was Julia's face. Clint was right. Julia was depending on him, counting on the fact that he wouldn't fail her. It was the police officer in him she needed now more than anything. His love for her would fuel the hunt for her, but the cop side of him was the only thing that could help her now. He gave his head a shake, flinging the remnants of the panic away from him. "I know. I'm good now."

At that moment, Kennel returned with the blankets and first aid kit.

"I'll leave you to it. Dany and I will go see what's happening upstairs." Clint dismissed most of the officers so that there'd be room for the forensics team to work. They couldn't begin to analyze whatever might be waiting for them to discover until everything in front of them had been properly photographed.

Dany scoured the shrine room from a distance while the photos were taken.

"How many layers of things do you think he has?" He muttered to Clint who stood beside him. "Looks like concert tickets. Photos. Newspaper clippings. Magazine articles. CD covers." He leaned closer to one wall. "Concert schedules?"

"No idea. And that's just the walls. Heaven knows what's on the table." They stood for a moment in silence, then Clint motioned with a hand for Dany to follow him. "Come on."

In the living room, they found a splintered coffee table. One of the forensics officers lowered his camera and turned as they entered.

"Go ahead. I'm done in here."

"I guess there's no wondering what happened here. Obvious temper tantrum," Dany said. "But, over what precisely?"

"I was here last night. He didn't seem flustered or anything by my visit – at least not any more so than I thought would be normal – but just before I left, I noticed a cut across the back of his hand."

"Oh?"

"Yeah, he said it was from when he was hanging lights. Speaking of which…" Clint walked out into the hallway, then abruptly headed upstairs. He checked each of the three bedrooms on the right – two kids' rooms and a master. "Nothing on the floors." He peeked inside the already-open closet in the master. "Nothing in the closet." Out of the master bedroom, down the hall to the door of the bedroom to the left of the stairs.

"What are you looking for?" Dany chased after him.

"Well, there's nothing to say that he doesn't have a secret stash somewhere, but last night he told me that he was Christmas shopping between the hours of 12 and 2 yesterday afternoon when he appeared at the Community Center, and so far, I've seen no signs of Christmas shopping."

Clint nudged open the door of the last bedroom to discover an array of recording equipment.

"Jackpot," Dany whispered, stunned. "And I'll bet that if we opened those blinds we'd have a clear view of Julia's house."

"You won't get me to bet on that." Clint backed out. "I don't want to touch anything yet. But sure looks like we've got our man."

Dany followed Clint back downstairs to the living room. With a gloved hand, Clint turned on the television, and then the DVD player.

"Let's see what the ol' boy watched last." Clint tapped a few buttons on the remote and Julia's face appeared on the screen.

"That was yesterday morning," Dany said. "I knew it! I knew he was watching. I couldn't see him, but I knew he was there."

Clint looked down at the coffee table. "I guess he didn't like what she had to say."

"I guess not."

"Well," Clint craned his neck around the room. "I think we've got our hands full with this one."

"Yeah, it's going to take us a while to go through all of this. But, there's nothing I've seen so far that gives us a clue as to where he might have taken her."

"You said her satchel was gone."

"Yes."

"But we haven't seen it around here."

"So, she must have taken it with her."

"Is it likely she might have her cell with her too?"

Dany thought for a minute back to when he'd arrived at her place to pick her up only to find the house eerily empty. "She may have. I don't recall seeing it at her house either." Dany whipped out his. "I forgot, I put it on silent mode when we went into the judge's chambers to get the warrant." Clint hovered over his shoulder. "Two text messages. The first one, sent at 12:10PM, 'I'm here' with GPS coordinates. Good girl! The next one at 12:30PM, 'I'm here' also with GPS coordinates."

"But that's it? Only two messages. It's been nearly an hour and a half since the last one. That's not much to go on."

"No, but it's a place to start. The first set of coordinates is not too far from here. Just around the corner. The second a few blocks away from that."

"Can't really tell much about where they're going. It's logical that he'd take her some place outside of the city, but that could be anywhere."

Dany looked up from his phone. "I know. But she's trying to leave a trail. I have to follow it."

"Alright, I'll continue supervising the clean-up here."

Dany stepped out into the cold, a couple of police officers following him. The GPS directions tracker led him to the left and down the street to the stop sign. As he neared the corner, the sun glinted off something at the side of the road. It could be anything. Most everything was snow white in the area after the dusting that had fallen overnight. He never would have noticed anything if it weren't for the sunlight.

As he stepped closer, he noticed a red label with white handwritten letters. A thought flashed through his mind and he ran the rest of the way. Standing over it, he recognized it immediately – one of the soda bottles Julia had bought the night before. But the sunlight didn't go all the way through. There was something inside. A message in a bottle. Dany tapped the open end of the bottle on his hand, but the paper had unrolled inside and wouldn't come out. He took a pen out of his uniform pocket and stuck it in the hole, as the other officers gathered around him. With a little wiggling he pulled the paper out and opened it.

voaa

"VOAA? What does that mean, sir?"

Dany looked at the other officer. "Voice of an angel. It's her message to me. A message only I would understand so I would know that the message was from her." He resisted the urge to hold the bottle to his heart. He couldn't get emotional now, and more importantly, the others couldn't see him get emotional. Julia was counting on him to stay focused, and he'd only be able to find her if he followed the adrenaline and momentum of the hunt.

"Do you think there's another one at the other coordinates?"

"I'd bet money on it. But let's take a cruiser."

Half an hour later, Dany found Clint in the shrine room. Clint looked up.

"Did you find anything?"

Dany waggled the bottles in their evidence collection bag. "She put messages in them."

"VOAA?"

"Voice of an angel."

"Voice of an angel? What does that mean?"

"She told me once that people would tell her that she had the voice of an angel. She knew no one else would get the reference. These messages were intended for me, so I'd know that she'd left them."

Clint examined the soda bottles. "The guys found soda bottle caps and pieces of a smashed bottle downstairs in that cold room. That's a good lead. Unfortunately, we've only got two of them. That's not much of a trail."

"She bought a six pack, last night, while we were out. Assuming, she had all six with her when she left the house this morning, that means she has three left."

"It's been long enough now that the next bottle would give us a better idea of where they're heading."

Dany let the unspoken thought between them settle – that there hadn't been a third message from her, which could possibly mean she'd been unable to send another message, and unable to drop the next bottle. He didn't want to think about the reason behind that.

"What have you found here?" Dany turned his attention to the room in front of them to distract himself from that train of thought.

"Well, as you can imagine, there's quite a lot of Julia McIntyre memorabilia." Clint waved a hand at the documents spread across the table sorted into various categories. "We haven't quite got through all of them yet."

"Anything in all this to indicate why he's been targeting her?"

Clint shook his head. "Nothing really obvious. We got most of the stuff off the walls. It's all music related except for this." Clint picked up a color photo of a woman.

"That looks like Julia, but that's impossible."

Clint turned the photo over. "Lila Connelly, 1988. It's her mother, I think."

"Her mother? What would he be doing with a picture of Julia's mother and what does she have to do with this obsession of his with her?"

"I don't know. But there's also this." Clint held up another piece of paper, issued by the city.

"Certificate of adoption for Peckton Marcus Oberman. Parents John and Millie Oberman dated November 1989." Dany paused as his brain started making the connections. "Assuming this means what I think it means, it still doesn't explain why he would want Julia dead."

"Well, let's finish off that set of shelves at the back of the room. Maybe there'll be more answers there."

After fifteen more minutes of sorting, it became clear that the shape unfolding before him was no ordinary set of shelves.

Dany took a couple steps back. "Do you see what I see?"

Clint joined him, and after a moment said, "It's an old upright piano."

Dany lifted up the keyboard lid and tapped a few notes. He cringed at the sour notes. "It sounds like it hasn't been tuned in a while." He flipped through a few of the sheets sitting on the deck just above the keyboard. Beneath everything were sheets of music, the pages curled and weathered. "Royal Conservatory of Music Grade 8."

"What do you make of all this?" Clint asked.

Dany stepped back to take in the whole room again and shook his head. "I don't know."

Chapter Twenty-Five

The car slowed, jolting her awake. A glance at her phone's display told her it was nearly three-thirty. She'd been asleep for two and a half hours. The amount of carbon dioxide and buildup of gas fumes had left very little oxygen. She needed air.

She had no idea where she was, but it had to be remote because her phone was on analog mode. Anything she did would use up extra battery power, which was already at the halfway mark. There was also no telling if P.O. would see her lift the trunk lid, or if Dany would even be able to find the next bottle. But she had to give him something.

She tucked two more rolled up notes into two pop bottles and tossed one out, taking great gulps of fallen-leaves-scented air as long as she dared to. They were obviously driving through a wooded area, but the bottle had landed with a clink and the ride was still smooth not crunchy, which meant they were on a paved road. She closed the trunk lid and tapped on her GPS. "Location not available." Must be pretty remote. Without the next set of coordinates, she wasn't sure if it would help Dany pick up on her trail or not, but she texted him anyway, "I'm here."

Not two seconds after she hit send, the car came to an abrupt halt. Julia hid the second bottle and her mobile in her satchel. She had just taken her hand out, when the trunk lid opened and she raised a hand to the blinding light. P.O.'s silhouette stood over her.

"What do you think you're doing in here?!"

"I-I needed air. The fumes from the gas were making me nauseous."

P.O. harrumphed. "Well, I suppose we're far enough out now that you won't be able to figure out how we got here or how to get back."

He waited until she was standing in front of him, then grabbed her arm above the elbow and led her to the passenger side and opened the door. He didn't seem upset that she was wearing his parka.

"Get in."

Julia did as slowly as she dared. They were indeed in a more wooded area. The road was one of many hundreds that roamed the nether regions of the province. It was impossible to tell where they were precisely, but she knew from the position of the sun that they were driving west. From London, that meant they were pretty close to Lake Huron, one of the Great Lakes.

As P.O. slammed the door and stormed around the other side, she wondered when she would be able to toss her next bottle without him noticing.

He was muttering as he got back behind the wheel.

"Thank you."

"Huh?" he growled.

"For letting me sit up here. This is much better."

He muttered and grumbled, clearly not accustomed to such a

simple thing as gratitude.

"What's your name? Your real name?" she asked as he pulled back onto the two-lane blacktop.

"Don't think you're going to befriend me. I've hated you this long. I'm not going to start liking you now."

She attempted to meet his attitude with attitude although she would never be able to match his level hatred. "I'm well aware of the fact that you hate me, but you at least know my name. If we're going to be spending the next however long together, and you're eventually going to kill me anyway, I'd like to know what to call you."

"Peck," he finally said after another long moment of muttering under his breath.

"Thank you. Where are you taking me?"

"Surely you don't think I'm actually going to tell you that?" he snapped as he negotiated the twisty road, the Cadillac's engine growling as he accelerated. Clearly he was trying to get somewhere fast, but his focus never faltered, and he was well in control of the car. Only a local would know these back roads that well, or at least someone who had travelled them often.

"I guess not." As she opened her mouth to say something else, he held up a finger.

"Don't even think about it. I let you up here so you wouldn't die before I had a chance to kill you myself. Don't drive me to the point of doing it earlier than I planned."

"Just one more question, then I promise I won't say another word."

He rolled his eyes. "What is it?"

"Why are you taking me to wherever you're taking me to kill me? Why couldn't you have done it back at your house?"

"I wasn't ready yet. Originally, I had planned to do it there. But Mariah found me and then that Dany-boy of yours. It was supposed to be my moment and I didn't want anyone else to get in the way."

"Like my brother did." He cast her a curious glance. The only name she could give the expression was annoyance. Was it annoyance at Michael's apparent interference, or the fact that Peck knew something that she hadn't figured out yet.

"Yes, precisely."

"What are you going to do to me?" Julia couldn't hide the tremor in her voice. There was no hiding his true intentions about whisking her away.

"My original plan was to stab you to death and leave you hanging in that little room with all my mementos to finally end my torment. I would have given almost anything to see the look on Dany-boy's face when he found you there." Julia wanted to curl up in a ball at the look of glee on Peck's face.

"But that didn't seem quite right to me. But don't you worry…" he turned and waited for her to look at him "…you will die. And this little escape will give me the time I need to decide precisely how I want to do it." She held his gaze a moment more, and wondered for the umpteenth time how so much hatred could have taken control of him out of anything she had ever done.

"Why? Why do you hate me so much? Until this week, I didn't even know who you were."

"Of course you know who I am! We've known each other for years, actually. You've just forgotten me."

Forgotten him? Known him for years? What was he talking about?

"That still doesn't tell me why you're doing this."

"Enough! I said no more questions!"

Julia mentally and physically bit her tongue to keep herself from asking more questions. Now, the only important thing was for for her to follow the path he was taking so that if the opportunity presented itself she could find her way back to some form of civilization. She had half an idea to call Dany and leave the line open, but there was no way she could do that without Peck noticing or at the very least hearing the beeps of the buttons. And with her phone on analog mode, it would drain her battery pretty fast before Dany even had a chance to reach her. Plus, since Peck apparently hadn't clued in that she still had it with her – or at the very least appeared not to care that she had it – she wasn't about to risk losing her only way of leaving a trail.

"Dany's coming for me. You know that, right? You won't get away with this."

Peck's hand slammed into her face, her head ricocheting between the window and the headrest, and with a stinging left cheek she blacked out.

Dany watched as Clint supervised the bringing in of the evidence from P.O.'s house. Boxes of eavesdropping equipment, DVDs, zip drives, a laptop. It had taken two hours to pack up what they wanted from the house and still no word from Julia.

They had sifted through every possible piece of paper looking for more clues to the certificate of adoption and the picture of Julia's mother, but there was nothing other than those documents. Given the inevitable conclusion the documents led to regarding the connection between Julia and Peckton Marcus Oberman, how could Julia not have mentioned the existence of another brother? She would have been 12 or 13 when P.O. was born. How could she have not remembered him?

The concert schedules and collection of memorabilia all dated back approximately two years ago, the exact timing of P.O.'s first messages to Julia.

He tapped an impatient foot on the floor, as the boxes floated by. Where could she be? Why hadn't she contacted him?

They had found car purchase documents for a 2010 Cadillac Catera in the name of Anthony Oberman, the same name that P.O. had given Julia when he tried to register for help at the Community Center. If he was born Peckton Marcus, who was Anthony Oberman? Julia had said that P.O. had used a driver's license to register with that name on it.

Dany glanced at his watch as his cell phone chirped again. His heart skipped a beat as he tapped a few keys.

"Another text message. It's about time! Whew. She's still alive. It was sent an hour ago."

"An hour ago?"

"She must be in a place that's not-cell-friendly. No GPS coordinates available. But we should still be able to trace it. Find out which tower relayed the message. I wonder why it took her so long for her to send this one? I'll get the records for this one, too. It's nearly four-thirty they could be anywhere by now. What about Craig? Has his piece aired?"

"They got it out as a BOLO message about the same time we hit Peckton Oberman's house. The video was pretty grainy, but hopefully with the description it will turn up something. No tips, yet, though. They just put out an update about the make, model, and license number of the car. An APB has also been issued. A Cadillac is not necessarily the most inconspicuous car he could have chosen. Our next step is to get a composite."

"What about Mariah? Any update from the hospital?"

"Not yet. You hold the fort here, I'm going to grab our graphics guy and head down to the hospital."

"Constables!" A voice called behind them.

"What have you got, Patton?"

"A hit on the name Anthony Oberman."

"Let's have it."

"He's in Australia, sir."

"Australia?!"

"He transferred there about two years ago as an expat for an oil company." Patton shoved a ream of papers toward them and Dany took them.

"Thanks, Patton. Let us know as soon as you find out anything else."

"Australia?" Dany met Clint's gaze, as the other officer trotted off. "What's going on here?"

"Don't know."

Dany flipped through a couple of pages on the report. "Born 1973. So 15 years older than Peckton." Dany looked back at Clint. "Big brother moves, and leaves younger brother in his house with his car?"

"Given the dates on the materials we've pulled from that piano room, Peck's obsession started with her about that time."

Dany paused and stopped flipping through the printed information as his mind churned with all the bits of information.

"Could it be," he started slowly, "that he didn't know about the relationship until then? Until his brother moved out. He started snooping through his brother's papers and discovered the adoption certificate and Julia's mother's picture. Or perhaps he suspected, but was only able to find the documents to prove it once big brother moved out."

"It's possible. His amended birth certificate he's carried since the adoption would only mention the adopted parents' names, not the original birth parents' names."

"I wonder if Julia would have any of that paperwork from her mother."

"She never mentioned her mother having had another child?"

Dany shook his head.

"How could she not have known? That would have been a pretty big event for her at that time."

Dany shook his head, again. "I don't know, but maybe, like Peckton, she never knew about it. But maybe she has documents that her mother kept and she just never looked at them. With her busy travel schedule and her grief and depression over Michael, going through old papers that appeared to hold no real meaning to her wouldn't exactly be a priority."

"Now, it may unlock part of this mystery."

Dany nodded, his heart burdened because he knew that would mean a violation of Julia's privacy. Regardless of the fact that it would be necessary to save her, he hated the idea. "It just might."

"Hey." Dany met Clint's intense, focused gaze. "You need to do this."

"I know."

"This stuff isn't going anywhere. It's also going to take a bit for the report to come back on her last message. Why don't you go back to her house, see what you can turn up? What time's it in Australia right now?"

"Nine o'clock tomorrow morning."

Clint nodded. "Obviously, you need to talk to the brother, but you still have time. I would see what you can find at Julia's house and then come back to this. I'm going to head over the hospital. Keep me posted!"

Dany drove back to Julia's house and let himself in.

He was a welcomed guest, but at this precise moment he felt like an intruder. Julia had invited him in, asked him to stay, and trusted him. Now, he was about to violate that trust. Without her permission. His mind argued the point that Peckton Marcus Oberman had made this invasion necessary, but even that didn't quite assuage his lack of comfort with this whole thing. He hoped Julia would forgive him in the end.

He looked around the house one more time without touching anything, maybe he'd missed something on his initial panicked whirlwind through upon receiving her phone message that she was turning herself over to P.O.. Panicked was putting it mildly. He'd had to resist charging over to P.O.'s house right then, but police protocol had won out, and he had returned to the station to plan the next step. His eternal frustration at the amount of time protocol took to get moving on a plan only increased when he discovered that the delay to get the warrant they needed had been long enough for P.O. to take Julia away to God-only-knew where.

Satisfied that he wouldn't be disturbing anything, he went back to the living room, and picked up the discarded food and dishes, tossed the food in the garbage, and placed the dishes in the sink.

He turned and looked at the table where he and Julia had eaten breakfast together. He recalled the moment she appeared in front of him freshly showered and looking stunning. Forget about the voice of an angel, she'd completely looked like one at that moment to him.

He gave in to the crippling heartache and dropped onto a kitchen chair. She really wasn't here. A part of him had hoped that it was all a trick, a bad dream, that she really was here somewhere. As he accepted the awful truth, the house seemed emptier, devoid of the life that she brought, lonely. He'd only been without her for 24 hours, and he knew he could never be apart from her again. But, unless he did his job, Peck might just make sure that they'd never be together.

That thought propelled him up from the chair and down the hall to her bedroom. He stood in the doorway for a few moments, his conscience battling with his duty until finally duty overpowered his doubt and he stepped into the room. He checked bedside drawers, clothing drawers, under the bed, and finally her closet. Tucked away in a corner of one of the upper shelves, he found a large, dusty shoebox. He brought it down and headed back to the kitchen, since he didn't feel comfortable being in her bedroom any longer.

He set the box on the kitchen table and lifted the lid. He sifted through lost first teeth and first-cut locks of hair, and other baby and school days memorabilia. He found three sets of hospital bracelets, three mother bands with the name Lila Connelly, one girl band and two boy bands – no names, but he knew now that Julia's mother had indeed given birth to another baby boy. Then three birth registrations; one, for Julia Connelly, born in Winnipeg, Manitoba, in 1976; another for Michael Connelly, born in Winnipeg, Manitoba, in 1978; and a third for Peckton Marcus Oberman, born in London, Ontario, in 1988. Oberman, not Connelly.

His knees buckled with the weighty implications of this information, and he landed unceremoniously in the chair he'd vacated earlier.

Peckton Marcus Oberman. She'd registered him with a different name. Why would she do that unless Oberman was the father's name? Why would she have given him to his father? Had the pregnancy been the product of an affair? Is that why she apparently kept it hidden from Julia? But, how did Julia not remember? She would have been 12 or 13 when Peckton was born. Certainly she would have remembered something like her mother being pregnant.

He turned back to the box. Marriage certificate, Lila Peckton to Simon Connelly. Death certificate for Simon Connelly, dated February 1985. A set of wedding bands. Two wads of report cards of various colors representative of Julia and Michael having attended different schools. He took the elastic band off Julia's pile of reports and shuffled through them. Several years of reports from a Winnipeg school, one report from a school in London, and the last few from a private school in Oakville. He flipped through Michael's pile and found report cards from the same private school. A private school? Julia's mother was a piano teacher. How could she have afforded to send two children to private school. Unless ....

The report on Anthony Oberman stated that he worked for an oil company, and was now working as an expat, and his father had been a construction foreman. The Oberman house was certainly worth a lot more than Julia's mother's humble house.

He placed the mother/baby bands in a Ziploc bag, as well as the birth registration for Peckton Oberman, the marriage registration to show the connection of the name, and Julia's report cards.

It was time to get back to the station. He needed to talk to Anthony Oberman. Time was running out for Julia.

Chapter Twenty-Six

Julia awoke alone in the car, the coldness and darkness of evening had already descended upon her and the forest around her. She shivered. The car had been off for a while.

She stepped out of the car, sparkles appearing in her eyes from the lingering effects of Peck's hand across her face, and she braced herself against the car with a hand. As her vision cleared, a two-storey cottage with a wrap-around veranda materialized in front of her. It was hard to determine the color in the dark. Lights were on inside, though, and smoke curled from the chimney.

She was alone. He obviously hadn't noticed that she'd woken up. There weren't even any discerning sounds of animals in the forest, the silence deafening. She could take advantage of the situation and try to head back to town. She looked down the driveway which curved out of sight a few hundred feet away. There was no way to know just how long it was back to the main road or even which way on the main road would take her back to civilization. They were in cottage country, a place people normally went to escape the daily grind, which also meant that the possibility of her escaping was highly unlikely. Even if she did try, it probably wouldn't take long for Peck to find her with his car, and even with his parka, she otherwise wasn't dressed well enough to get very far in the winter cold.

But there was one thing she could do. She removed the fourth bottle from her satchel, walked to the start of the first curve, and hurled it as far as she could. She had no idea where the bottle landed, or if it had rolled into the ditch. She only hoped wherever it was that the stark red label would be noticeable. She pulled out her mobile, and sent Dany another text message. They were so far into the boonies that there was a chance this message would never reach him. The message cost her the last of her battery power, and the indicator light flashed red.

She sent up a silent prayer that Dany had enough information that he could somehow figure out where she was.

Peck was likely to come out and check on her any moment, so she needed to move quickly. She shuffled around in her satchel for the last two bottles, and only came out with one.

Only one left? But, she had bought six. She and Dany had finished two, then she and Mariah had finished the last four … and used one to try to dig their way out. She looked at the last bottle in her hand. If Peck took her anywhere else – she had a sneaking suspicion that he wouldn't actually kill her in the cottage – she wouldn't be able to leave another bottle. It didn't make sense to keep the last bottle with her either, as she would have no way of leading him to it and the chances of him finding it if Peck took her somewhere even more remote were extremely low. She stuffed it into the pile of leaves festooning the verandah, so that the label was just visible and angled so that it looked like it had been raked up along with the leaves. Of course, it was entirely possible that with any snowfall the bottle wouldn't be visible at all by the time Dany found her.

Best I can do. She put the last note in her pants pocket. She'd have to use it wisely.

A gust of damp, frosty wind blew off the lake and blasted through the outer and inner layers of the parka around her as if they weren't even there, sending her body into fits of deep, chilled-to-the-bone shudders. No sense staying out here.

She ran up the front stairs and stood in front of the screened door.

Would it be open? Or had he decided to just leave her outside to freeze to death? Seemed kind of unlikely given how much he appeared to want to kill her with his own hands.

She had just opened the screened door and was reaching up to knock on the inside door when he opened it.

"There you are. Finally." It wasn't a happy statement. "Was just coming out to make sure the cold didn't take you."

Julia shook off his bitterness, as she eagerly jumped inside. She didn't have it in her nature to be hostile and mean back.

"It just about did," she replied, good-naturedly, as she rubbed her arms. "That wind off the lake is brutal."

She couldn't tell if his snarl was his reaction to her positive attitude or something else.

"Well, you might as well come eat. It's just hot dogs."

"Sounds fine to me." No sense playing difficult to get along with. Besides she was famished. She'd probably have eaten dog food if that's all he had in the cupboard.

As he led her to the kitchen, she admired the updated, but quaint cottage. The front foyer led to an open-concept living room and dining room area, and then the modernized kitchen to the right with an island. The floors were a charcoal-shade laminate, but had the grainy pattern of real wood, with matching kitchen cabinets. The countertop was butcher block, leading around and to stainless steel appliances.

But what really drew her gaze was the old white upright piano sitting against one wall. Searing pain tore through her and it took every ounce of her strength to remain on her feet. As if drawn by a magnet, she drifted over to it. It was just as she remembered it from a lifetime ago. Barely able to touch a piano in the last few months, her hands tenderly brushed the keyboard lid and caressed the dented corners that she knew so well.

"H-how did you come to get this?" she asked the shadow that had passed over her.

"I got it from *your* mother when she died." It was the first time she'd heard tenderness in his voice. Her mother had taught many students over the years, and nearly all had loved her as dearly as she had.

Julia nodded as her mind wandered back. She didn't remember much about that time. She had been on the road when word had come of her mother's death of a stroke. Her mother had been alone in the house and a neighbor discovered her when she didn't appear for a planned outing. Both she and Michael had been so blinded by grief at the time. Julia vaguely remembered having been left everything in her mother's will except for the piano. She'd been heartbroken, but given her concert schedule and grief, it wouldn't have made sense for her to fight to keep it. Her mother had obviously thought well of the person she'd bequeathed it to. Who was she to argue with her mother's wishes? She hadn't thought of it since … until she walked into this cottage and there it was.

She took a deep breath as she shook the memories aside. "Well, I'm glad it went to someone who was going to take care of it. It looks just like I remember it." She looked back at Peck and tried to smile, but she knew it didn't quite reach her eyes, and Peck still glowered at her, though not quite so hatefully as before. He obviously had loved her mother dearly if the memory of her had broken through his hatred of her for just a moment.

"You're hungry, right?"

Sigh. The attitude was back. How much more of his negativity would she be able to tolerate?

"Yes, thank you."

She followed him back to the kitchen where he had laid out several hot dogs and fixings on the island. He sat on the kitchen side, she took a stool on the dining room side. As she looked back at the living area from the kitchen, she noted the absence of a television, but that there was a phone sitting on a side table beside one of the chairs. There was likely no cable or Internet, but hopefully the fact that there was power for the lights and the appliances meant that there was phone service. She would have to look for any opportunity to get a message out. But, for the moment, she didn't want Peck to pick up on the fact that she had noticed the phone.

So, with her face turned away so he couldn't see her, she closed her eyes and imagined Dany's voice and face to counter the swelling terror that threatened to make her curl up in a ball. It wasn't just the renewed pain over her mother's and Michael's death, but her loneliness at being separated from Dany. He felt a million miles away right now and there was no guarantee that she'd see him anytime soon, or at all – if Peck had his way.

"This is a beautiful cottage," Julia said as she reigned in her emotions, and selected a hot dog.

Peck grunted.

"I've always dreamed of having one. Never really got around to it with traveling and touring. Perhaps I should look at getting one. It's always nice to be able to get away. I'm sure this is a lovely spot in the summer." She squirted mustard down the middle of her dog and took a bite.

She let the silence settle in between them. She didn't really expect him to respond anyway.

"How long am I going to be here?" she asked once she'd finished her first hot dog.

"Haven't decided yet. I haven't even decided how I'm going to kill you, yet."

"You're still set on that, are you?" She defiantly met his gaze. She knew the only thing that could save her mentally was meeting his hatred with composure. She had to know why he was doing this and keeping her composure was the only way she was going to be able to keep herself alive long enough for Dany to find her. She didn't expect Peck to return her attempt at civility. His hatred of her obviously seemed have taken him beyond the capacity to forgive whatever it was that he believed she had done. Perhaps a moment would still materialize for her to try to reach him, but she sensed now wasn't the right time.

"Absolutely."

She swiped the crumbs off her hands over the counter. "What have I ever done to you to make you hate me so much? You said in the car, that we've known each other for years. Now, that I know what you look like, I recognize you. We've lived on the same street all our lives. I've watched you grow up in that house. I knew your father and your mother. I seem to remember you had an older brother, as well. Can't remember his name though or what he's doing.

"Anyway..." she waved a hand "...what does any of that have to do with any of this? Why is it enough for you to want to see me dead?"

His brown eyes darkened from cappuccino to dark roast, and Julia wondered if she'd pushed him too far.

"You really have no idea who I am, do you?"

"Up until this afternoon, I didn't even know your name, Peck."

"Which is short for Peckton."

A little bell jangled in her mind. *Couldn't be. No way.*

He smiled a crooked, knowing smile that was probably as close as he could get to showing happiness.

"Let me prove it to you."

He wandered over to the piano, flipped up the lid, and started to play. Melody after melody with flourishes, chord progressions, and arpeggios impeccably placed. While she was an accomplished pianist in her own right, she had never been able to play like that. She knew of only one person who could. She raised a hand to her mouth. *No way. That's impossible.* She tried to convince her mind otherwise, but as the melodies floated unheeded through his dancing fingers, it became more and more clear to her. His musical style was unmistakable.

She burst into tears and ran up the stairs next to the kitchen, chose a bedroom, and flung the door shut behind her as she threw herself on the bed and sobbed into a pillow.

Chapter Twenty-Seven

Dany surrendered to Clint's office with the cell phone records in his hand and the details about Anthony Oberman. It was 5 AM and his body and mind felt like jelly. The original adrenaline surge that had propelled him through most of the previous day had faded as fatigue and lack of progress started to set in.

They'd worked through the night sorting through all the documents, and formulating a working strategy to set into motion once they knew where they needed to go. The first cell record for Julia's first remote message had come through just as he returned from her house. Really nothing specific they could act on. The hours waiting for her next message and the location tracing information on that were agonizing, and they still had little to work on without being able to pinpoint exactly where she was in such a remote area.

The mobile phone records only showed the towers that relayed the SMS message, but the remote location required a relay of the message from tower to tower. The trail ended in the small town of Port Franks, Ontario. Why would he have taken her there? It was a cottage-y area. The local economy boomed during the summer, but dwindled down to just the locals in the winter. Assuming that there was a family cottage or some type of summer home up there, why would he choose such a remote area? Was it just another diversion, a chance to plan his final moments for Julia before he moved her somewhere else, or did he really intend to kill her there?

It would be useless to go out there without knowing what he was looking for and where he should look for it. There were so many back roads and twists and turns it would be impossible for him to find the cottage, if that was in fact where he had taken her.

He hadn't yet had a chance to look at the information provided on Anthony Oberman, but he knew it likely held the key to where Julia was. He knew this was the only way to find out the answers he needed. Who was this Anthony Oberman? Who exactly was Peckton Marcus Oberman? What did this all have to do with Julia? And where had Peck taken her?

It was nearly 9 PM in Australia, as good a time as any to call.

Dany scoured the information Patton had given him before picking up the phone and dialing. He anticipated getting an answering machine, so he was caught off guard when a voice repeated, more sternly...

"May I help you?!"

"Oh, sorry. I'm looking for Anthony Oberman."

"Can I ask what's this about?" Was it his wife? Housekeeper? So tricky not to give away too many details, but enough for whoever to understand the urgency.

"I'm calling from Canada. It's extremely urgent that I talk to him right now." Dany introduced himself then gave a brief description as to the reason for the call.

"Just a minute please." An agonizing five minutes later, a male voice came on the line.

"I'm Anthony Oberman."

"Mr. Oberman, thank you for taking my call."

"What's this all about?"

"Sir, we have reason to believe that the person currently living in your house has been involved in a kidnapping. I'm hoping you might be able to shed some light on the situation for us."

Dany wasn't sure if the silence that followed was out of fear that he'd finally been caught, or shock.

"I see. Constable Howard, that is my house. I grew up there, and later, started to raise my family there. Instead of selling it when I took this position two years ago, I let my younger brother live there. He was old enough to be on his own and look after himself, but had never been quite right in the head, if you know what I mean, since our mom passed. To my knowledge, he's never been involved in any crime, though. I just didn't have the heart to kick him out on the street when we left, and the house was paid for anyway…."

There was another pregnant pause.

"What's happened? Is he okay?"

"What's your brother's name?"

"Peckton. He goes by the short form Peck. Is he okay?"

"Physically, we think he's fine. Emotionally is another thing."

"What do you mean?"

"I mentioned that we believe your brother was involved in a kidnapping."

"Yes."

"Mr. Oberman, do you know who Julia McIntyre is?"

"I seem to recall the name. Wasn't she that singer whose brother was killed during a concert or something?" Another pause. "You're not suggesting…?"

"Yes, Mr. Oberman, we have reason to believe that he's taken her somewhere and intends to kill her."

"My God." Another pause settled over the airwaves. It was a prayer, not meant as an expletive.

Dany's instincts told him that Anthony was struggling with the idea of telling him about Peck. He didn't want to betray his brother's trust.

"Mr. Oberman…"

"Tony, please."

Dany smiled and hoped it came across in his voice. "Tony, as part of our investigation, we have searched the house and found documents that seem to indicate an affair between your father and Julia's mother, and the birth of a child."

"I know. I was 15 at the time. My father was a widower and met Julia's mother, Lila Connelly, when he signed me up for piano lessons from her. They lived across the street from each other so that also made it easy."

"I have to tell you that Ms. McIntyre never mentioned her mother being involved in a romance or being pregnant during the course of our investigation."

"That's because she and Michael were at boarding school."

"Boarding school? But how could…?"

"My father paid for it. Lila thought that Julia and Michael would be upset over the relationship, so he paid to send them. They never knew."

"They never knew about the baby either."

"No."

"So, what happened when the baby was born?"

"Lila gave him up. She'd actually called off the relationship months earlier before she found out she was pregnant. She had a hard enough time raising two children on her own. Although my father was willing to support her and the family, she thought it was best to sever all those kinds of ties, although he continued to pay for their education. They, Lila and my father, agreed that he would take the baby when it was born. By then, my father had met and was planning to marry another woman, our step-mother, Millie, and they arranged to adopt the baby."

Dany settled against the back of the chair as his mind tossed this information around.

"Do you have any idea why he would want to kill Julia McIntyre?"

"No idea. To my knowledge, aside from occasional contact, he and Julia never really interacted. I know my father and mother kept in touch with Lila, though, about baby milestones and such. By the time he was old enough to start taking piano lessons, Julia's career was starting to take off and she'd already met Martin."

"Did your brother know he was adopted?"

"No. Well … I don't think so. That is, no one told him. I had left home by the time he started school, but it was pretty obvious by that time that his physical stature and features were different from my father and me.

My father was in construction and I was starting a career in the oil industry. Peck was wiry, with brown hair that our mother could never seem to tame. He tended to look to the arts, music in particular, instead of sports and industry. The only time he really seemed happy was after his piano lesson."

"You think Lila had something to do with that. Maybe she fostered a bond there?"

Dany heard the rustle of a shrug.

"Perhaps. I think it was the only place he was truly happy. My father was never one to push Peck to do get into construction or oil or something, once he recognized Peck's musical talent. So, he never interfered with that."

"What about your step-mother?"

"Millie? She was a good mother. It wasn't an easy situation to come into … me an ornery teenager, my father a widower and the baby being carried by another woman on the way. But she took us on and we never felt – or at least I never felt that she resented the burden placed on her. My father and she clearly loved each other, and she loved me and Peck as if we were her own."

"So, what do you think happened? You said that he wasn't quite right in the head after your step-mother's death."

"Yeah, he took her death pretty hard. Of course, I remembered the death of my mother, Joan. Her maiden name was Marcus, by the way, so that's where Peck's middle name came from. Most everyone called him Marcus, though. But, this was the first time he'd lost someone that close to him. I was married by that time and not living at home, but dad would tell me that the only time Peck would venture out was to his piano lesson. Then Lila retired from teaching piano. I still think he went to see her. But when my father took sick and I moved everyone back into the house, it was pretty obvious how Peck had changed. He was never what I would consider a happy kid, but it was like the life had gone out of him when she retired.

"He was the one who found her on the floor after the stroke."

Dany let out a breath through pursed lips. A kid who felt like an outsider all his life, had found the only refuge he had, and bit by bit the walls started crumbling. Pretty standard downward spiral of a life for a killer, but that still didn't explain why Peck had targeted Julia in particular. There had to be a reason.

"How did you say you found out about the adoption?"

"We were acting on a search warrant after we gathered sufficient evidence to convince a judge that your brother was holding Julia and another woman in the house, a news reporter. We found a piano room plastered with documents and photos relating to Julia's touring schedule along with the adoption certificate and a photo of Lila Connelly."

"He found them after we moved to Australia."

"That's what we're assuming. The touring schedules and other things dated back only about two years."

"You said he was holding another woman. Is she alright?"

"He'd kept her in an old cold storage room, so she was suffering from hypothermia when we found her, but we managed to get her thawed out and she's expected to make it."

"Whew. That's good to hear."

"Any theories as to why he's targeting Julia?"

"Not at all. Your guess is probably better than mine. I haven't spoken to my brother much in the last two years."

"You said he'd never been involved in criminal activity before."

"No. I never heard of any, but perhaps he did and just never got caught."

"The last text message I received from her was traced back to a cell tower in the Port Franks area."

"Ah, yes, my family has a cottage in that area. Has for years."

Dany's heart soared. *Bingo!*

"So, he would know that area well then."

"Yes. And if he's taken Ms. McIntyre there, he'll be pretty hard to find. He would disappear for days on end. We never knew where he went, but he'd always turn up eventually."

"Well, it's a place to start anyway. Can you give me directions…?"

Chapter Twenty-Eight

When Julia awoke, daylight was streaming through the closed blinds on the bedroom window. Without her cell phone she didn't know what time it was, but assumed it to be about nine o'clock.

The house was quiet outside her door.

Why hadn't Peck woken her earlier?

She pushed herself off the bed and padded across the floor to the door. Surprisingly, it was unlocked and she headed down the hall to the bathroom until she remembered she'd left her travel toothbrush in her satchel downstairs. She could see over the lower level of the house and Peck was definitely not there. It would be a stretch to think that he would have left her an avenue of escape, but this would be the perfect time to investigate the place.

At the bottom of the stairs, she turned towards the kitchen, the only area of the house she couldn't see from the upstairs landing. A couple bagels and cream cheese sat on the island with a note.

Don't go anywhere. I'll be right back.

She laughed at the absurdity. She sliced one of the bagels and dropped one half in the toaster, then headed out to the front door. It was locked with a double bolt, so it would need to be unlocked with a key from the inside. And there was nowhere obvious for a key to be hidden. The flooring was laminate and not tile, and nothing was loose enough to lift up. There were coat hooks on the wall in lieu of a closet. He'd probably taken the key with him.

The scent of toasted bagel lured her back to the kitchen. Again, her gaze was drawn to the piano. That beautiful piano. Hour upon hour she had spent at that piano. Sometimes on her own, sometimes with her mother gently coaching from behind as she mastered scales, arpeggios, concertos, hymns. She wrenched her mind from the flood of memories, notes, and voices. She couldn't afford to let them take over her attention. There was no telling when Peck could return and she still had other areas to search.

She wasn't getting out through the front door, but perhaps she could get a call out before Peck came back. She didn't remember Dany's cell number, but there had to be emergency services of some sort out here. She sat on the couch next to the table with the telephone and found the phone book in the drawer. Not surprisingly, the local emergency number page had been torn out. She picked up the receiver and put it to her ear. No dial tone. Again, not really surprising.

The bagel popped up and she headed back to the kitchen to add the cream cheese, then carried her plate with her to the back door while she munched. She tugged on the handle. Locked. It was a double key lock like the front door. While her mind still toyed with escape options, she admired the admittedly beautiful scenery. The property spread out behind the massive deck. A line of nearly naked trees formed a boundary at the end of the property. It was hard to see even through the bare trees, but Lake Huron lay beyond the boundary. Imagining the trees full of leaves, she could understand why people escaped to places like this.

If she were actually on the shores of Lake Huron with its rolling hills, beaches and dunes, Peck could have gone anywhere. Assuming he'd grown up here, he probably knew every square inch of forest. The Ausable River and Pinery Park area was known for its hiking trails in the summer and cross-country ski trails in the winter, when snowshoes and skis, and not snowmobiles, were the main method of transportation. Conservation efforts had severely restricted snowmobile use in the area. Snow was late in falling this year, though, so the ground lay covered in a thick blanket of red maple, chestnut and other leaves.

Pinery Park followed the earlier path of the Ausable River which had once formed a sharp curve in Grand Bend, a beach community to the north obviously named after the bend in the river, and flowed back down to Port Franks, 25 kilometers away. The river's path had been altered by early settlers to try to create a harbor of sorts in Grand Bend and in Port Franks while also trying to alleviate yearly flooding in the area. The result was that a segment of the original river still remained, but there was no water source except spring meltdown and rainfall, the riverbed dried up over the summer and provided a coveted combination of hiking-perfect forests and swimming-perfect beaches and dunes.

In the winter, the area turned into the ideal area for snow-enthusiasts around February. About this time of year, though, late fall/early winter, the park hosted an annual aboriginal deer hunt about and the park was closed off to the public. There'd be fewer people in the park than usual, but still people who would be likely to help her if she could get out, and avoid being mistaken for a deer.

With the two main doors accounted for, she checked the windows only to find that they, too, were locked.

Nothing for her to do, but to finish off her bagel and think about what she could do next. What kind of message could she leave for Dany and where could she leave it so that he would see it? With only one note left she had to make it count.

She looked at the piano. Would he think to look there? What were the chances that Peck would want to play before they left? Before she knew it she was sitting on the bench and had lifted the keyboard lid. She took the last note from her pocket and set it on the music rack before her where hundreds of pieces of music had once been set. She ran her fingers lovingly over the keys. Would the music ever flow again? If her mother's piano didn't make her want to play nothing would. She closed the lid.

To say that she had been stunned to see her mother's piano here was an understatement. She never remembered the name of the person named in her mother's will. That whole time was such a blur. She remembered feeling shocked that the piano had gone to someone else, but didn't have the energy through her grief to contest it. She didn't even get to reminisce about where it used to sit against the wall for nearly 30 years because Martin had immediately begun renovations so that would her grand piano would fit.

There was no denying who Peck was. Peckton had been her

mother's maiden name. And the entire time he'd played last night, all she saw were visions of her mother sitting at the piano. Their styles were virtually identical. Each pianist had their own style even if they were taught by the same piano teacher. Some styles, however, seemed to be hereditary. No one really knew why. Her mother had always mentioned how different her and Michael's style of play was, and she'd always wondered why she, Julia, never quite sounded the same as her, no matter how much she practiced. It became clear over the years that her musical voice differed from her mother's and that she was destined for something else.

Peck was her mother's son. But how? All those years at boarding school. She never questioned how her mother on a piano teacher's salary could have afforded to send her and Michael away, and never questioned why they'd been sent to the boarding school. It had been an excellent school, chosen for her and Michael likely because of the emphasis on the arts. Now these questions ran roughshod through her mind.

She stood and walked around the perimeter of the room, mindlessly running a hand over the smoothness of the wall until she felt a small indentation almost in line with the sofa. She turned her hand, and the wall opened up to present a large screen TV with every media and video player imaginable tidily sitting beneath with an army of videos and DVDs lining sections of shelves beside it.

She skimmed the titles and found several unnamed disks. As she shuffled through them, she discovered one with "JULIA, February 10, 2000," written in her mother's hand on it. The date was the week before she died.

Julia remembered seeing a remote control inside the drawer beneath the phone. She hit the red button and everything glowed to life. She found the DVD player and put the disk in, then sat back on the arm of the couch.

Her mother's face appeared on the screen. She hadn't seen her mother too much while she'd been on tour those last months, and the sight of her sunken appearance broke her heart. How many times had she wished she could have spent more time with her mom, even with the impossibility of her schedule?

"Julia, dear. I have a lot to tell you. I know you're busy and traveling and I want you to know how proud I am of you and I want you to have no regrets for the path your life has taken." Tears erupted over her eyelashes at her mother's gentle voice. "I know my time is growing short. I've chosen not to tell you because I didn't want to worry you. But I really feel you need to know this. Peck, from across the street, whom you have met on several occasions, is really good with these recording things and has agreed to help me. Such a good boy.

"Actually..." her mother's eyes glowed "... he's so much more than that to me. Come around here for a moment." She waved to someone off screen. "This is Peckton Marcus Oberman. Your half-brother. You won't remember him because you weren't here when he was born.

"See, when we first moved here, I met John Oberman across the street and we fell madly in love. We tried to keep it secret from you and Michael because I didn't think you'd be happy about it. I worried that you would feel like I was betraying your father's memory. John agreed to pay for you and Michael to go to boarding school. I regretted sending you away the moment you left, but you and Michael did so well there it turned out alright. But the guilt over sending you away was too much for me, and I eventually broke it off with John, but by then I was already pregnant.

"John and I eventually decided that he would raise the baby. By the time the baby was born, he'd already met and married another woman. I was very happy for them, and they adopted Peckton as soon as they were married. We kept in contact over the years until Peck was ready to take piano lessons and it was very obvious that he was my son. John and Millie took good care of him, don't get me wrong. I never told him he was my son." She glanced up from the screen to the young man looking over her shoulder and beamed. The love clearly returned in the gaze. "But I never stopped loving him."

"A woman's life is full of secrets, and this is one I really felt I needed to tell you and him before I pass on."

The man left the screen, and seconds later the recording stopped.

Her half-brother. Well, that confirmed what Peck had implied last night. Still, it didn't explain why Peck hated her and wanted her dead. There was only one person who could answer that question.

"Enjoying the walk down memory lane, are we?"

Julia startled at the sound of Peck's voice. He stood just inside the patio doors.

"H-how did you get this? Why did you never give it to me? It was her last message to me."

"It was her last message to me, too." He didn't bother to remove his outer winter clothing as he approached her.

"Of course, she died the next week."

Julia wasn't sure what to make of his responding smile. She couldn't help the feeling that he knew something she didn't know, again. Now that she knew that he was her half-brother, what other secrets could he possibly be hiding from her?

"Of course. Come on. Come get dressed." He opened a hidden cabinet beside the back door, and tossed a thick jacket at her. "Time to go. No doubt Dany-boy will be banging on my door any moment now."

"What is it you're not telling me? Where are we going?"

"Nowhere you know."

"Just tell me why you're doing this. I understand that hearing what she said would have been a shock to you. But, what does that have to do with me and Michael?"

The change in his facial expression--darkening eyes, pinched eyebrows, and deeper scowl than normal--made her wish she'd never asked. She shrank away from him until she felt the wall against her back.

"Did you hear her? You were the reason she sent me away. You were the reason I lived my entire life being different. You got sent to boarding school while I endured the ridicule of the bullies in public school because I wasn't the star athlete. It was your mother who called off the relationship. It was your mother who cursed me with music."

"But, when all that happened, you didn't even know about me. You didn't know you were adopted. What's the point of blaming what happened in the past?"

Another one of his glares, as bone chilling as the wind off the lake. "Let's stop pretending you had nothing to do with that past, shall we?"

"From what I understood, your parents were good people. You were raised in a loving home. Even though you were someone else's child and, perhaps, visibly different, you were treated like you belonged. That's the kind of life a lot of children dream of. Why can't you be thankful for that? I understand how horrible the bullying must have been, but you know what they say isn't true."

A side of his mouth quirked upward. "Hmm. Nice try. Distract me so you can delay the inevitable and so Dany-boy will get here in time to save you."

"But who's going to save you?" She was pressing her luck and she knew it. Any second now she expected another hand across the face, but it was a chance she was ready to take. Not just to delay whatever plans he had for her, but to try to make him see that though his lot in life had been tough, there was a way to turnaround on the path he'd chosen.

The fury in his face lessened as he took a step back. "What do you mean? Save me?"

"Yes, save you. I see a man in front of me who's acting out the anger and hatred he has towards the kids that were mean to him, and the feelings of not belonging. You have to remember, I didn't always go to that boarding school." Julia sat on the couch in an attempt to defuse him more. Instead of feeling like he was being confronted and putting him on the defensive, perhaps he would finally be convinced, somehow, that this wasn't the right way to deal with whatever he felt about his past. Perhaps she could convince him that he could change what he was doing. Perhaps he would see her as someone who accepted him for who he was.

"Before I went to that boarding school, Michael and I were part of the artsy group too, never accepted by the jocks, never part of the popular crowd. Our faith also set us apart from a lot of kids. We were teased about it, me not so much, but Michael was. I don't know what it is that people think that boys are too tough to need faith. That having a faith is a sign of weakness. We were well-respected and admired by the teachers for our talents and our small circle of friends, but we never really felt like we truly belonged. While the other kids were out doing their sports, we were home practicing."

Since he was still standing, she stood again and walked over to the DVD player and removed the disk. She hoped that her talking would actually distract him so that he wouldn't realize she was trying to setup the scene for Dany. She put the DVD back in its case and then set it on the side table, label side up, then stood straight to face him.

"We're really not that much different, you and I. People who are given gifts and talents like you and me are not usually appreciated by others. I chose not to focus on those people, and focus instead on what I wanted to do with my life and that was to be on stage, singing, making people happy. That's where I found I belonged. People loved me, loved my music and were drawn, I hope, to a deeper faith.

"There is a place where you belong. You're part of my family. There's no one else left." He didn't flinch when she touched his arm, but didn't return her smile either. "Let me guess that when you were at my mother's house, you felt like you belonged there even before you knew you were her son."

He nodded. "Yes."

"That's because you're one of us. You always were. Michael ..."

Peck's head snapped up, fire in his eyes, and terror plummeted to the pit of Julia's stomach, as he grabbed her by the throat and forced her up against the wall. She clutched at his hand as she gasped for air. She'd briefly hoped that she'd be able to talk around the wall of jealousy he'd built, but there was nothing stable or kind in him. He didn't know anything but the feeling of rejection and jealousy over the life he believed was given to her and Michael, and wasn't offered to him.

"You want to talk about Michael? I was never one of you. Maybe to mom I was, but never to you and certainly never to Michael. Michael, the brother who never talked to me when we would pass on the street. Saint Michael, the boy could do no wrong in your mother's eyes. Especially when he took over as your stage manager. You and Michael were all she talked about. She never talked about me.

"You'd think I'd be accepted by my own mother, who appeared to love me, but all she talked about was you and Michael, how well you were doing. Your latest CD. Your latest tour. Her house was filled with stuff from your career. I was merely a blip on her radar. It didn't matter how much I practiced, she would always talk about you.

"And, you know what? I realized I was never going to be accepted by her, and I was tired..." his teeth grit together "...of living in your shadow. You really want to know how your mother died?"

Julia's eyes widened, as she continued to gasp for air. *What did he mean?*

"Yes, someone found her. Except I didn't 'find' her. I was with her. I decided it was time to shut her up. So I would never hear another Michael and Julia story. She was playing the piano at the time. She never saw it coming."

"No." Julia managed. Tears streamed down her cheeks and she was close to blacking out.

"Then, there was Michael."

"No."

"Oh, yes. Everyone thought I was targeting you, but what I was really doing was targeting both of you. I just couldn't send hate mail to the two of you. Just one was enough. Everyone thought I was aiming for you. But I knew he would try to protect you. All I had to do was aim at you and I knew he would come. Good, faithful brother that he was, that mom was always telling me about. She made it so easy to predict Michael's reaction and protectiveness of you, and he did exactly what mom said he would do, die to protect you."

"Nooo." Her last vision before the darkness swarmed in was of Michael falling to the stage floor at her feet.

Chapter Twenty-Nine

Kathump! Kathump! Kathump!

Dany thought his heart was going to burst through his ribcage as the caravan of cops inched down the gravel drive. The access to the cottage was narrow and the large vehicles barely fit. It had taken them a gut-wrenching two and a half hours to get there. This time they hadn't needed to wait for a search warrant, since Anthony Oberman had given them permission to enter and search the premises, but they did have to get a warrant for Peck's arrest, which fortunately hadn't taken as long as he had feared. They were able to race along the main highway and the smaller county roads pretty good, but the weaving in and through the backwoods access roads had slowed their progress. His insides screamed for them all to go faster.

He hadn't received any more texts and that worried him. One part of him said that it was likely due to the fact that her cell battery had died. It wouldn't have taken long for that given the remoteness of this location. This warred with the part of him that said that Peck had done something to her so that she couldn't respond and that they were too late. He had to coax himself out of panic mode. This was no time for it. If something had happened to her, he needed a clear mind.

Dany thought it unlikely that Julia was still in the cottage, and that Peck had taken her somewhere else. Peck had to have known that the police were breathing down his neck. He was growing weary of the cat and mouse game. Every time they got close, Peck was always a step ahead of them, having anticipated their moves. And without her phone, he hoped she had found another way to leave the next bread crumb for him because he didn't see how he was going to be able to find her otherwise.

He took his eyes off the winding road ahead of them and looked into the surrounding forest. Most of this area was considered Carolinian forest which meant the trees in it were deciduous, leafy trees like oaks, maples and hickories rather than pines and such. Along this part of Lake Huron, even though it was early December, snow hadn't fallen yet and so the ground was still covered in a pretty thick blanket of various types of leaves. Without their plumage, the trees just stood tall and straight around the laneway, their leaves forming deep skirts around their trunks creating a safe haven for many forest creatures.

A flash of red caught his attention. A bright red, not the dark rich red of the fallen leaves.

"Stop!" He was out the door before the vehicle stopped completely. It was a Coke bottle. He knelt down on the side of the road and reached into the ditch where the bottle rested on top of the leaves. Dany rolled it over in his hands, then after a few taps was able to stick a finger in and pull the paper out.

Clint appeared at his shoulder.

"What is it? Another bottle?"

"Yep." If Clint hadn't been right there, he likely would have succumbed to a bit of a pity party. His heart ached inside his chest, it grew hard for him to breathe. He mentally shrugged it off and switched back into cop mode after a few deep, steadying breaths, focused on their mission. "That means we're on the right track and that there's one more."

"Well, let's keep going then."

The vehicles continued rolling once they'd settled back in and after one last twist in the road the cottage appeared before them, with the white Cadillac parked in front.

Dany almost hollered in victory. *I've found her.*

Clint barked orders for the car to be processed for evidence, then organized two teams to sweep the property, while the rest of them set up in front of the door. Two men crouched, weapons aimed at the door, giving them a direct line of sight, while three men stood over them weapons aimed in the same direction. Dany stood on the doorknob side and Clint on the hinge side, with one officer ready with the battering ram.

"Ready?" Clint asked at a whisper.

"Ooh, yeah."

Clint opened the screen door, and Dany knocked on the main door, then bellowed, "Mr. Peckton Marcus Oberman. This is the police. We have the place surrounded and a warrant for your arrest. Come out now with your hands where we can see them."

No answer. He didn't really expect there to be any. He bellowed the ultimatum again and when there wasn't any response the second time, made way for the battering ram. With a swing, the frame splintered, and the door banged open. The house was eerily silent as they inched their way in. Dany had half expected a blazing gunfight, but there was none of that. There was nothing.

"We're clear out here, sir," came the report moments later from the troop outside over the radio.

Dany waved for his group to head upstairs. They found three bedrooms and one bath. In the first room they happened upon, it looked like someone had slept on top of the bed rather than in it, leaving the covers all wrinkled and out of sorts. One of the other guest rooms hadn't been used, and the master suite at the end of the hall had been used, too, but the bed was tidily made and there was nothing out of place.

Dany felt Clint approach behind him as he stood over the bed where she had been.

"She was here. Where has he taken her?"

"Don't know. Perhaps she left us another clue downstairs."

Dejected but determined, Dany followed the others downstairs. Now that the intensity of getting into the house had passed, he tuned in to the gut instinct that every cop seemed to have when gathering evidence that blocked out every emotion so that logic, experience and training took over. His gaze was drawn to two things, the large, white upright piano and the 50" flat screen TV with the requisite media equipment beneath.

Dany wandered over to the TV. He noticed a remote and a DVD case with Julia's name on it and date of February 10, 2000, on the side table and smiled. It was highly unlikely that Peck had placed it there. *Good girl.* He opened the case, carefully removed the DVD – who designed those things in the middle? – and slid the DVD into the player. The TV turned on instantly and an older version of Julia appeared on the screen.

"Well, that answers a lot of questions," Clint said when it was done.

"Yes, it does," Dany replied reflectively.

"What are you thinking?" Clint said after a few silent moments.

Dany popped the DVD out and looked at the label again. There was something about that date. He radioed dispatch to let them know of the situation and then, "I need Constable Orin to find me the cause of death for Lila Connelly, as well as any police record if there was anything reported about the officers who responded to the 9-1-1 call."

"What are you thinking?" Clint asked again.

"I have a hunch, just a hunch, mind you, that Lila Connelly didn't die of a stroke."

"But that's what Julia told us."

"I know. Perhaps that's what she was told and in her grief, she didn't think to question it. But my hunch is that his deep hatred of Julia wasn't limited to Julia. And if that's the case, then Julia wasn't Peck's target on stage that night – Michael was."

Clint whistled. "Why?"

Dany's mind flashed back to the reams of documents they took off the piano room wall, including framed Royal Conservatory certificates issued to Marcus Oberman, not Peckton, which would explain why he didn't initially make the connection with P.O. until he discovered the birth certificates.

He knew from his own high schooling that there was often a divide between the artsy crowd and the jock crowd. The artsy, musical group was kind of frowned upon and teased as not being as tough as the jocks and not very popular. Anthony had mentioned that Peck had been smaller in stature and had different overall features than he and his father, though still clearly John Oberman's son.

He turned to look at the piano, then back at the now-black TV.

He stared blankly down at the floor as his mind processed everything and he attempted to explain his thoughts to Clint.

"My guess would be jealousy. He was an outcast at school. Part of a family, but obviously different. There are bullies in every school. His small build compared to his brother and father, plus his musical abilities would have made him an easy target. Plus, his father paid for Michael and Julia to attend that boarding school which was known for its arts program, Peck went through the public school system. Perhaps he's upset over the fact that his father never did that for him, saving him from the bullies and, in some strange way, allowed him to study music the way he really wanted to."

"Why would that be strange?"

"Because I have a hunch, he clashed with his musical talents. Anthony said that Peck seemed happiest after he came back from his piano lesson. So, that was obviously a place where Peck felt he belonged, where his talent was accepted and encouraged, and on one level was jealous of both Michael and Julia because they were able to use their music as a career. Perhaps he feels like he was never given that opportunity, although his father and family completely accepted and recognized his talents. Add that to the bullying and he might have seen his talent, eventually, as more of a curse than a blessing."

"We found this, sir."

Dany looked up, as one of the officers approached with a stack of DVDs.

"They were all together. No labels."

"Why would someone have so many without labels?" It was a rhetorical question and Dany looked at Clint as he continued his thought. "Probably because whoever made them didn't need labels. Let's try one."

Dany chose the last one on the right, assuming that the disks were recorded and stored chronologically which would mean this one would be the most recent, and hopefully reveal something about Peck's obsession with the Connellys.

After a few moments of black screen, a man appeared, back to the camera sitting at a piano, not the white piano, but the brown one from his brother's house. Dany knew immediately from the slight shoulders and thin frame that it was Peckton. A few seconds later, hunched over the piano, Peckton began to play. Not a classical piece from the Royal Conservatory, but a haunting melody that, as he continued to play, Dany knew Peck had composed himself. He had to admit it was one of the most beautiful pieces he'd ever heard, with interesting chords and flourishes. Dany felt entranced by the music. The last time he'd felt like that was when he was watching one of Julia's videos and listening to her play.

Music had a way of speaking to the soul in a way that nothing else could. One could express him or herself through pretty much any style and connect with the audience. The song was definitely a glimpse into the heart of Peckton Marcus Oberman, a man who had been bullied most of his life for the ability he demonstrated, who had never really felt he belonged anywhere, perhaps even in his own family despite their acceptance and love, because of his extraordinary ability on the piano. A man who, if his hunch proved correct, had set on murdering the three people he hated most in the world. A sudden thought hit him – what if there weren't only three people he hated most in the world. If Peck hated the world enough to plan and carry out the deaths of Lila Connelly, Michael Connelly, and had targetd Julia all this time, could he not also have taken his anger, hatred, jealousy out on the other two people in his life who had been part of his pain?

Millie had accepted Peckton as if he were her own son. Anthony had said that. Normally, one wouldn't think there'd be resentment there, but where Peckton was concerned, the man was anything but normal. Even if Millie had died of natural causes – or at least was not caused by someone else – once she was out of the picture, Peckton would have had open access to his father. Dany was beginning to believe that Peckton knew far more about the adoption situation than anyone gave him credit for. What if he found out, by looking through his dad's papers or something about him paying for Julia and Michael's education? An education in music that he never got. Peck's skill and talent on the piano was extraordinary, and yet Julia and Michael got all the attention, all the opportunity. He'd already explained the possibility of Peck's love/hate relationship with his ability to play.

The man on the screen played with extraordinary passion and

demonstrated a true talent that most piano players wished for. The kind that could mesmerize people and make listeners feel the joy, sadness, or in this case, torment of the person playing. Perhaps Peck had secretly wanted a career in music like Julia and Michael had. Yet, instead of turning his energies into working that out for himself, he let the jealousy take over and, if Dany was right, had killed two people, probably three, had likely been responsible for the eventual death of another – and possibly one more if he didn't find out where he'd taken her.

Dany stood as the song ended. The room settled into a stunned silence. The kind that usually follows a brilliant performance. And it certainly had been that. But the music had been so haunting and expressive of the torment inside Peck's soul that an oppressive darkness had descended upon the cottage and sucked the love of life out if it. The only weapon against such negative emotions was positivity, hope and love. Given the darkness that had happened in his own life, the only light Dany could hold on to was Julia. The man on the screen had focused all his hatred and anguish on Julia, and her family, whose only apparent crime was to try to bring a little bit of light into a dark world. A source of light, perhaps, that Peck couldn't fathom and only served to push him deeper into his own living hell, so that the only way out was to kill his way out.

On the video, Peck turned to face the camera.

"Well, this will be my last video diary for a while. I know from past experience planning and carrying out justice will take all my energy. With mom and dad and now Lila taken care of, that leaves Michael and Julia – and I have special plans for them." A twisted smile. "Very special plans.

Marcus Oberman signing off."

Another stunned silence settled over the group as Dany stared at the screen in disbelief. Peck had just confirmed all that had been going on in his head. He had planned the death of Lila Connelly, his mother and father and Michael. Systematically, eliminating everyone he felt had betrayed him. He hated to consider what Peck would do next if they didn't find him in time and he managed to slip away again. Would he try to find some of those who had bullied him, teachers, principals, Anthony … anyone he felt was complicit in ruining his life.

After a few long silent moments, the men started to stir again, waiting for their next course of action.

"What do you want to do?" Clint asked.

"Do you have access to a chopper?"

Clint nodded.

"Let's get it up in the air. We need to know everything we can about this area to figure out where he might have taken her. We can't possibly do that on foot."

Clint nodded again, and radioed dispatch.

"What's next?"

"Well, we don't need all these guys in the house and I highly doubt he's going to come back here. They didn't take the car, so they went somewhere on foot. Assuming Julia went with him willingly, they could have gone--" he looked at his watch "—at an average foot speed of 3-4 km/hr. If she didn't go willingly, he'd have to carry her or drag her, which means likely a foot speed around 2 km/hr. Obviously, we can't know how long they've been gone, but I'm guessing about 2 hours that means they could be about four kilometres away in any direction. So, I would send them out to do a forest sweep before we lose all our daylight, first looking for anything in the yard or foliage on the ground that might indicate more than one set of footprints or how he carried her – that might give us a trail.

"With our luck, the boys will probably come upon something by the time the chopper's here, but we can't just sit around and wait."

With another nod, Clint, like a mother duck gathering her ducklings, waved the men outside to instruct them.

Dany turned back to the now-black television screen, his mind churning with all the information. He needed to talk to Anthony Oberman, too, and find out what he knew about the deaths of his parents. He needed to figure out how Peck had killed Lila Connelly, and wondered how long it would take for Orin to call him with the information on Lila Connelly's death.

An idea hit him and he reached for the video disc with Julia's name on it.

"What are you thinking?" Clint appeared beside him.

Dany shook his head. "Not sure yet. Another one of those hunches."

He paused the replay once she came into view.

"What's that behind her?" Dany asked.

"A white..." the last word they said together "...piano." They both turned to face the white upright piano against the wall. Dany saw something flutter on the music stand and then fall to the floor.

Dany walked over and picked up the note as Clint peered over his shoulder.

"VOAA. Voice of an angel. This was her last note."

"You don't know that. She may have taken others with her."

"Perhaps. But I'm going on the assumption that she made one note for each bottle and realized later that she only had five bottles."

"What are you thinking?" Clint asked again as Dany's mind played out a vision of what happened the last time Lila Connelly saw this piano.

"I'm thinking we need fluorescein and to cover these windows."

"You want to do the whole house?"

"No, just the piano."

Clint gave a curt nod and waved for the couple remaining officers to follow him.

Lila Connelly had spent most of her life at that piano. It was where Peck had found acceptance in a world that never really fully appreciated artists. And, he suspected, it's where the conflict in Peck began. Lila Connelly was probably not able to hide her love for her son and, even though she may not have outright told him until he was older, he probably had figured it out. Perhaps she had also talked about Michael and Julia and their successes, particularly when Julia's career took off. In a mind like Peck's, those stories had likely cultivated resentment and jealousy. In a twisted sort of sense, Peck wouldn't have been able to stop going to Lila's house. He'd likely grown to love her, as many piano students develop a bond with their piano teachers, and that love was returned, although a part of him would dread always hearing about the half-brother and sister and knowing he would never have a hope of reaching the same esteem in her eyes.

What had been the catalyst, though? What had set him off and made him decide to start killing? If his hunch proved correct, Peck had actually killed his mother, and had somehow contributed to the death of his father. Peck would have been in his early twenties perhaps when he killed Lila Connelly, that would have meant he was younger when his parents were killed. Anthony had come back when his father had taken ill. Perhaps it was just a big brother thing, and he suspected Anthony had been given power of attorney over his father's affairs. He stayed just long enough to get all that settled before he headed off to Australia, leaving Peck alone in the house and never suspecting anything untoward had happened.

How had Peck managed to keep the secret? And how was it that no police investigation was opened in these cases? To do that, Peck would had to have staged what the emergency responders found to make it look like an accident or natural causes – anything but a murder. Julia had been told that her mother had had a stroke. With all the revelations turning over in his mind, Dany was more convinced than ever that Lila Connelly didn't die of a stroke. But then who would have told Julia it was a stroke?

As Clint and the other men returned with the materials for revealing latent blood stains, Dany's phone rang.

"Yes," he barked.

"Sir, Constable Orin, here. I've got the information you wanted on Lila Connelly."

"What've you got."

"Well, there's something strange about that, sir."

"Let me have it."

"Her recorded date of death was February 10, 2000."

Dany looked up at the woman on the TV screen. That video was the last anyone saw her alive.

"Cause of death?"

"Blunt force trauma to the head after a slip and fall."

Julia was told and clearly believed her mother had died of a stroke. "That is strange."

"That's not what I mean, sir."

"Oh?"

"I pulled the medical examiner's full report. There was no autopsy performed at the request of the family so the only notes are from the ME's external examination."

Curious.

"The date on the report is February 17, 2000. And the ME describes the circumstances as, 'Deceased reportedly found dead on the floor of her home after having been discovered by a neighbor. Findings of external examination consistent with time of death of a week before examination.' "

Although Dany had suspected as much, it was still a shock to actually hear about such planning to deceive the police.

"I pulled the 9-1-1 report, too, and the person who called it in February 17, 2000?"

"Yes …."

"Marcus Oberman."

Bingo!

"Do you have any information on the deaths of John and Millie Oberman? I imagine it would be with the information we took from Oberman's house."

"Yes, sir. Just a second."

Dany waited through a few moments of rustling. They had spent an enormous amount of time meticulously sorting all the documents into categories and bagging like documents together. It was just the matter of finding the right bag and sifting through the documents in it. Constable Orin had been part of that sorting process so it wouldn't take him long to find the right bag.

"Got them, sir. John Oberman, complications associated with pneumonia. Millie, trauma to the head after fall. Do you want the medical reports on them too?"

"Yes. One more thing before you go and do that, I need a number for Martin McIntyre."

Chapter Thirty

Julia woke up in darkness, and to the smell of dampness and old wood. Something like an old library or church. She tried to move her arms and legs, but when she tried, something cut into them. In the pitch blackness she couldn't tell what.

As her eyes adjusted, with the help of limited moonlight eking through the windows, she was able to make out shapes in front of her – two columns of benches reaching from the front to the back of the room. A stand or podium-looking shape stood in front of her, but she seemed to be looking down on it, as if she were … hanging.

She looked up at her arms. They were drawn out to her sides, hands slightly above her head. Again, something cut into her wrists when she tried to move. Her legs were drawn together, with her ankles secured to the wall, side by side so that her ankles touched. She wasn't sure exactly what was holding her, but she had a hunch. It wasn't string or twine. It was thicker than that, and sharper than that. She would have probably escaped from those. No, she was pretty sure it was some kind of wire, piano wire. And, from the layout of the room in front of her, she guessed she was in some kind of meeting room or chapel.

Her stomach grumbled, the sound seemingly echoing in the open space of the room. The last thing she'd eaten was a bagel about mid-morning. Given the darkness, it was probably only early evening, perhaps five-thirty, six o'clock.

A door opened a few feet to her right, and a Peck-shaped silhouette stepped inside.

"Ah, you're awake. S'about time." He sounded almost chipper, giddy. "Do you like it?" He twirled around in front of her, arms spread wide. "I'm sorry you can't see it in all its splendour. This building doesn't have any power right now. I thought it was very appropriate, given your career and faith. I wanted you to see what it was like to hang there. And there's just as little hope of you getting yourself down than there was for *him* 2000 years ago."

Julia had rarely been struck dumb, but as the realization of what he had done to her settled in, she really didn't know what to say. Peck obviously thought he'd done something akin to genius, proud in his use of the symbolism of everything she stood for to finally exact his revenge upon her.

"And the wonderful thing is your mother is here with us." He moved closer so that his stinky breath puffed in her face. "Those wires holding you are out of her precious piano." Julia's heart plummeted to her toes as he took a small step back and laughed, apparently pleased with himself. "I really hadn't decided what to do with you until I caught you watching that video, and then I thought, how appropriate?"

Words would not come to her, except in the form of a screaming prayer inside of her that Dany was getting closer.

"What? Don't you have anything to say?"

"Y-you don't have to do this," Julia finally managed, her throat clenched with emotion.

"What do you mean? Of course I do. You're meant to die this way, don't you see? Dying the same way as the Jesus you revered so much. Wish I'd thought of it for mom and dad and Lila as well. Nothing much I could do with Michael though. I wouldn't change a thing about that one."

Julia choked on a sob, the weight of her memories and his obvious hatred, physically pulled her down, putting pressure on the wires cuffing her wrists and ankles.

"Y-you killed your parents, too?"

"Oh, yes!"

"W-why? They loved and cared for you and raised you?"

He stepped further away and twirled once in front of her again, then paced back and forth, fuelled by anger and jealousy.

"Because they're part of this whole problem, don't you see? Instead of sending me to a place where I'd be accepted and would actually be able to play the piano without ridicule, they kept me at home. They saw – or really, dad saw you and Michael as more important than me, and mom went along with it."

He stopped pacing and turned to face her.

"I didn't even really plan mom's death. That just sort of happened. A moment presented itself after I killed Lila."

Julia shivered at the disdain in his tone when he said her mother's name.

"I had confronted her about the adoption and everything. To her credit, she never denied any of it and maintained that she had loved me and raised me as her own child, but I wasn't having any of it. Any parents want what's best for their child. They didn't give me that. They gave it to you."

"W-what about your brother?"

"He was already married and working by that time. He was always the perfect son. Followed in dad's footsteps. Has a good career. Is quite wealthy. Married. Two kids. Someone I could never measure up to in their eyes. But, yeah, he's next on the list after I get done with you. You guys are front and center the people who have ruined my life, that's why I had to get rid of you first." He said it so nonchalantly Julia could hardly believe her ears.

"But mom, she was right there," he continued before she could say anything, and started pacing again as he retold the story. "I was so tempted to just shut her up, just like Lila. Just put my hands around her neck and squeeze." He brought his hands up in front of him as though they were actually around someone's throat. "But I was smart enough to realize that I couldn't have the police snooping around. I hadn't figured out what I was going to do about dad and you and Michael at the time, so I couldn't risk someone interfering with whatever I came up with. I had to make it look like an accident.

"But she actually made it so easy. We were arguing in the hallway and she tripped over my foot as she turned to go down the stairs. She was a rather petite woman with some osteoporosis. Her neck snapped on the way down." He smiled a sick, twisted smile. "Kind of ironic, don't you think?"

"How can you talk about killing your family as if it were fun?"

He turned suddenly and stepped toward her in one swoop so that he was nearly nose to nose with her. "Because it was! Don't you see? I finally started to see the freedom. No more reminders of all the people who were better than me. With you all gone, I don't have to hear about how awesome and successful you all were. How well you did at the school that I should have gone to. I never again had to see the disappointment in dad's eyes when it was very clear I didn't have the aptitude for construction or oil."

"But you're not free at all."

He stared at her, dumbfounded. "How do you figure that?"

"You can kill as many people as you think are responsible for the path your life has taken. You can blame as many people as you want for not making the decisions you wished they would have made. Sending you to a school that favored the arts. Supporting you in whatever career you wanted. Dealing better with the bullies who sapped your joy and love of music so that you saw your talent as a curse.

"You've been given an amazing gift. A chance to do speak to people's souls in a way nothing else can -- that's music. You have a unique way of looking at the world shaped by your experiences. You could have used your struggles and experiences as inspiration for your music … which I actually assume you have … so that it could help other people find a way to get through their difficulties. Don't you understand the power of the gift you have? And instead of using that and turning something negative into a positive to help others, you've turned to murder.

"The problem isn't the people around you whom you feel haven't accepted and appreciated you. The problem is *inside* you. You've let hatred completely take you over so that you feel murdering your family is the only escape. But you'll only end up digging your prison deeper. Because no amount of killing will make that hatred and conflict inside you go away, because it's not about all those people. Your purpose in life is not about people finally appreciating your talents and uniqueness. It's about using the talents you've been given to help ease and lift the hatred and conflict that others feel. Instead of focusing your efforts on doing that, creating a career for yourself and persevering with what you knew was right even in spite of what others said, you focused on punishing them.

"You say you found freedom, but you're in a bigger prison now than you were when you started."

His eyebrows clenched together quizzically.

"I'm not talking about a prison with metal bars. I'm talking about the prison of hatred and of trying to find a reason for living. So long as you choose to focus on all the darkness in the world and lash out that way, you will lose out on the impact of being able to make a positive difference in someone else's life. We're all here to help one another through life. It's so easy to become jaded by some of the attitudes other people have developed through their own life struggles and give up. But we're all learning how to cope with things, and I think it's our duty as fellow human beings to help others along in their journey by sharing what we've learned and how we've learned to overcome those life struggles that happen in our own lives.

"We're not meant to live life alone. It's easy to become lost in some of the terrible things that can happen in our own lives and the world around us. But I believe we're meant to help each other. We're meant to be there for each other as fellow human beings. No, the things that happen in this life aren't always pleasant, and we don't always understand right away why they happen, but in the end if we can use our experience to help carry someone else or lighten their load, I think the experience is worth it. I wouldn't wish what has happened to me on my worst enemy -- not even you."

He hissed at her and started pacing again, this time like a stalking animal. But he was actually listening to her, she had to keep going.

"I'm sorry for all the unhappiness you've felt. And, believe it or not, I'm quite familiar with the feeling of not being accepted. Kids at the other schools saw us as being out of their league, as being weird to want to focus on music rather than sports or romance or the latest Hollywood gossip. I'm sorry the opportunity of going to that private school wasn't offered to you. I obviously can't say why your parents didn't decide to send you to that school, but just because that part of your life didn't happen the way you would have liked doesn't mean that this is the only path for your life can take. You've always had a choice. Perhaps you didn't have anyone in your life to encourage you to make better choices. If you didn't feel accepted by your mother and father, I can see why you might not talk to them about your feelings.

"But whatever happened back then, you still have a choice. Living at peace means that you acknowledge the past hurts and terrible things happened, but that you start making choices so that you don't make the mistake of taking out that hurt out on other people. You're going to make choices that will actually help people who may have lived through similar bullying experiences that you have. You could encourage other students interested in the arts to follow their hearts and stay true to who they are.

"We never know from one day to the next who will need to know the message of hope, encouragement and reassurance in our hearts. Even though there may not be the exact peace in the world around us, we can have peace inside us."

After a few moments, she continued. "People don't have to die for you to be at peace. The peace and freedom you're looking for can't happen by killing all the people whom you see as doing you wrong. That kind of peace is never enough. It will never satisfy your soul. It will never make your heart stop hurting from all the things the world has done to you.

"The people and the things of this world will always disappoint us in one way or another. And everyone is struggling to find the same peace and freedom as you are, and everyone has to make the same choices … give in to the hatred and try to satisfy the lust for revenge, or choose a different path.

"Like for me right now. You have done some pretty terrible things to me and my family. I can choose to hate you for the rest of my life, and many people would probably say that I'd be well within my right to. But I don't have it in me to hate. Not even you. You will face the justice you need to for all you have done, but I refuse to let your hatred take me over and do terrible things to other people because of you.

"Peckton Marcus Oberman, I forgive you."

He moved so fast that Julia hardly blinked and he was standing in front of her again, with his hand around her throat, her skull cracking against the wall behind her with the force. The action pulled against the piano wires around her ankles and wrists and warm blood trickled down her arms.

"I'm about to kill you and you're talking about forgiveness?! What do you think I can do with that?!"

Julia gasped as his hand closed tighter, and darkness swirled over her.

"You … still have … a choice. I … made mine. What's yours?"

Chapter Thirty-One

Dany marched back and forth across the front of the kitchen island, mobile attached to his ear.

Damn being on hold. Time was running out and everything was ready for the latent blood test on the piano. The chopper had arrived and was scoping out the surrounding area. The men who'd been sent into the forest earlier, had returned to the house after the shrinking daylight had forced them to call off their search. They'd sent another couple teams to canvass other local cottages, but no one was home. Of course, that didn't preclude the fact that Peck hadn't broken into one of them and was using one without the owners knowing. But their circle checks of the houses revealed no possible entry points and without sufficient evidence that he had done something like that, they'd decided to pull everyone back to the house and wait for the results from the helicopter search.

"Martin McIntyre." Finally! "What can I help you with?" No nonsense kind of tone, annoyed at someone interrupting whatever else in his life he considered more important.

"Mr. McIntyre. I'm Constable Daniel Howard with the London Police Services in Ontario."

"Ahh, I thought you might be calling me."

Curious. "Why is that, sir?"

"Well, it's all over the news that Julia's been kidnapped by her stalker. I figured sooner or later you'd be calling me."

Hardly the confession Dany'd hoped for. He hadn't expected Martin to admit that he'd obviously lied to Julia about her mother's death. It seemed farfetched that Martin had known Peck in any way and could have participated in the killing. His only crime, at the moment, appeared to have been not telling Julia the truth about the real cause of her mother's death. That and being the man who'd abandoned Julia in her darkest hour. But, a part of him had hoped, however unlikely, that Martin would just come out with the story instead of him having to dig for the truth. He didn't have much time or patience to play 20 questions.

"You obviously haven't found her, yet."

"No."

"Well, I haven't seen her, and no one's contacted me to tell me where she is."

Dany had never wanted to punch someone in the face so much than he did at that moment. Dany turned to face the white piano which was now lit up with luminescent blood spots and looking like an eerie night sky. The blood spatter patterns on the piano keyboard, keyboard lid, and music stand created a kind of halo around where Lila had been sitting playing when she was struck, several times, and sprayed out in decreasing-in-size droplets towards the top and sides of body of the piano. Completely consistent with Dany's hunch that Lila Connelly had been murdered there.

The patch of blood found on the corner of the piano bench did not have the spatter pattern of someone who had slipped and fallen and struck their head there, suggesting instead that she had been placed there, staged for the police. Lila Connelly had not been killed by blunt force trauma due to a slip and fall, but by having been struck from behind with a blunt object. The fact that only the fall had been noted in the police report told Dany that Peck had likely cleaned up the blood on the piano, but left the blood on the corner of the piano bench, staging what he did and didn't want the police to find.

Dany schooled his mind back to Martin.

"Actually, I'm calling on a slightly different matter."

"Oh?" Martin's tone was one of slight intrigue with a strong hint of "Yeah, whatever. What does that have to do with me?"

The hairs along the back of Dany's neck stood on end. What kind of man was Martin that he didn't appear to care that the woman he was once married to could be dead? As much as he wanted to hear Martin's explanation of what happened, Dany wasn't looking forward to finding out just how despicable a man this guy was.

"Mr. McIntyre ..." Interrogation tone. "...tell me what happened to Julia's mother, Lila Connelly."

Silence, Dany suspected the stunned kind.

"She died of a stroke about 10 years ago."

"Are you sure about that?"

"Yeah. Why wouldn't I be?"

Dany decided to let that go for the time being. He didn't want to get Martin on the defensive, yet. He needed Martin's co-operation to get the information he needed. He had to be very careful with his line of questioning.

"Well, the investigation into who kidnapped Julia has brought some evidence to light that it may not have been a stroke."

"Oh, really?"

The cottage around him was abuzz with the dismantling of the equipment and materials needed to get the latent blood prints. Dany walked to the opposite corner of the room. Clint followed him, trying to eavesdrop over his shoulder.

"Mr. McIntyre, the records we have indicate that she died of blunt force trauma to the back of the head as the result of a slip and fall. Our records also show that the medical examiner's determination of time and date of death to have been a week before her body was discovered, supposedly by a friend. The name on the 9-1-1 report is Marcus Oberman. He lived at that time with his mother and father in a house just down the street."

"That wouldn't be all that unusual. Lila taught piano for many years."

Curious response. "What do you mean?"

"This Peckton fellow was probably one of her students reporting for a lesson."

Dany smiled. Martin McIntyre's wall of lies was about to come crumbling down.

"Mr. McIntyre, we're fairly certain that Mrs. Connelly had retired from teaching piano at that time."

An exasperated sigh came across the line. "What's your point, Officer Howard?"

"Okay, let me lay it out for you. We've discovered latent blood spatter on Lila's piano, which happens to be in the cottage owned by Peckton Marcus Oberman's brother, Anthony. This is in addition to the blood that we found on the corner of the piano bench."

"Well, it wouldn't be unusual for blood to travel that distance with a significant enough impact."

"No. No it wouldn't. Except our analysis of the blood indicates that she was killed while sitting at the piano before being moved to where she was found. The finding of her body was staged."

"So, what does that have to do with me?"

"Well, the thing is, moving a body with that kind of trauma to the head would be kind of messy. And there was no report from the responding officers of any blood found along the floor. We also found several receipts for housing renovations. The first ones dated February 12, 2000, for hardwood flooring." Silence. "Julia had mentioned that you had renovated the house after her mother's death. Vancouver Police have been notified of our findings and are on their way now."

"What exactly are you accusing me of? I don't even have to answer any of your questions without a lawyer present."

"Ah, you've been watching too many American TV shows, Mr. McIntyre. That rule does not apply up here. As to what exactly I'm accusing you of, I'm accusing you of tampering with evidence. You can and will be arrested for that." Time to go in for the kill. "What I can't arrest you for is lying to your wife about the circumstances of her mother's death. Why did you lie to her? Why did you help cover up the fact that her mother was murdered?"

Martin didn't talk for so long that Dany feared he might have hung up.

"Mr. McIntyre?"

"She was on tour at the time. With a performance that involves as much emotion as hers do, she's approached by hundreds of people after every concert and she talks to every single one … it's what made her shows so special and why people paid to see her. Peckton called me, although he called himself Marcus, and passed himself off to me as the neighbor who had discovered her body and that she had fallen. Julia didn't need any more stressors in her life than she already had. I really, honestly believed it was better if she didn't know. So, I told her it was a stroke.

"I really, honestly didn't believe she'd been murdered. But I didn't bat an eye when Marcus asked for help cleaning the place up. I knew if Julia ever went back there, even with her mother having died of a stroke, it would be painful for her, so I thought it would be better to wipe the slate clean, as it were. As it turned out, Lila's will bequeathed the piano to Marcus."

The regret and grief were genuine.

"You have to believe me. I never knew she'd been murdered. I was managing things from a distance. I was afraid for Julia's career. We had to cancel three shows as it was because I couldn't get her to move from her hotel room."

"So, you just threw money at the problem afraid your well would run dry if Julia knew the truth."

"Please, it wasn't anything…"

"Don't tell me that. With all due respect, Mr. McIntyre, you don't come across as an unintelligent man. You had to know something wasn't quite right … a neighbor finds your wife's mother dead and you lie to your wife about that and then destroy any evidence of what really happened."

"I didn't even think of the possibility that she'd been murdered."

"Well, you'll have to convince a judge of that. Right now, I have to find Julia. Time is running out for her."

"For what it's worth, I really hope she's found okay."

The emotion of the statement surprised him. He didn't believe for a second that Martin acted completely out of concern for Julia's best interests. He only made money when Julia did and if Julia shut down emotionally and wasn't able to perform, then he lost money. Money was the driving factor here. Not love.

His phone beeped, indicating a call waiting.

"Me too. Me too. Thank you for your cooperation, Mr. McIntyre." He tapped a couple of buttons to connect with the incoming call. "Howard speaking."

"Constable Howard. Anthony Oberman. I'm en route to you. I should be landing at Pearson in a couple of hours. Something just told me there's more going on here and I needed to be at home to assist in any way I can."

"Fine. Should I send a cruiser for you?"

"No, I'll have a car waiting for me. Where should I go?"

"Downtown. As soon as you can get there."

"I'll let you know when I've landed."

Dany disconnected and shook his head. "Wow."

"What is it? I didn't quite catch all of it." Dany related all that Martin had said and Anthony Oberman's call. "Wow."

"Seems like quite the understatement, doesn't it?"

"Constable Howard. Constable Davis. We have something from the chopper, sir. A camp, sir. Less than 10 kilometers from here, kind of buried like many camps are in the back roads so we would never have found it. There are two heat signatures coming from one of the buildings."

"Let's roll out now!"

Chapter Thirty-Two

Julia opened her eyes. The room was still dark, though darker than before, and she was alone.

She had no idea what time it was or how long she'd been out, but even if there was any sort of moon up tonight, very little of its light shone through the windows, suggesting that the moon had moved behind the tree line or been covered with clouds. She was barely able to make out the podium structure in front of her and the first row of benches.

Cold had descended, as well, so that she shivered, the piano wires cutting into her wrists and feet. Peck had apparently not thought to put a coat on her before he hung her up here. She wouldn't last long in the cold. Ordinarily, she'd probably last longer inside than outside, but if she stayed inside, Peck would kill her. If she found a way out, she'd probably freeze to death. But Dany was looking for her. It had been long enough, he should at least have found the cottage by now.

A deep *whomp-whomp-whomp* sound passed overhead. Was that a helicopter?

If it was, surely Peck had heard it. Where was he? Dany was closing in. He didn't have much time, and neither did she. She needed to get out and take her chances.

She couldn't really see her hands, but she knew that he had to have mounted the piano wire on some kind of screw in the wall, wrapping it around a hook. He couldn't have just used a few nails. Those would have just pulled right out if she tugged on them. She imagined three huge eye-hook screws.

She twisted one hand so that her palm faced the wall, more blood trickling down her arms, her hand falling precisely over one of the giant eye-hook screws. She started twisting, every move the piano wire dug deeper into her flesh. Peck had already killed her voice, by the time she was done escaping, her hands would never be able to play another note, as well.

Finally, the bolt was loose enough that she stopped turning it and just grasped the eye-hook and tried to wiggle it out the rest of the way. Eventually, it did and she fell toward one side. Now that her weight wasn't completely supported, she was unbalanced. She needed to free her other hand next, which would mean she would likely fall over her feet. But, Peck would likely appear at any moment. She was a sitting duck. She had to keep going and live with whatever the wires did to her. It would be better than dying here.

She reached her free hand up to the still-hanging hand and found the eye-hook, her twisting pulling on the wire at her feet. Shortly, that bolt was free and she braced herself with her sliced up hands against the floor as she fell. Then she pushed herself back up against the wall so that her nose almost touched her toes, trying to put all her weight on her wire-cut hands instead of her feet. With one hand supporting her, she used the other to unscrew the bolts at her feet. Once her feet were free, and the wires gone from around her hands and feet, she crept along the wall to the door, and peeked out through the window. She couldn't see much.

Was he out there waiting for her? Would she even be able to get very far? Finally, the draw of freedom won out, and she opened the door and with a quick glance around in the pitch blackness, turned to the right. She turned the corner and there he was.

In an instant his hand was crushing her throat again.

"Not going anywhere, are we? I'm not done with you yet."

Julia drove one of her free feet between his legs and he dropped her. As she started to run, he grabbed her ankles and pulled her down. The next moment he was sitting on her chest with a piano wire stretched across her throat.

Whomp-whomp-whomp.

"Time to silence the voice."

"Sir, I see them."

"We're just entering the camp now," Clint radioed up to the chopper.

"She was stationary for a long time and is now on the move. They're not in the building anymore they're outside and appear to be having a struggle."

"Where are they?"

"They're behind the chapel. We've got the spotlight on them now." A million-candle-power beam from the chopper lit up the whole area, focusing on the forest to their right. Now that their presence was announced, would Peck run like a frightened animal, or finish the job he'd given himself?

"Clint, stop the vehicle."

With a stomp of the brake, the Suburban slid to a halt on the soft ground. Dany was off and running toward the light as Clint barked orders to his various teams before following.

Whomp, whomp, whomp. The blinding light from above. Dany was here.

She wanted to fight back, but couldn't feel anything, partly from the cold, partly from the shock of everything, but mostly because of Peck's weight on her chest and however deep he'd gotten with the wire. And the fact she feared if she rolled over, she'd bleed out all over the ground. She had started focusing on other things to distract her mind from what was happening. Then she heard Dany's voice.

"Peckton Marcus Oberman. Get up now! Hands above your head."

Rustling footsteps surrounded her. Her soul cried out a "Thank you" as Peck got off her chest, but her body was spent. She couldn't move. Blood gurgled in her throat as she gasped for air.

Peck stood with his arms wide, almost like an invitation.

"Well, look at that, Dany-boy's arrived."

Julia was barely moving. Maybe he'd arrived too late. He knew

Clint had sent a couple of teams around the other side of the building so that Peck would be surrounded. He had no way of knowing how badly she'd been hurt. One side of him screamed to get to her now. The other side reminded him he still had a job to do.

He aimed his weapon at Peck's chest. Memories flashed, drawing his focus away and threatening to swarm him, but with a quick prayer for focus and a shake of his head, the panic attack abated and he focused all his attention on the murderer in front of him.

"You're under arrest for kidnapping, attempted murder and the murder of Michael Connelly and Lila Connelly. Turn and face the building."

"No, I don't think I will." He sounded like some lunatic supervillain from a movie.

Dany took a few steps closer, hoping he'd be able to physically force Peck against the wall or the ground, whichever.

"Up against the wall now."

"So, Dany-boy, you figured it all out."

"I know you murdered Lila Connelly and asked Martin to cover it up by renovating the house before reporting her death."

Peck smiled. "Ah. So smart of you." He tilted his head over his shoulder without breaking eye contact. "Your commandos are behind me, now, aren't they? You want me to surrender because there's no possible way for me to escape. Well, you have to know I have nothing to lose now."

Peck lunged forward, piano wire in his hand in a kind of eerie slow motion. Dany's gun discharged and Peck dropped in a heap on the ground.

He'd done it. It was over. Dany looked at his gun in a state of almost disbelief.

Clint ran up beside him and put a hand on his shoulder. "Good job, man. I'll take care of this. You better go check on her. Medivac is en route."

Dany put all police protocol aside and ran, pushing through the group that had gathered around her to tend to her injuries. He gasped at what he saw. Blood trickled from her wrists and ankles and throat, just below the jaw. Peck really had been trying to silence the angel.

His heart crumpled as he knelt down beside her and cradled a hand under her head.

"Julia?" Had he made it in time? Peck hadn't gone all the way through with the wire, but he may have done enough. "Julia, can you hear me? It's Dany. I'm here." No movement, no response at all.

The Medivac arrived and hovered overhead, two attendants were lowered down with a cage-looking kind of stretcher.

"It's time to get her out of here, sir," one of the attendants said once he'd landed.

He nodded, then stood aside for them to care for her. He'd done everything he could, but the last part of the battle was still hers.

Chapter Thirty-Three

"Are you ready?"

Julia looked up at her front door, shivering not just because of the cold but also with anticipation of coming home. The doctors had said it would be highly unlikely that she'd make it home for Christmas, but she had been determined not to spend Christmas in the hospital if she could help it.

She gave a curt nod.

"I'm ready." She cringed at the scratchiness of her voice.

Dany smiled as he opened the door.

"Welcome home!"

Julia blinked in surprise at the chorus of people in front of her. All the volunteers from the Community Center, Sammy's cheerful voice bellowing over all the others while he carried a bowl of mashed potatoes. Mariah Colverton was there too. Martha was the first to step out from the group and hug her. Mariah was next, then Constable Davis.

"You did all this?" Julia looked up at Dany.

"It's Christmas Eve. It's time to celebrate. You're home. You're free." He knew he didn't have to say what she was free from. He knew from her eyes that she had finished the statement in her mind "...from Peck's prison."

Everyone seemed to sense they wanted to talk, so the crowd dispersed to different areas of the house.

Julia reached a scarred hand up to touch his face. "Thank you. I wish I could have saved Peck though. I did try."

"I know you did." He took her wrist in his hand and kissed it just below the palm. "I wish I could have gotten there sooner."

"I know you do. But you got there. You did your job. You found out the truth. And, you proved you could step into the line of fire again and do what you had to do." She managed a smile before she had to cough to clear her throat. Despite the happiness around her, her eyes welled up with tears.

Dany led her through the bustling kitchen to the music room.

"Don't go to-a far. Dinner's-a ready," Sammy called after them.

Dany turned before he closed the doors. "Please tell the others to go ahead. We'll join them in a few minutes."

He led Julia to the sectional and settled into a corner of it with her snuggled against him.

"You didn't tell them, did you?" She managed through the tears.

He shook his head. "No. I wanted this to be a happy moment. You've gone through so much, I didn't want that to overshadow everything."

"I so looked forward to singing every Christmas. Now, there won't be any more singing at Christmas, or any other time."

Dany hugged her close and kissed the top of her head. "There's really no way of rehabilitating your vocal chords?"

"No. Not with all the scar tissue."

"I should have gotten there sooner."

Julia sat up a bit and looked at him. "Stop beating yourself up. You got there. Peck was bound and determined to shut me up."

"But look at what he did to you." Dany took her wrists in his hands again.

"Please, don't let them remind you of what you wished you'd done differently to stop him. Let them remind you of how you got there just in time, just like I knew you would."

"You did, huh?"

"Never doubted it for a second."

Dany smiled. "Can I ask you to do one thing for me?"

"What's that?"

"Stop beating yourself up over the fact that you can't sing. I really, honestly, understand how devastating it is for you, but there's so much more to you than the voice. The voice may be what you're best known for, but now's the time for them to hear your voice in other ways."

Tears tumbled down her cheeks again. "How?"

Dany shook his head. "I don't know. We'll discover that together. Besides, you still sound like an angel to me." He kissed her long and hard until they were both breathless. "Now, no more tears tonight, 'kay?"

"Okay."

He took her hand and led her back out to the living room where everyone mingled over their plates of turkey, mashed potatoes, veggies, and gravy.

Later on in the evening, with the meal finished and people full and relaxed, Dany reached down under the tree.

"Did you put presents down there?" Julia asked from behind him.

"As a matter of fact…" he popped back up then turned "…I did." He held a small square box in flat on his hand. "For you."

Julia stared at him, agape. Her heart soared as the love in his eyes beckoned her to open it. She gingerly unwrapped it, still kind of in shock as to what he'd done, then open the velvet lid. Inside was the most beautiful ring she'd ever seen. A simple gold band with a single diamond in the center surrounded by two large wings … angel's wings.

She put a hand to her mouth. "Dany…."

"Julia…" he got down on one knee "…I want to spend the rest of my life with you. I need to spend the rest of my life with you. Will you spend the rest of your life with me?"

Tears of joy coursed down her cheeks as she looked into his beautiful face. She knelt down in front of him.

"Yes."

She hugged him more tightly than she ever imagined she could. All she knew in that moment was the scent of him, his secure arms and shoulders, his hands crushing her against him, and the growl of his voice as he murmured in her ear. All she wanted was for him to never let go, and she knew from the strength of his arms around her he never would.

Chapter Thirty-Four

He watched, hidden behind a tree, as the woman knelt in the grass at the graveside. Her body shook with sobs as she placed a white rose on the mound of dirt.

He looked at the white rose in his own hand. It now seemed inadequate given the level of her grief.

Now that he was back in Halifax, their meeting had to have happened sometime. And it wasn't all that surprising that it happened today, the one-year anniversary of the moment that had changed his life--and hers--forever.

He wanted to go to her and try to bring what comfort her could, but was afraid of any backlash she might hurl his way. He was an intruder here. Finally, her grief compelled him out from behind the tree. He stood over her for a few minutes, careful to maintain his distance. She didn't react to his approach.

"I knew you were there." Her voice deep with grief.

Her confession stunned him.

"I-I had to come," he said when he found his voice. Several moments of silence stretched between them, and he struggled to voice his grief and regret to her. His lower lip quivered and tears slid down his cheeks. "I know, it must come as little comfort to you, but I still see his face every night in my dreams. My heart still grieves over the life that he will never get to live because of me."

She turned and looked at him then, but didn't move from her knees.

"I will live the rest of my life wishing I could take that bullet back."

She rose then, fury in her gaze. "So will I."

"I know no amount of apology will ever be enough or can ever bring him back,and I wanted you to know that as long as you carry this burden, I will carry it too. I will never forget him."

Rage and grief warred across her face with compassion and relief.

"I may never come to a point where I can offer you my forgiveness, but I appreciate that you came here today." She turned again, this time to look down on the grave. "I'd tried so hard to keep him away from the gangs and that kind of crowd. Every day that boy would go out and I would wonder if he would come back to me."

"That's what my wife and foster son wonder every day about me when I report for duty."

She cast a glance over her shoulder. "I suppose they do."

"I think there's a way we can work together so that Jayson's life and death wasn't in vain, that may also help bring some peace to both of us. And I hope it won't come across as some cop trying to assuage his guilt, but as someone who really does want to try to help."

She turned back to him. "What do you mean?"

Dany took a deep breath. He'd had a whole year to think about what he was going to do and really hadn't decided until this moment.

"I want to help kids like Jayson. I want to help keep kids like him out of the gangs, off the streets, out of the jewelry stores so they never, ever have to face the barrel of a gun either from a cop or from another gang member."

Her widened eyes told him he had her attention.

"I would like you to help me run a drop-in center for teens like Jayson. A safe place for them to come and hang out. A place where they could be mentored to keep them out of trouble and help them with the decisions they're faced with as teens and pre-teens."

She stared at him, stunned.

"I will help fund it and work on getting some of the guys to volunteer. We won't be able to stop all of them, but I'm hoping we can help most of them know there's another choice for them. I want to see those kids grow up to live the life that Jayson now can't. I figured we could name the center after him."

She shook her head as her eyes closed and tears flooded down her cheeks.

"Will you help me save other kids like Jayson?"

She nodded.

Dany took a deep breath. "Good. Come around and see me next week. I work until 8 all week."

She looked up again. She couldn't decide if she should smile or cry.

She nodded again, then reached up and touched a hand to his cheek. "I know I said earlier that I might not be able to offer you my forgiveness, and I'm not sure I still can, but this is certainly a step. Thank you."

With that she walked away.

He didn't know how long he stood there, tears drying on his cheeks, before he finally crouched and laid his white rose across hers. Then he turned on his heel, and headed back to the car.

A gust of warm salty Atlantic air blasted across the beach, swept through the small town, and up the perch upon which Nan's House sat, the sun just starting to touch the horizon in the summer evening sky.

Dany followed the melodious sound upstairs and stopped just outside the bedroom door with a smile. It wasn't quite the same as her stage-performer's voice -- it was much, much better. The voice of an angel indeed. Months of training had helped her work past the scarred tissue and rediscover the voice she thought she'd never hear again. She had not only gained her physical voice, but, more importantly, her inner voice. A voice that was no longer shrouded by fear and grief, but set free and full by love.

Julia rose from the side of the bed, then stooped to give the boy one last goodnight hug.

When she turned from the bed, her gaze met Dany's, and her cheeks flushed.

"You were listening?"

"Of course."

"It's still not quite the same." She let him settle his arms around her waist, as their foreheads touched.

"Maybe not, but you still have the voice of an angel to me. And it seem that little boy thinks so, too." Dany cast a glance at the boy.

Julia did the same. "Yeah. I guess so."

Dany waved for her to follow him downstairs.

"What did you and Weldon do today?" Dany asked once she was nestled against him on the sofa.

"We spent most of the day on the beach. He's fascinated by the tidepools and the caves. I had to drag him away kicking and screaming to get him to come home and eat." Silence fell for a few moments as she ran her hand along his chest and he kissed the top of her head.

"How about you? Did you go this morning?"

"Yes."

She lifted her head and twisted so she could see him. "What happened?"

"She was there." Julia listened intently as Dany told her.

"Well, that's good. I'm really glad for you and for her that this is going ahead. I think will make a bigger difference in those kids' lives than either of you could possibly imagine."

"I'm sure it will."

She settled back against him and didn't say anything for a few moments, absorbed in thought.

"Who ever thought we would be here? I can hardly believe I'm here. So much has happened in the last year. I never imagined I'd be remarried and now be a mother. Twelve months ago…." Her voice faltered at the emotion flooding through her, still fresh and raw, and his arms tightened around her. "I'm sorry," she said after a while.

"Don't ever be sorry." His breath was in her ear and sent shivers down her spine. "This has not been an easy time for us, both with Peck and the shooting, but we've had some pretty amazing things happen. The last six months being married to you, moving back to Nova Scotia, I'm back on the force, we adopted Weldon, and you've found your voice again. Doesn't mean all that other stuff didn't happen. If it hadn't, all this good, amazing stuff wouldn't have happened."

"You're probably right. How was your day, anyway?"

"You know what?"

"What?"

"Let's not talk shop, okay?"

"Okay. What shall we talk about?"

"How about whether or not you've heard from the hospital?"

"I was out with Weldon all day."

"Come on, Julia," he nudged her playfully. "Don't keep secrets. That's highly unfair. Tell me what they said."

Julia stood and wandered across the living room to stand in front of one of Nan's umpteen knickknack shelves even though she instantly missed the warmth of his body next to hers.

"They said they absolutely loved the idea of Voice of an Angel Ministry and want me to start first thing next week. They're going to rotate me through NICU, ICU and palliative care, anywhere else they feel musical therapy would be good. I'm not allowed to sing directly Christian songs, unless the patient specifically requests, but the impact of music is just the same."

Dany lept off the couch. "That's wonderful! You still don't quite believe in yourself, do you?" he said as she looked bashfully at the floor.

"I don't know if it's only that. I mean, it's not like the crowds I've sung in front of before. This is about the impact of music itself. Being able to reach someone's soul and, hopefully, bring them the comfort that only music can. It's somehow much more personal, much more humbling, almost, to know that sharing my heart will have such an effect on a person whose only desire at that particular moment is company, a little bit of peace and solace in the midst of their pain, suffering and loneliness. It's an honor to serve that way."

Dany brushed away a lock of hair and curled it around her ear. "You're doing what you're meant to do." His grin grew wider.

"What is it? What are you up to?"

He took her hand. "Come with me."

She followed him into the kitchen. What's he done now? She gasped as the table came into view with a huge bouquet of long-stem roses and a bottle of sparkling green apple juice, in lieu of champagne, and two glasses. Not exactly five-star, but certainly good enough for Nan's house.

"They're beautiful!" She touched a velvety petal and bent to drink in the scent of the blossoms.

Dany took the bottle of sparkling apple juice, opened it and poured a couple glasses, then handed her one.

"I kind of anticipated their answer … well, actually," he scuffed a toe at the floor, "I called them this afternoon and asked if they'd made their decision."

"You what?!"

He shrugged. "I just couldn't wait."

Julia whacked him playfully on the shoulder. "You knew all along?!"

"Ow. Yes."

Julia stared at the roses. "I'm sorry, this is still taking some getting used to."

"Well, get used to it. We need to do something else. Come."

"What? What is it now?"

He led her by the hand out the front door onto the covered veranda, then to the swing. "As far as I'm concerned, this is the only place to have our drinks on a night like this. This is our night to celebrate."

"Celebrate what?"

"To next steps." He raised his glass. "To rediscovering what we thought was lost forever, but was never really gone."

From their vantage point, a vast canopy of stars followed the expanse of the ocean so far that it was difficult to tell where the ocean ended and the sky started.

On instinct, a song rose to her throat in a hum and eventually grew to her full voice, though hushed in the evening air.

When she finished, Dany tilted her head up so that her lips met his. "See what I mean?"

The story continues…

Be sure to check out the devotional companion – *Finding Your Voice: When Life Seems to Have Stolen Yours* and the journal companion – *The Connected Voice Journal: Connecting Your Voice with God's*

Acknowledgments

First word of thanks needs to go to my cover designer and long-term BFF Catherine Howlett. This is the first cover she's ever done for me and they all look awesome! (Check out the devotional and journal covers as well.)

Thanks also to Pat Hauldren for her proofreading and input on the blurb. Why are those things always so dang hard to write? To London Schade who also provided input.

To Lanico Media House for believing in me, and Jesse Kimmel-Freeman for all her hard work in getting this book out to you.

To my kids, Chris and Brent. Brent in particular endured a lot of mornings with mommy sequestered away in the kitchen "writing my stories."

To my God and Heavenly Father for his patience and enduring love which I will never in a million years comprehend, who has given me every word of this book. It's hard to explain to those who don't know the power of inspiration and still small voice that guides my fingers. This story didn't start out in my head the way it appears here in your hands -- and I can't take credit for that. Plus, he's been orchestrating *Voices of Angels* all my life. You can read more about that in the devotional companion *Finding your own Voice.*

Enjoy this first journey with Julia and Dany! (Yes, there will be more to come.)

About the Author

Darlene Oakley is a Marketing Coordinator for Next Century Publishing, and has been a freelance writer, editor, and transcriptionist for 15 years. She has written over 200 articles that have been published online, and edited over 25 books. Her first title, *Inner Sanctum* (Dystopian Fiction) was released in 2014. *Voices of Angels* (Romantic Suspense) is her second fiction title.

Sources

Miller-McIntyre, Barbara. (n.d.) St. Martins – The 'best kept secret' along the Bay of Fundy. Village of St. Martins. Retrieved November 13, 2014 from http://stmartinscanada.com/history.htm.

Carolinian Forests and Carolinian Species & Habitats. CarolinianCanada.ca. Accessed: Sept 7, 2015. Caroliniancanada.ca/legacy

The Fluorescein Method of Latent Blood Detection. Tomboc, Ricardo. Crime-Scene-Investigator.net. Accessed: Sept 7, 2015. http://www.crime-scene-investigator.net/fluoresceinmethod.html

61617881R00186

Made in the USA
Lexington, KY
15 March 2017